Twins of the Twenties

Bright, young bachelors find love in New York

Brothers Patrick and Connor McCormick aren't alike in just looks—their rebellious spirits mean they've both left the prestigious family business behind to forge their own paths in life...

New York cop Patrick devotes his life to helping others, but the one woman who can help *him* overcome his demons is on the wrong side of the law!

Businessman Connor's playboy reputation precedes him and there's not a woman in New York who can tempt him to settle down... until his high school sweetheart returns!

Join these bachelors of the Roaring Twenties as they take New York by storm in

Scandal at the Speakeasy

Available now

And look out for Connor's story coming soon!

Author Note

Welcome to the first book of the Twins of the Twenties duet, where you'll meet twin brothers Patrick (Mick) and Connor McCormick. *Scandal at the Speakeasy* is about Mick, a police officer from Rochester, New York, who finds himself falling in love with a speakeasy owner from Missouri.

I hope you enjoy Mick and Lisa's story!

LAURI ROBINSON

Scandal at the Speakeasy

HARLEQUIN
HISTORICAL

HARLEQUIN®
HISTORICAL™

Recycling programs
for this product may
not exist in your area.

ISBN-13: 978-1-335-50610-8

Scandal at the Speakeasy

Copyright © 2021 by Lauri Robinson

All rights reserved. No part of this book may be used or reproduced in
any manner whatsoever without written permission except in the case of
brief quotations embodied in critical articles and reviews.

This is a work of fiction. Names, characters, places and incidents
are either the product of the author's imagination or are used fictitiously.
Any resemblance to actual persons, living or dead, businesses,
companies, events or locales is entirely coincidental.

This edition published by arrangement with Harlequin Books S.A.

For questions and comments about the quality of this book,
please contact us at CustomerService@Harlequin.com.

Harlequin Enterprises ULC
22 Adelaide St. West, 40th Floor
Toronto, Ontario M5H 4E3, Canada
www.Harlequin.com

Printed in U.S.A.

A lover of fairy tales and history, **Lauri Robinson** can't imagine a better profession than penning happily-ever-after stories about men and women in days gone past. Her favorite settings include World War II, the Roaring Twenties and the Old West. Lauri and her husband raised three sons in their rural Minnesota home and are now getting their just rewards by spoiling their grandchildren. Visit her at laurirobinson.blogspot.com, Facebook.com/lauri.robinson1 or Twitter.com/laurir.

Dedicated to Pat Bruchert for being an amazing fan since my first book.
This one is for you, Pat!

Chapter One

1927

As the other passengers climbed off the train with the same jubilance that they'd boarded it with back in Kansas City, and headed toward the train depot building, Mick McCormick walked around the caboose to the baggage car and waited for the porter to collect his bag.

He'd been in small towns up and down the East Coast, but this was a far cry from them. Junction, Missouri, wasn't just small—his first glance made him think of a fabled old ghost town.

The road was hard-packed dirt and there was hardly a tree in sight, other than a tumbleweed that rolled across the road a block ahead.

Tony had told him that Junction was small, but a good town. A fine place to raise a family.

Mick wasn't so sure.

"Thanks," he said, taking his bag with one hand and tipping the porter with the other. "Where is the best hotel?"

Short, with a black toothbrush mustache, the man

laughed. "There's only one." With a nod, he gestured toward the road. "A block up the street. That red building."

Mick nodded, taking another glance up the street, where the red building, being a story higher than the others, stood out. "Thanks."

The train whistle blew. As soon as the porter jumped on board, the locomotive slowly chugged away, heading south and leaving the small train station empty.

So was the street.

Silent, too.

Mick glanced around. There wasn't a single person in sight. Unless they all had boarded the passenger car again, the other people who'd gotten off the train had disappeared.

Curious, but not so interested that he moved closer, he glanced at the open door of the depot. A small one-story brown brick building, that from what he could tell, was empty.

If he'd been on a case, he'd have investigated where all the people had gone, but he wasn't on a case. This was a promise. To find Tony Boloney's daughter and take her back to Rochester, New York.

Carrying his bag, he headed up the road to the hotel.

The entire town, all the buildings, the road, the landscape, looked old and worn-out. Sun-faded and chipped paint covered the buildings. A grocer, a hardware, a clothing store and what looked like it used to be a saloon lined one side of the street. The other side was the post office, a restaurant, with a closed sign in the window, and a pharmacy. The next block was the hotel and another restaurant, which looked to be open. He hoped. He was hungry.

There were a few other buildings across the street from the hotel, a feed store and butcher shop, but he'd yet to see another person. Houses filled the street to the edge of town, which didn't appear to be too far away. The sun was still out, so it was hard to say if any lights were on, but no one was outside of those houses.

There was a total of two cars. Both parked in front of the hotel.

It appeared as if Junction, Missouri, rolled up and tucked away by seven in the evening. Rochester, New York, wasn't that way. Life, and crime, went on just as much during the night as it did during the day, spring, summer, fall and winter.

It was spring now, and the April air was warmer here than New York, making him think that he should have taken off his suit coat.

A little overhead bell jingled as he pushed open the door of the hotel, and an older man, wearing a pair of brown-and-green-striped pants pulled so high up on his waist they made him appear to be overly tall and spindly, walked out of a wooden door on the right as Mick was still closing the front door.

"Good evening," the man greeted.

"Good evening. I'd like a room," Mick replied.

"Just one?"

Mick scratched the back of his neck at the oddness of the man's question. "Yes. Just one."

The man pointed to a book on the high counter, while turning around and taking a key off a square board on the wall full of hooks with keys hanging off them. "Just one night?" he asked.

Mick nodded. It could be two nights, but he wouldn't know that until tomorrow. "Can you tell me where the school is located?" In a town this size, finding Tony's daughter would be even easier than he'd imagined.

"You with the state board of education?" the man asked.

"No." Mick never shared more than people needed to know.

"Oh, well, then." Smiling, the man pointed toward the front door. "This is Main Street. Go two blocks north to Myrtle Street. Turn west. The school is two blocks up the road, on the north. Can't miss it. A big brick building. Got a brand-new swing set and slide for the kids to play on beside it." Frowning, he added, "But it's closed now. School goes from nine to three."

Mick nodded at the information and laid down the pen, having signed his name while the man had been speaking. "How much?"

"Four dollars a night."

The price seemed steep, but everyone needed to make a living and he doubted the hotel was overly busy any day of the week, or year. He pulled his wallet out of his pocket. "Do you know if the restaurant next door is open?"

Glancing at the clock on the wall, the man nodded. "For about another fifteen minutes."

Mick laid four dollars on the counter.

The man handed him the key. "Top of the stairs. Second door on the left."

Tossing the key in the air, Mick caught it. "Thanks."

"My pleasure."

The room was clean and the bed soft. Mick left his bag on the chair and headed to the restaurant next door. It, too, was clean and the waitress said they had roast beef tonight. Mick ordered it, ate it and left before closing time, but didn't head back to the hotel. He'd been the only customer at the restaurant, but the kitchen had been full of activity.

A man's instincts were something he either learned to trust, or learned to ignore. Mick had learned to not only trust, but depend on his instincts years ago. This town was odd, and too quiet. The depot was where he'd find the answers, and that's the direction he went.

He scanned the outside of the brick building and the surroundings while walking closer. Nothing looked out of the ordinary. Far off, across a field of brush and tall grass, there was a house and barn. Too far away to make out much more than that. There were a few other houses along the road that continued out of town, and, like on the north end of town, they looked quiet.

He walked to the front of the depot, read the train schedule, four a day, two southbound and two north-bound. The door was still open. He entered. There was a ticket booth, but no one manning it. Other than a couple of benches and a back door that led to the outhouses, there wasn't so much as a fly buzzing around.

He walked behind the teller cage to a door that he was sure would be locked. Every depot had an office.

The door wasn't locked and it wasn't a back room. It was a hallway. A short hallway, with doors on both sides. The first one he tried was a depot office, complete with a desk, but without an attendant. He closed the door. The second one opened to a set of stairs leading down into a basement, with a flickering light bulb hanging overhead.

The steps were well worn, with grains of sand on each step. Off the shoes that had walked down them. Or up them. At the bottom of the steps there was a small room with another door. He opened it and found a tunnel, with a line of light bulbs hanging from a single electrical line hooked to the railroad timbers supporting the ceiling.

Railroad timbers reinforced the walls, too, and the floor was as hard packed as the Main Street of town.

The tunnel curved a few times, but all in all, his instincts said it went in the direction of the house and barn he'd seen past the overgrown field. As he walked, he began to pick up faint sounds.

Laughter.

Music.

A speakeasy.

He knew them well.

Rochester, as well as Buffalo, Syracuse, New York City and nearly every other town, was full of speakeasies, and though they were disguised as something else, everyone knew what they were. For the most part, the police ignored them. It was the bootleggers, sneaking booze in from out of the country, and the manufacturers they busted. The mobs. They were the ones that were getting rich while making prohibition deadly. Despite what others thought, the police were concerned about the death rates that had increased during prohibition more than anything else. If anyone was to ask him, the law had been doomed to fail from the moment it had passed.

The tunnel was well constructed and included vent holes overhead every twenty-five yards or so, and ended at a solid door with a small sliding wooden window. The laughter and music were louder. Much louder. Mick now knew where all the people off the train had gone, and why they'd been so boisterous.

He knocked on the door.

The window slid open.

Recalling what he'd heard repeated by some of the crowd on the train, Mick said, "Two bits."

"Do you have a card?"

For a town this size, this was a pretty sophisticated joint. "Need a new one," he said.

"Five or ten?"

Mick took out his billfold, pulled out a five-dollar bill and slid it through the slot. "Five."

The door opened and a guy with dark curly hair who looked like he threw bales of hay, one in each hand, all day long, every day, handed him a slip of thick paper with ten red x's drawn on it.

Mick took the paper. "Thanks." Ten drinks for five bucks. Plenty of places did this. Sold cards. One of the x's would be crossed off each time he ordered a drink. The idea behind it was that the speakeasy wasn't selling drinks. They merely sold "cover charges" for entering the joint, claiming it was for the entertainment—which at times was nothing more than a pig or chicken in a pen.

"Got a magician tonight," the husky guy said. "And Rudy's on the piano."

Mick nodded as he walked past the guy and pushed open a second door. The place was big, and packed. A wooden bar ran the length of one wall. At the far end there was a piano in one corner with a man pounding on the keys, producing music for people to dance to on the floor near the far wall. Tables filled most of the room, with people gathered around them, talking, laughing and drinking beneath the strings of light bulbs hanging overhead.

Recognizing several from the train, Mick shouldered his way to the bar and handed another big man the ticket he'd purchased.

"How's life?" the bartender asked. Another good-sized farm boy type of guy with slicked-back blond hair.

"Can't complain," Mick replied.

"Beer, hooch or cocktail?" The bartender's barrel chest was so large, the buttons on his shirt were strained. "Any one of them will make life better."

All three of the beverages were sure to be homemade, so going with the safest bet, Mick said, "Beer."

The guy filled a mug from one of the kegs on a shelf behind him, slid the mug across the bar and crossed off one of the x's on the card before handing it back.

Mick stepped away from the bar and then up against the wall at the end of the bar, giving room for the bartender to assist other customers, never making anyone wait a fraction of a second longer than necessary.

There were two other bartenders. Another big and young guy, who looked like the one he'd paid the five bucks to, was behind the other end of the bar and a young woman with a string of white pearls looped through her brown hair was behind the middle of the long bar.

He tried not to stare, but couldn't help it. She was pretty, very pretty. But it was more than that. There were shelves of shot glasses behind her that she'd grab by the bases four at a time, fill them while still holding them in her palm and slide all four onto the bar without spilling a drop. She was so quick, so graceful, it almost looked like a magic trick.

A better trick than the guy dressed in a black tux, red shirt, and black and red cape who was walking around, slipping cards out from the cuffs of his shirt sleeve and pretending to pull coins out from behind the ears of those watching him. Not much of a magician, but it didn't take much because the entertainment wasn't why people were here.

They were here for the hooch. That's what the woman was pouring in the handful of shot glasses she slid onto the bar nonstop. She also appeared to be the one running the joint. All questions from customers and the other bartenders were directed to her, and she had the answers. From where things were located to the magician's name and that the entertainment tomorrow night would be a juggler named Beans who could juggle four bottles. Full ones, which evidently were harder to juggle than empty ones.

Mick had no idea if that was the case or not, and because his curiosity had been solved about where everyone from the train had gone, he took the last swallow of his beer and set his mug on the bar.

"Another one, mate?" the bartender asked.

Mick considered it, because the beer had been good. Not overly bitter like a lot of the joints back home. Prohibition had changed a lot of things, and whether he was an investigator for the police department or not, he appreciated a decent beer now and again. However, none of that had an iota to do with why he was here. He gave the bartender a one-finger wave. "No, thanks."

Chapter Two

Lisa Walters had been keeping one eye on the bull since he'd walked into the joint. She could pick out a cop from a mile away, and that slick-dressed fella at the end of the bar was definitely one. He had on a three-piece black and gray pinstriped suit rather than a uniform, looking all air tight, but the way he watched the room, the way he stood, straight back and stiff, she'd swear on her mother's grave that he was a bull. What she couldn't figure out, was how he'd got past Myers. She paid the ticket master to stay at the train depot until midnight, when the train would haul the majority of her patrons back to Kansas City. Those groups of city slickers were her bread and butter. She'd worked hard to make the Depot *the* happening place that people were willing to ride a train for half an hour to have a night of fun, and that work had paid off. Thursday, Friday and Saturday nights were standing room only.

Fred Myers knew what to look for as far as suspicious patrons, and in the three years since she'd hired him, he hadn't let anyone who so much as resembled a cop enter the tunnel. He knew, as did most everyone else in Junction, what would happen if the Depot was busted. The entire town benefitted from the guests she brought to town. When prohibition had hit, her stepfather, Duane Kemper, had thought all he had to do was pretend to sell food upstairs and open a speakeasy in the basement of the saloon he'd operated on Main Street for years. Even back then, she'd known that wouldn't work. Missouri was too close to the Bible Belt for that, but her stepfather wouldn't listen to her.

It had worked for almost three years, before the state police busted Duane. He'd been out of jail within a couple of weeks, with little more than a hand slap, for running a speakeasy, but had realized that if the police had found his manufacturing site, he'd have been doing serious time. He also understood if he was caught again, they wouldn't go as easy on him and had finally listened to her ideas. If he wanted a speakeasy, it had to be hidden, and it had to be guarded. As hidden and guarded as his distilling site, and because people didn't trust him, he couldn't have anything to do with running the joint—other than collecting money of course.

Lisa had created the Depot, and loved the fact that she was in control for the first time in her life. She enjoyed knowing the town of Junction, the people and businesses that her real father had known and loved, were once again thriving.

The bull had set his mug on the counter, refused a refill and was now walking toward the door. The place was hopping tonight—standing room only, as most Thursday nights. Leaving Buck and Toby to tend bar on their own would slow down the drinks, but things were going too good right now for her to take a chance at getting busted.

"That guy tell you his name?" she asked Buck while filling four glasses of hooch.

"No."

After sliding the glasses onto the bar, she set the empty whiskey bottle in the crate beneath the bar. "Mark their cards. I'll be back."

Lisa wasn't sure what she was going to do, but she had to do something. She squeezed between Buck and the line of beer kegs on the back wall, and lifted up the hinged section of the bar near the wall, where the bull had been standing.

He wasn't yet to the door, and she rushed in that direction, caught his arm just as he reached for the door handle.

"Hey, Rupert." It was the first name that popped into her head. "You aren't leaving without dancing with me. You promised and this is my favorite song."

He turned, stared at her with a frown that wrinkled his forehead.

Her mouth went dry. Up close, he was handsome. So. Very. Handsome. She forced down a swallow, irritated at herself for being caught off guard. Especially by a man's looks. He was handsome all right, in that turn a woman's head sort of way. That wasn't her. No one ever turned her head. She knew a cake-eater when she saw one, a man who thought he was a real lady's man. Other women, those who liked flashy billboards—men who were too handsome for their own good—would have their heads turned by him. Due to how his brown hair was cut short on the sides, but longer on the top, combed to one side so it fell over one of the dark brows that arched over his deep blue eyes. But not her. His hair or eyes didn't matter to her. She was immune to men.

"I'm not Rupert," he said.

She had to swallow again, just to bring about her senses, then forced out a giggle, a silly-sounding one.

"I guess you aren't, but this is my favorite song." She tugged on his arm. "Dance with me."

His frown increased. "Who is going to pour drinks while you're on the dance floor?"

The fact he recognized her from behind the bar didn't surprise her. A bull would be looking to see who was pouring drinks. That's what he was. A bull. One she couldn't let bust her place. "The guys have it covered," she said, tugging harder. "A gal needs to have some fun." Men said that to her all the time, and she refused them all the time.

He remained still. "You'll have to find Rupert." Taking hold of her hand, he lifted it off his arm. "I'm leaving."

To keep from balling her hand into a fist at how it burned from his touch, she grabbed the long string of pearls she had tied into a knot near her breast bone and swung the beads in a small circle, while batting her eyelashes at him. She hated flirting, and didn't do it very often, if ever. This situation called for whatever she had to do. "But you just arrived."

"I've been here long enough," he said, twisting toward the door.

"Wait!" She grabbed his arm again, desperate. Trying to come up with another reason, she said, "The magician hasn't started his show yet." Stepping closer, she lifted her chin, grinned at him. "He's supposed to be magnificent."

He glanced over her shoulder. "How do you know that?"

She twisted her neck, spied the magician. "Because his name is—"

"Rupert the Magnificent," he said dryly.

Horsefeathers! No wonder that name had popped into

her head. Why hadn't she realized that before saying it? She'd been the one to hire Rupert the Magnificent! This bull just had her so flustered!

"It's embroidered on the back of his cape," he said, mockingly.

She knew that! Dagnabit! If there were two things she hated, it was bulls and being wrong. It took all she had to hold on to her temper. To keep from telling him that she knew the magician's name and that she knew he was a bull, but not a state policeman. She knew the ones who patrolled this area, they were regular customers. That meant he was a fed. A Federal agent was one of her greatest fears. She couldn't get busted. And wouldn't. Not by him. Mr. High and Mighty Bull.

"Good night," he said, while removing her hand from his arm once again.

This time she had to ball her hand into a fist. Both hands. She waited until he'd walked out of the door and was sure he'd crossed through the checkpoint before she wrenched open the door. Thad was reclined on his chair. She slapped the table beside him, making him bolt upright. He and Toby were brothers. Buck was their cousin. She depended on the bulk and brawn of the three farm boys regularly. Toby and Buck behind the bar with her and Thad guarding the door. "We are going to follow that guy," she said, walking to the second door.

Rising to his feet, Thad asked, "Why?"

She pushed back the sliding piece of wood and peered through the opening. "Because I said so." He even walked like a bull. Purposefully. With his shoulders squared and his back straight. His head upright. A cocky swagger in his step. The overhead light bulbs in the tunnel made his dark hair glisten. His suit, too. Like the pinstriping was made of silver threads.

Just looking at him made her mouth go dry again. That had never happened to her before. Why did it now?

Why did he do that to her?

Because he was a bull!

What was he doing here? That was the question she should be asking!

The Depot hadn't been on anyone's radar, her sources would have told her if it had been. He had to be after Duane. That's what the feds were after. The distilleries.

"When?" Thad asked.

"As soon as I say." She was waiting for the bull to turn the first corner, so he wouldn't sense the door opening. Bulls were like that. They could sense things.

She could, too. Her insides were steaming like the brewing pot of a still. Every bubble that popped said she wasn't about to let this fed bust her. No way in Hades or hell.

He turned the corner and she counted to five before pulling open the door and stepping into the hallway.

On the tips of the toes of her patent leather shoes, she rushed forward, and then held her hand up, telling Thad to stop behind her as she paused near the wall and slowly leaned around the curve to peer down the tunnel. It was empty and she waved her hand so Thad would continue to follow her. Silently.

She paused again at the next curve, peered around the corner and frowned. The tunnel was empty. That bull must be running in order to be so far ahead of her. Her temper rose. She wanted to catch him in the tunnel. Justifying that might not happen, she concluded that the depot building would be just as good. Fred Myers would be there. Not that she'd need more help than Thad, but she'd be able to find out why Fred had let the bull enter the tunnel in the first place.

"Where'd he go?" Thad asked.

"He's fast, and slick," she answered. Federal agents were like hound dogs and foxes rolled into one. "Fred will see him at the top of the stairs."

"But will he stop him?"

Blast it! Fred wouldn't stop him! He'd let him in and wouldn't think twice about letting him out. She bolted forward.

"Why are we after this guy?" Thad asked, running beside her.

"He's a bull."

"Didn't look like one to me. He knew the password."

"Half of Missouri and Kansas knows the password," she hissed while sliding to a stop at the door to the basement of the train depot.

"How do you know he's a bull?"

"I just do!" She opened the door, and, like the tunnel, the basement was empty.

"How?" Thad asked.

She held up a hand to silence him and walked to the stairs, peered up them. Empty. The door at the top of the steps was closed. "Go back to your station."

"You don't want me to go up there, find him?" Thad asked, towering over her and looking up the stairway.

"No." There was no need. The bull was gone. She doubted Fred would have given him a second look, but still started up the steps. "I'll be back after talking with Fred."

"What if—"

She cut him off with another wave of her hand. "I'll be fine."

Forcing herself to stay strong, keep her back straight and her head up, she marched up the stairs. She'd had to learn to assert herself when she'd started running the

Depot. Her stepfather had said that she'd fail straight off, and she'd been determined to prove him wrong. Because she was short, small boned and a woman, other men besides her stepfather had thought she didn't have what it took to manage anything, let alone a speakeasy. As if size or gender had anything to do with it.

She'd learned to bark orders, demand action and expect results, all the while completing a handful of her own tasks. It hadn't been easy, and at times she hadn't liked it, but she'd forced herself to do whatever it would take to make the Depot successful.

People listened to her without question now, knew she was the one in charge. There were nights when she'd take the cash box up to her house that she couldn't believe how successful she had become. More than she'd ever imagined, and she certainly wasn't going to let a nosy, spiffy-looking federal agent take away everything she'd worked so hard to achieve.

Not by a long shot. The town needed her to keep Duane in line so they could succeed, and she wasn't about to let those people down.

Fred Myers was in his office across from the basement door, feet up on his desk and reading a book. Her lips pursed as the air she drew in and let out through her nose grew hotter with every breath.

Fred glanced up, saw her and dropped his feet to the floor. "Trouble brewing?" he asked, shooting to his feet.

Holding her composure because calm seriousness got her further than out-of-control mad—which was how she felt—she asked, "Where is the man who just left?"

"What man?" Fred adjusted the temple stems of his gold wire-framed glasses. "I didn't see anyone."

"Tall, brown hair, wearing a black and gray pin-striped suit."

Fred rapped his knuckles on the top of his desk. "Nope. Ain't seen no one fitting that description, and I've been here the whole time."

"What about half an hour ago, when he entered?"

Sticking his thumbs behind the black suspenders over his yellowed, once white, shirt, he shook his head. "No one's entered since the train arrived. Was he one of them? From Kansas City?"

"You've been here the entire time?"

"Yes."

Fred knew the importance of his job, and hadn't failed her in the past. He and his connections with the engineers of the trains between here and Kansas City were major pieces of how well everything was working right now. "You haven't left this office since the train pulled away?"

He nodded, then shrugged. "Except for going across the street for a sandwich shortly after the train left. Hilda has turkey ones today."

Fred always went to the grocery store across the street for supper. That bull must have been watching, knew exactly when to sneak in, and snuck out just as quietly.

"Why? Who is he?"

She sucked in a breath so deep it made her lungs hurt. "A federal agent."

"No?"

"Yes."

Chapter Three

Mick watched the depot from across the street, in the shadow of the awning of the brick grocery store that also gave him a clear view through the open depot door. The woman had followed him all the way through the tunnel, and now stood in the hallway, talking to the agent who'd been sitting in the office reading a book when Mick had snuck past him and out the door.

Pretty didn't describe her appropriately. She was more than pretty. Her eyes were so dark blue he'd almost been able to see his own reflection in them. Her lashes were thick and dark, and not because they were coated with mascara. Her face had been so flawless, so pretty, it had taken him aback for a moment, like catching a glimpse of a movie star's photo on the cover of a magazine, where he had to take a second and third look, because they looked too perfect to be real.

She was real, and she'd been as nervous as a dog in a thunderstorm when she'd stopped him at the door, on the pretense of dancing. He didn't dance. But he was an officer of the law, and she knew it. He'd recognized a certain alarm in those dark blue eyes. It was impossible to explain exactly what it was, but people got a certain tremor in their eyes when they realized they were talking to a cop. They couldn't hide it, either. Especially those who had reason to be afraid because they knew they were about to be caught in some form of action that was against the law.

Running a speakeasy was against the law. He could have saved her the worry. Told her he wasn't here to bust anyone. He had considered it for a split second, but had decided it was better if she remained afraid, because someone as young as her shouldn't be that deep in illegal activities. It could ruin her life. He wouldn't be around to see it, but what she was doing was putting her on a road to nowhere.

He didn't like that idea.

He wasn't overly sure why she'd followed him, either. Had she thought she could overpower him? The goon who'd been selling tickets at the door had been with her in the tunnel, but it would take more than that to intimidate him—he was from Rochester, New York. A farm boy goon was nothing compared to the mob torpedoes he'd encountered in the past. The only reason he hadn't stopped, hadn't confronted them, was because then he'd have to follow through, and that speakeasy was none of his business. He was here to get Tony Boloney's daughter. Nothing more.

The woman disappeared, and, certain she'd gone back to the speakeasy, Mick left the shadows of the awning and walked up the road to the hotel. The sun was setting now, and, oddly enough, even though the closed signs were on the doors and shades were pulled, there were lights on inside the stores.

Maybe that wasn't so odd. The entire town seemed peculiar to him.

Back at the hotel, he took a bath in the bathroom at

the end of the hall, and then returned to his room, more than ready to get a good night's sleep.

The sheets smelled like sunshine and the bed was comfortable, but sleep evaded him as his mind circled back to the speakeasy woman. She was far too young to be running a joint. He'd be surprised if she was twenty. The top of her pearl-encircled head had barely reached his shoulder. Her dress had been a dark purple silky number, trimmed with fringe and decorated with that long set of white pearls she'd twirled like a lasso while batting that set of long dark lashes at him.

He grinned recalling her flirting, and her blunder over the magician's name. That had flustered her. Maybe he should have played along, shown her how dangerous her snake charmer game could have been. Would be when the day came that she encountered someone with less restraint than him.

Later, while he was still waiting to fall asleep, still thinking about why a girl that young would be running a speakeasy, noise filtering in through the window drew his attention. A glance at the clock said it was eleven thirty. Tossing back the covers, he rose and pulled back the curtain. It was dark, but streetlights shone down on every corner, and several lit up the depot.

There were now several cars parked along the streets and tables were set up all around the depot building, like it was some sort of marketplace. More tables were being taken out of cars and trucks and carried toward the depot, along with crates, baskets and bags.

This town really was strange, and too curious not to check it out, he slid on his pants, socks and shoes, and his shirt. By the time he arrived at the store across the road from the train station, people were trickling out of the depot building. People he recognized both from the train and the speakeasy.

Once again, he stayed under the awning, watching as people wandered through the makeshift bazaar, buying sandwiches and other food to eat, as well as other wares being sold at each of the tables.

A short time later, a bell rang. So loudly that had he been asleep, it would have woken him. Within five minutes, what appeared to be the entire speakeasy emptied out through the door of the depot and those tables were overrun with customers picking the tops clean. The sound of the train whistle caused a frenzy of last-minute buyers scarfing up anything that was left.

Mick stayed, watching as the train filled up and the market vendors packed up their tablecloths, signs and cash boxes into their crates and bags. As the train pulled away, heading north toward Kansas City, the vendors carried their tables, bags and boxes toward their vehicles and stores.

He'd searched the crowd for the bartender, but hadn't seen her, or her farm boy helpers. They must still be at the speakeasy, cleaning up and counting their money like the outdoor vendors.

In his mind, this town was now a mixture of peculiarity and shrewdness. It had taken an enterprising spirit to come up with this idea. People were hungry after drinking all night, and it wasn't hard to convince an ossified man, or woman, they needed to spend their money on other things, too.

Mick walked back to the hotel, where several people were now checking in. Still somewhat in disbelief, he shook his head and went up to his room. There, he undressed and climbed back into bed. This time, he forced himself not to think about that cute bartender, or anything else he'd seen since coming to this little town.

The following morning, having slept well considering all, he had breakfast at the café and then walked toward the school. The town was livelier this morning than last evening, but nothing compared to the bustling marketplace at midnight. That was still circling in his mind. How the entire town took advantage of the customers the speakeasy drew into town. Definitely enterprising, and he was a bit in awe by having seen it.

Kids were out this morning. Plenty of them, rushing up the road to the school building. A big brick building with a large metal tubular fire escape slide attached to the second story and a good-sized playground where children had already gathered, taking their turn on one of the swings or going down the slide before it was time to attend classes.

Several boys shot around him, running toward the playground, but the last one, younger and trying hard to keep up, lost his footing and would have fallen if Mick hadn't caught him by the arm.

"Whoa, slow down there, young fellow," he said, holding on to the boy until his small feet were firmly on the ground again.

"Sorry." Towheaded with freckles covering his nose and cheeks, the boy slumped and kicked at the dirt as he looked at the playground. "Aw, shucks! I never get a swing."

"That's tough," Mick said.

"It sure is." He huffed out a sigh, then frowned. "You going to school?"

Mick nodded. "I'm looking for a teacher."

"Mrs. Goodall?"

"No. Miss Walters. Do you know her?"

The boy shook his head. "No." His face lit up. "I know Lisa Walters. Everyone does. She runs the Depot. My brother Edwin says she's hotsy-totsy."

Runs the depot? That had to be the name of the underground juice joint. Mick's spine quivered. Tony Boloney's daughter wasn't a schoolteacher, she was running a speakeasy! He should have considered those odds. Birds of a feather. Tony had been a mobster for years, before he'd turned and provided Mick with the information that had led to one of the biggest busts in the history of the Rochester police department.

"Ma washed Edwin's mouth out with soap for saying that," the boy said. "You ain't gonna tell my ma I said it, are you, mister?"

"No," Mick answered. "I'm not going to tell your mother."

"Good! Her soap tastes awful!"

"I'm sure it does," Mick answered, grinning. His mother's soap had tasted awful, too. Both he and his brother Connor had tasted it more than once. "You best get on to school now."

"All right. Bye, mister."

"Bye." Mick shook his head. Running a speakeasy. This certainly was an interesting turn of events. Tony had said she probably wouldn't want to see him, and Mick had been prepared to convince her that she did want to see her father. That just became easier. If she refused to go to New York with him, he'd simply arrest her.

Lisa rubbed her eyes and let out a groan as she rolled her head enough to see the clock. Ten in the morning? No one knocked on her door at ten in the morning. It took her until after three in the morning to get the Depot cleaned and restocked after everyone cleared out. Despite the train leaving at midnight, there were always stragglers that hung around until the one o'clock closing time. By the time she had the joint in order, the tunnel doors and barn doors locked, and the money counted and stored away, it was always close to four before she was able to take a bath in order to wash away the smell of cigarette smoke and crawl into bed.

The knock came again, and she huffed out a breath before dragging herself upright and tossing back the covers. Duane, her stepfather, was the only person who could be knocking. He came every Sunday morning to collect his share of the weekly proceeds.

Irritated, because he knew she didn't get to bed until the wee hours of the morning, yet it never stopped him, she grabbed her housecoat off the foot of the bed. "I'm coming!"

After shrugging into the housecoat, she released her hair from the loose braid she'd plaited it into after her bath and before crawling into bed and finger combed the tresses while walking out the bedroom door.

It was times like this that she really wished she'd been able to follow her childhood dream of becoming a schoolteacher.

The knocking came again as she walked down the stairs from the second floor. Someday, she was going to tell Duane off. Tell him off good. He wouldn't be making anywhere near the amount of money he was without her. He acted as if it was the other way around. He boasted that she'd be nowhere if not for him. That, too, was the other way around. If not for her and the Depot, he wouldn't have enough money to put gas in that big car he drove around, acting like the big cheese of Junction.

Arriving at the door, she turned the key and wrenched open the door. Recognition struck instantly. The man on her porch wasn't her stepfather. Shocked, frozen, it was a moment before she could react. Then she did the only thing she could do. She slammed the door shut.

"Good morning, Miss Walters," he said through the door.

She fumbled for the key, but it was gone. Had fallen out of the keyhole when she'd slammed the door shut. Searching the floor, she saw it, near the edge of the rug, too far away to reach.

Horsefeathers! How had she forgotten about him? The bull from last night. It wasn't Sunday! It was Friday and he was the reason she hadn't fallen asleep until the sun had been coming up.

"I would like to speak to you," he said.

She didn't want to talk to him. Ever. Turning, she put her back against the door, holding it shut if he tried to open it, and stretched out one leg, trying to reach the key with her toes.

"I can see you through the curtain," he said.

Of course, he could see her through the curtain! She was leaning against it!

Why hadn't she looked through the curtain before opening the door? She stretched further, almost reaching the key with her big toe. Just not quite. Keeping as much weight against the door as possible, she stretched her leg to its limit, and touched the key with her toe.

Yes!

Now to slide it toward h—

The door jarred. She tried pushing against it, but lost her footing and went down on the floor, one leg stretched out so far, she yelped at the pain of thigh muscles being pulled.

He poked his head around the door. "Morning." Seeing her on the floor, he frowned. "You all right?"

She scrambled to her feet, picking up the key in the process, but it was too late. He pushed the door all the way open. Wearing the same suit as last night, he looked just as spiffy. Just as handsome. "Get out of my house!"

"I'm not in your house. Yet." He stepped over the threshold. "Now, I am."

He sure thought he was smart. Standing there, grinning. Staring at her. She pulled her housecoat tighter across her front, covering her thin nightgown, and tied a knot in the cloth belt as goose bumps assaulted her from head to toe. "Get out!"

"Can't." He shut the door. "Not until we talk."

The one time she needed Thad, Buck or Toby, they were nowhere near. She couldn't overpower him by herself, that was obvious. Not about to admit that, she'd have to fake it. "I have nothing to say to you." Lifting her chin, she leveled a glare at him. "And one of my men will be coming through that door at any moment."

"One of the farm boys from last night?" His grin showed off his pearly white teeth. "Nice try, but I don't buy your bluff. You're here alone."

Thoroughly frustrated, she asked, "What do you want?"

"To talk to you."

Was he crazy? She had no interest in talking to him about anything.

"It's about your father."

Horsefeathers! She'd been right! All of Duane's boasting had come back to bite him. That's what had gotten him busted years ago. His mouth was just one of his flaws. Just one of the things about him that had driven her crazy since the day her mother had married him. "He hasn't lived here for years. Since before my mother died."

The bull folded his solid arms across his chest. "Not your stepfather. Your real father."

Her insides froze at the same time an old loss, old pain, rose up inside her. Which irritated her even more. The gall of this man was unbelievable. "I don't have a *real* father."

"Yes, you do. Anthony Walters."

Her spine stiffened and she had to tell herself to breathe. "Tony—Anthony Walters died years ago. In the war."

"No, he didn't."

Gritting her teeth against the pain, she seethed, "Yes, he did. He left for the war when I was eight. When I was nine, we got a telegram that he'd died in Europe." For years she'd wished that wasn't true, even dreamed of it not being true. But it was true.

"And you received his telegram last month. The one saying he wants to talk to you. I know you did, because I got confirmation of it being delivered."

She'd thought she'd heard of every dirty trick in the book, but this guy took the cake. Trembling, she flicked her hand toward the door, telling him it was time for him to leave. Past time. "Get out. Now."

Chapter Four

Mick wasn't going anywhere. He couldn't tug his gaze off her, either. Thankfully, she'd pulled the front of her purple, flowered housecoat closed. The thin nightgown beneath had been too close to see through for comfort. His comfort. She'd been cute last night, but this morning, with her long honey-brown hair disheveled and her eyes slightly puffy from sleep—or lack thereof—she was the prettiest thing he'd seen in a very long time. If ever, and she stirred things inside him.

He glanced down at the floor to get his thoughts back in line. He wasn't here to determine just how pretty she was, and it wasn't his place to say that Tony had come home and found his wife married to someone else. Tony could share the particulars. Mick had other things to tell her. "Perhaps you'd be more comfortable getting dressed before we discuss the details," he suggested.

"Details? There are not any details to discuss, and I'd be *more comfortable* if you left."

She'd erected a battle shield last night, and it was still there this morning. He understood why, considering the business she managed and his occupation. However, her battle shield had become a solid brick wall the moment he'd mentioned Tony's name. Her eyes had glassed over and her body had gone stiff. Shock maybe. That he was here, following up on the telegram he'd sent. He'd sent the message via a telegram rather than a letter, just to be sure she got it. And that's why he was here, because she hadn't responded to it.

She could lie all she wanted to. As far as Mick was concerned, it was between her and Tony to let bygones be bygones. His issue was getting her to New York, and if he had to arrest her, he would. Life was too short to die with regrets. He had firsthand knowledge of losing a parent without being able to settle things, to say goodbye. It still haunted him.

"I can't leave," he said. The living room had a bright yellow upholstered sofa, matching chair and wooden rocking chair, all placed upon a bright red-and-gold rug. He walked over and sat in the rocking chair.

"What do you mean, you can't leave? The door is right there. Just get out of *my* chair and walk to the door! Walk out it. Out of *my* house!"

"The house you inherited from your father, Tony."

Her blue eyes widened and turned colder. "Why are you doing this? Tony Walters died twelve years ago."

Her acting was good. She was almost believable. He pushed a foot against the floor, set the rocking chair in motion. "My name is Mick McCormick. Patrick Mc-Cormick, but everyone calls me Mick. And as you surmised last night, I am an officer of the law. A detective in Rochester, New York. That is where Tony is currently residing."

"I don't give a rat's ass what your name is!" Her lips quivered as she drew in a breath. "My father, Tony Walters, is dead, and I want you out of here. Now."

He shrugged. "Can't." Standing, he glanced toward

the doorway that led into a kitchen. "Do you want some coffee?"

"No!"

"I do." He walked toward the kitchen. Those quivering lips could lead to tears and he needed a distraction. "I'll make it."

"No, you won't make coffee or anything else."

He ignored her and walked into the kitchen. Like the rest of the house, it was tidy, clean and modern, fitted out with the latest conveniences and appliances. Ground coffee was in a small tin canister marked Coffee sitting on the counter, right beside an electric percolator.

She had followed him into the kitchen, and as he filled the pot with water, he told her, "Go get dressed. Then I'll explain all I can."

"I said—"

"I heard what you said, but I also saw your reaction. Your father is alive, and whether you admit it or not, I know you received the telegram and chose not to respond to it." He set the pot down on the counter. "You don't have the choice not to listen to what I have to say, because if you don't, your establishment will be busted, tonight."

Her eyes narrowed as she lifted her chin. "You don't have any jurisdiction in Missouri."

She was putting on a show of bravery, although she was fully aware of what he was capable of. A part of him had to admire her courage. "One call, Lisa, and this place will be swarming with bulls who do have jurisdiction. It's your choice. Talk to me here, in your home, or from the other side of cell bars."

Her eyes welled with tears, but they didn't flow. "You're so rotten you stink." She spun around, walked out of the room. "I hate you, Mick McCormick!" echoed in her wake.

"I'm not here for you to like, Lisa Walters!" He plugged in the percolator, found cups and then searched the contents of the refrigerator for something to feed her.

By the time she reappeared, wearing a sleeveless knee-length blue dress with white polka dots and a white scarf tied around her forehead, he had a plate of scrambled eggs and toast on the table. She glanced at the plate, and at him.

He leaned against the counter, drinking his coffee, that tasted better than the cup he'd had at the café this morning, and nodded at the table. "Eat. Then we'll talk."

"I'm not hungry."

"I didn't ask if you were hungry. I said eat, and then we'll talk." Because she obviously needed to know he was in charge, he flashed the badge on the inside of his lapel at her.

She sneered at him. "You can flash that badge all you want. It doesn't mean anything."

"Really? Should I go flash it around town? To all those business owners who had tables set up at the depot last night. Let them know you're the reason I'm here?"

Her eyes widened and her mouth gaped before she plopped down on the chair and made a show of sticking a forkful of eggs into her mouth.

Satisfied that she'd finally figured out she had no choice but to listen to him, he set his cup on the counter. "Join me in the living room when that plate is empty." She had to know that he was in control. That he was always in control.

Lisa glared at him as he walked out of the room, wondering exactly what this guy was up to. Claiming that her father was alive, and that she knew about it? That was ludicrous. She had not received a telegram, because there was no telegram. He was here to shut down the Depot. That's what this was about. He must be using Tony as a ploy to get her to talk about Duane, and his distillery site.

Dagnabit! A bull flashing a badge was the last thing she needed. Duane would… Or was Duane behind all this? That would be just like him. Trying to get rid of her any way he could.

Poking a forkful of eggs in her mouth, she was surprised at how light and fluffy they were, and how delicious. She was hungry. Usually, she ate after coming home, but had been too frustrated last night, worrying that the bull would be back, but had thought he would be at the Depot. Not here, at her house. She would talk to him, all right. Let him know that she knew what he was trying to do. He wasn't the first bull to take the side of bootleggers, and wouldn't be the last. Every man was out for himself. Bull or not.

Trickery. That's what he was up to. Using lies about her real father to do so, while being in cahoots with her stepfather. That angered her beyond a level she'd known. When Tony Walters had left for the war, she and her mother had cried, for days, weeks. They had missed him so much, and then… Lisa shook her head, dispelling the thoughts.

She wouldn't put herself through memories filled of pain, years of hoping Tony would come home and save both her and her mother from Duane.

Swallowing the last bite of eggs while pushing away from the table, she washed the eggs down with a swig of coffee and then walked into the living room. "I know what you're trying to do, and it won't work. There was no telegram. Tony Walters is dead, and shame on you for using a dead man in your scheming."

"No telegram?"

"That's what I said. No telegram."

"Yes, there was," he said. "I got confirmation it was delivered to you."

"Not to me."

He was sitting in her rocking chair again, pushing one foot against the floor and making the chair move in a slow, steady motion. He barely glanced her way as he dug in his breast pocket, pulled out a picture and handed it to her.

Lisa's heart constricted inside her chest as she recognized the family in the picture. Her, her mother and father. "Where did you get this?"

"From your father."

Disgusted, she glared at him. "You mean my stepfather. The man who put you up to all this."

"I've never met your stepfather, and I got that from Tony. He'd carried it with him since he left for the war. That's why it's so tattered. He said the doll you're holding was one he'd given you for Christmas, you named her Marie."

Lisa grabbed the back of the sofa with her free hand at a wave of lightheadedness. The picture was tattered and faded, and Duane wouldn't have known, or cared where she'd gotten the doll or what she'd named her. "He can't be alive." Her throat burned. "He would have come home."

"You really didn't receive the telegram?"

She shook her head, not able to speak.

"I'm sorry," he said kindly. "One was sent and I received confirmation that it was delivered."

Confusion over so many things had her mind spinning. "It wasn't delivered to me. If he is alive, why didn't he come home?"

"He'll explain that to you."

She couldn't pull her eyes off the picture. It was taken on the front porch of the house, shortly before her father had left for the war, and the doll, Marie, was on the shelf in her closet. "He really gave this to you? He's really alive?"

"Yes, and yes. He gave it to me in New York. That's where he's at."

It was so hard to believe that her father was alive. Impossible to believe. "Is he in trouble with the law?"

"No. He's not in trouble with the law. In fact, he helped my department bust a major bootlegging mob."

She sat down on the arm of the sofa. "Is he a cop, too?" A brief moment of hope rose up inside her, then shattered. Duane would be furious to learn her father was alive, and no one, not even a bull, would be able to help her. She was in too deep. Furthermore, the town needed her. It had been on the verge of drying up and blowing away when she'd opened the Depot.

"No. Tony's not a cop."

Lisa swallowed hard and slid off the arm of the sofa, onto the cushion. "Why are you here?"

He stopped the chair from rocking, and settled a gaze on her that was so direct, so intense, her insides shivered.

"Your father is dying, Lisa. He has cancer."

There was an odd ringing in her ears, and she held her eyes wide open because if she closed them, tears would form.

She'd already cried for years. When her father had left, when she'd been told he'd died, and for years afterward, wishing that he hadn't left and that he hadn't died.

That was enough. More than enough crying over one man—any man.

Even her father... Her mind, still spinning, went down another route. The Tony Walters she knew, the father she remembered, would have come home. A shiver rippled her spine. This bull wasn't on the level. One single picture wasn't enough proof for her to believe he was telling her the truth. He had to be in cahoots with Duane. There was no other reason for him to be here, to be doing this to her.

Controlling her every movement as strongly as she was her emotions, she rose. "Thank you for telling me." She walked to the door, wrapped her hand around the knob. "You may leave now."

He rose.

She kept her eyes on the rockers of the chair, how they continued to move back and forth as he walked closer. It kept her focus off the pain trying to enter her heart. But it didn't work. Unable to stop it, the pain from her childhood sprang forth, at how badly the death of her father had hurt.

Mick stopped directly in front of her and leaned one hand against the door. "I'm here to take you to New York, to see him."

"New York?" Her emotions released in the form of a laugh. That happened when she was nervous, scared, hurt, but it also helped. "I'm not going to New York. Not now, not ever."

"Yes, you are. So you can hear directly from Tony what happened, and so he can say his goodbyes."

A new wave of anger filled her. Duane was trying to get rid of her. That's what was going on here, and she wasn't about to let that happen. "Tony said his goodbyes years ago, when he left for Europe."

Mick looked at her oddly. That was fine. He could think whatever he wanted about her. She hadn't bought his lies and wasn't about to, but she was going to find a way to get rid of him. Now. And prove to Duane that he couldn't get rid of her that easy. He wanted the Depot, and all the revenue it brought in. Had since the beginning and hated the fact that she'd put her foot down back then, had said that the only way he could use her property was if she ran the joint. He also hated how she shared her success with the town.

"Tony deserves the opportunity to make things right. It's weighed heavy on him for years."

Lisa kept her head up. He was good, trying to pull on her heartstrings. If only he knew the kind of weight she'd lived with for years. The child of the town's hero. That was a hard role for a kid, it kept his death, his absence front and center, and alive.

And then there was her stepfather. Duane had practically run this town into the ground with the ruffians his saloon had brought to town. The past three years, she'd worked at changing all that.

At first people couldn't believe she'd gone into business with him, but then she'd proven how it could help everyone. And it did.

Come midnight on her busiest nights, every business owner was there, selling their wares at the train station.

The money she donated to the school was appreciated, too. Playground equipment, books, chalkboards, desks—whatever they needed, she'd supplied it the past two years. Just last week, the city council had received a letter from the state board of education, commending them on supporting their local school and stating they could expect a visitor from the state board soon to present them with an accolade.

Duane was keen on taking credit for the accolade, even though he constantly criticized her for all she did for the school and community.

Duane had to be behind all this, and wasn't going to get away with it.

"...tomorrow."

She shook her head. "What did you say? About tomorrow?"

"I said we'll leave tomorrow. That should give you time to get things in order here. Someone to take over during your absence."

"What part of *I'm not going to New York* didn't you understand? I don't know how I can say it to make it any clearer than that. I'm not going anywhere." Finding someone to take over for her was just as ludicrous. No one could run the Depot like she did.

"What part of we are leaving tomorrow did you not understand?"

He still had his hand on the door, otherwise she would have pulled it open. He wasn't like anyone she'd known. He was stubborn, but there was more to it than that. He was... She couldn't put her finger on it, but he was different. He wouldn't take no for an answer, but it went beyond that.

He was confident. That's what he was.

Well, she was, too.

"Or maybe," he said, "I should have asked, what part of the Depot being busted, tonight, did you not understand?"

She understood that, but it wasn't going to happen. She wasn't going to New York, either. Time was what she needed, just a few moments to figure out a plan. Releasing the doorknob, she walked across the room, trying to engage her mind. Issues, trouble, came up all the time—she was used to finding solutions quickly.

Yes! Turning, she nodded. "I'll call him. He can say his goodbyes on the phone." There was no way her father was alive. Problem solved.

"No. He needs to see you in person."

He certainly was stubborn, and stuck on lying to her. She might as well lie back. "I truly don't care what he needs. There's no reason for me to see him. He had his chance to be a father and gave it up by not coming home."

She questioned if she'd finally gotten through, because Mick nodded and took a hold of the doorknob.

"I will expect you to be at the train station at noon tomorrow." He opened the door. "Good day."

The door shut before she could respond.

Not that she'd had a response prepared. She was speechless.

Her brain was working though.

Who did he think he was? Telling her what she was and was not going to do. That did not happen. She told people what they were going to do. Not the other way around. This was all a ploy that she wasn't going to fall for.

That was something Mick McCormick from New York was going to figure out. She walked into the kitchen and lifted the earpiece off the wall phone. "Sarah, ring Buck Hendrick."

The line crackled and sizzled, then a far-off ring echoed. When Buck answered, Lisa said, "I need to see you boys now. At the barn."

She hung up. There were four trains that rolled through Junction. Seven in the morning and seven in the evening that went south. Noon and midnight that went north. Mick McCormick would be on a southbound one. Tonight. She'd see to it. A slow smiled formed on her lips. Before he woke up, he'd be in Texas.

Chapter Five

Thanks to Twila O'Neil, Mick never let his guard down when it came to a woman. Twila had happened his first year on the force, when he'd been a rookie beat cop, covering the streets on overnight shifts. She'd been an actress at one of the playhouses and appeared so sincere and innocent—his first mistake, trusting. She'd been beautiful, with short blond hair, big brown eyes and a body that curved in all the right places—mistake two, attraction. She'd claimed she'd never met anyone like him—mistake three, gullible.

That had been him, five years ago. He'd trusted her, been attracted to her and had been made a fool by her. For the first time in his life, he'd had time for himself, time to date women. Up until then, he'd been too busy, first following in his father's footsteps, and then becoming a cop.

He'd learned a solid lesson from Twila, and would never fall into that trap again. Into any woman's trap.

Therefore, when he noticed a beat-up truck roaring through Junction while walking to the hotel after leaving Lisa's place, and recognizing the three men in the truck—two in the front and one in the back because all three of the farm boys wouldn't fit in the front—he knew what he had to do.

Mick proceeded to the hotel, collected his bag and turned in the key. Next, he went to the train station, bought two tickets and left his suitcase to be loaded on the noon train with the ticket master, a different one than the one who'd been sleeping in the office last night. From there, he crossed the field to Lisa's house. The truck was there. Red and black and dented everywhere a vehicle could be dented.

Having scoped out the house this morning before knocking, Mick snuck up behind the barn. The gin joint was beneath the barn, and though the building had been locked earlier, the door was open a crack right now. All he could see was a huge stack of hay bales, some so old they were turning gray. By the worn path to the stack, he could imagine that behind those bales were crates of whiskey bottles and kegs of beer to be hauled downstairs. A door to the speakeasy was most likely behind that hay, too.

He didn't push the barn door open any further to check, because of the voices. One particularly.

"No one, and I mean no one, can know about this," Lisa was saying. "Not even Fred. I don't have to tell you what Duane will do if he finds out."

There were mumbles of agreement and then footsteps. Mick eased away from the door and then around the building to the backside where he stayed until the truck drove away and Lisa walked back into her house.

It was a good thing he never underestimated anyone. He didn't know exactly what her plan entailed, nor did he care. His would overrule hers.

Mick walked to the house and entered the back door.

She was in the kitchen, and spun around, eyes wide. "What—"

"Pack a bag."

"What? I'm not packing anything!" She tried to shoot around him.

He blocked the door and crossed his arms. "You either pack a bag or we leave without one. It's up to you."

She planted her hands on her hips. "I'm not going to New York or anywhere else with you."

"Yes, you are. Now pack a bag."

"No, I'm not. And I will not pack a bag."

Tension was building in his neck. He really didn't like dealing with women. The faster he got this over with, the better. A suitcase was a minor detail. He'd just been trying to be kind. That was over. She'd had the last chance he was going to give her.

"Suit yourself." He grabbed her wrist with one hand and the handcuffs out of his pocket with his other hand.

"What are you doing? You can't handcuff me!"

"Yes, I can, and I will." He held the cuff over her wrist. "Either you agree to go to New York, or I'll arrest you."

"For what?"

He lifted a brow.

She huffed out a breath. "I'm not going—"

"Going anywhere with you!" he mocked. "I've already heard that, and you are going with me. To New York."

"Why?"

"To see your father!" He shoved the handcuffs back in his pocket. He'd had no intention of using them and noting a purse on a table near the door, he picked it up. As he started to hand it to her, he paused. Knowing her, she'd just hit him with it. Concluding she might need something out of it along the way, he hooked the handles of the purse over the wrist of his free hand, locked the back door, then motioned her to go to the front door.

Once outside, she turned and glared at him.

"If you don't let me go right now, I'm going to scream and the whole town will come running."

He shrugged. "If you scream, your stepfather is going to know you're gone before the train leaves, at which point I will have to explain to him that the state police are on their way to bust the gin joint the two of you have beneath your barn."

Her eyes grew wide. "You called the police?"

He didn't lie, and wouldn't, not even in this instance. "Not yet. But I will from the train station if you don't cooperate."

"Cooperate? Why would I—"

"Fine." He locked the front door, dropping the key in her purse. "I'll call the police. I'll also be sure to tell them about your scheme to have your farm boys knock me in the head."

"How do y—?" She stopped midword and pinched her lips together.

"I may have been born at night, but it wasn't last night."

She huffed out a breath. "They weren't going to hurt you, just—"

"Get rid of me?"

She glared at him again. "Yes, and they will, too."

He paused, and although he didn't want to give her the benefit of any doubt, he saw something raw in her eyes. He understood what he saw, too. She was too stubborn to believe anything that he'd told her. "You still don't believe Tony is alive, do you?"

"I know he's not alive. He would have come home if he was."

Mick glanced over toward the barn. Tony had told him far more than what he'd needed to know, but all of that was for father and daughter to hash out. His debt was to Tony. Mobster or not, Tony had gone above and beyond in order for the Valentino Family to be busted. Based out of Buffalo, the *Family* had been the major manufacturer and supplier of booze in the region, and had been attempting to set up a branch in Rochester, and Mick owed Tony for how he'd helped get the Family arrested. He had to convince her to come to New York any way he could. "How old were you when you fell out of the barn loft?"

He felt the way she shivered.

"How do you know about that?"

"I know that your father caught you, and when he put you down on the ground, to check to make sure you weren't hurt, all you did was laugh, and ask if you could do that again." Mick nodded as she stared up at him. "It's one of his favorite stories about you," he said. "I've heard it several times."

She shook her head, and blinked as if fighting off tears.

He looked away, not wanting to see them. "Your father is alive, Lisa, and he wants to see you, to explain things. It's his dying wish."

Mick couldn't help but wonder if this could also be a wake-up call for her. One that might make her realize that she couldn't live her entire life on the wrong side of the law. Her little gig was sure to get busted sooner or later, and if half of the things that Tony had said about her stepfather were true, she'd be the one to go down.

That angered him, deeper than it should. "It won't

take long. Three days to New York, you'll see your father, talk to him, then return."

"Why didn't he ever contact me?" she asked softly.

Mick had to look at her, and his gut took a punch at the pain he saw in her eyes. "He's the only one who can answer that."

She closed her eyes and bit down on her bottom lip so hard it went from pink to white.

Mick clamped his back teeth together to keep from saying more as he waited for the battle she silently fought to come to a conclusion.

Far off in the distance, a train whistle sounded.

"That's our ride," he needlessly told her.

She stood stock-still, and if there ever was a time that he wanted to know what someone was thinking, it was now. That battle was still going on inside her, and he didn't know her well enough to guess which way she'd go.

Lips pinched and her blue eyes shimmering with unshed tears, she lifted her chin. "Fine. I'll go to New York, but there's something you should know, I'm not a good traveling partner."

A bit surprised, he handed her the purse, glad to not have to get on the train with it on his wrist. "Traveled a lot, have you?"

She snatched the purse out of his hand. "No, but don't expect me to even talk to you."

"Nothing would please me more."

She sneered at him.

Caught somewhere between his mistrust of women and understanding her frustration, was an odd sense of respect. He did respect her. She'd been through a lot and came out on top. There was admiration in that.

They had to hurry and she marched along beside

him, head up. He wanted to know what had changed her mind, but would wait to ask until after she was actually on the train. The stubbornness she'd displayed earlier said she could still bolt before that happened.

The porter was putting his suitcase in the baggage car as they approached the station. Pulling out the two tickets, Mick waved them at the porter and escorted Lisa onto the train. No one else boarded, and the few people that were on the train were all near the back.

She chose a bench seat near the front, and he sat down on the seat across the aisle from her.

There wasn't much to see as the train pulled out of the station, yet she kept her head turned, as if staring out the window. He told himself that he was fine with that. Would be fine if she held true to not talking, as well. The sooner all of this was over, the happier he'd be.

That part was true. He'd be happy when this was all over.

The part that wasn't true, was that he wasn't fine with the way she was staring out the window. It made him want to sit next to her, comfort her, and that was unusual for him. Disruptive to all he knew about himself.

"Tickets."

Mick handed them to the porter, who punched holes in each one, marking the first leg of the long journey ahead of them. The porter handed the tickets back to him, glancing at Lisa several times.

"Thank you," Mick said, pulling the porter's attention off Lisa and then tucking the tickets back in his suit pocket.

The porter nodded and walked away.

Mick scooted to the edge of the seat and leaned across the aisle. "Does he know who you are?" he asked her.

She shrugged.

He wondered what the town would think about her absence, but not so much that he was overly obligated to worry about it. "Well, word will get out one way or the other," he said.

She made no response, verbally or physically. Maybe she would hold true to her threat of silence. If she did, it would be a first. He'd never known a woman who could keep silent for long.

He was a bit surprised that she did keep silent during the half hour train ride to Kansas City, and while they departed the train and boarded the one to Chicago.

The passenger car was nearly full, but at least the seats were padded on this one.

With eyes watching their every move, they found an open bench in the center of the train. He waited for her to sit down, near the window, then sat beside her. Once again, she stared out the window.

"Do you have enough room?" he asked.

She clutched the purse on her lap, leaned back and closed her eyes.

He glanced around. She was keeping her promise of silence. It wasn't as enjoyable as he'd thought. Not that he expected any of this to be enjoyable. She was just distracting, and he hadn't expected that. He wasn't easily distracted.

Others on the train were. There was hardly a pair of male eyes that weren't finding their way toward her.

Mick relaxed against the seat. Let them look. She was pretty. Eye-catching pretty. He could admit that. It didn't change anything. She was Tony's daughter and he was taking her to Rochester.

The train began chugging forward and he dug in his pocket as the porter started collecting and punching tickets.

It was the scarf, he concluded while waiting for the porter to make it to their bench. The reason men kept looking at her. The scarf was fetching. Made her fetching, the way it was tied around her head, with the long ends hanging down, over her shoulder, amongst the waves of her honey-brown hair. The blue and white polka-dot dress was fetching, too. The way it exposed the smooth skin of her arms and legs, and the scooped neckline showed a hint of the creamy skin covering her collarbones.

One man, with a derby hat and brushy black eyebrows, had yet to look away from her, and that was inching up Mick's irritability. He leveled a glare at the man, and when the man's gaze shifted slightly to him, Mick opened his suit jacket, just enough to flash the badge pinned on the inside of his lapel at the man.

It was enough to make the man look away. It also caught the porter's attention.

Holding out his hand for the tickets, the porter asked, "Do you need any additional accommodations?"

Mick gave the man the tickets. Some railroad lines allowed law agents to transport detainees for free and would provide special accommodations as needed. Lisa wasn't a prisoner and he didn't believe that anyone needed to know the truth behind their travels whatsoever. "No."

The porter punched the tickets and handed them back. "Let me know if that changes."

A sense of defensiveness rose up in him as Mick nodded and tucked the tickets back in his pocket. He had no personal interest in Lisa, other than delivering her to Tony, but he didn't want others to think she was the worst sort of criminal, either. He'd flashed his badge to deter the man from staring, not so the porter would think she was under arrest. That was a sure way to spread rumors. This train would take them all the way to Chicago. With all the stops in small towns, though, they wouldn't arrive until well after midnight.

Mick twisted and touched the porter's arm, who was punching tickets of the passengers in the seat behind them.

"Yes, sir?"

"She's not a prisoner," Mick said for only the porter to hear. "We're just traveling together."

The man nodded. "I see. I'm sorry if I offended her." He then leaned across Mick, and said to Lisa, "My apologies, ma'am."

Lisa nodded at the porter, and then turned to Mick, wondering what he'd said to the porter to make him apologize.

"I told him that you weren't a prisoner," Mick said quietly.

She'd said she wouldn't speak, so she couldn't ask why the porter would think that.

"He'd seen my badge," Mick said.

She turned and looked back out the window. Whether someone had seen his badge, or thought she was a prisoner, was the least of her worries at this moment in time.

She still didn't believe her father was alive. He couldn't be. The man who had caught her when she'd fallen out of the hayloft had loved her, and her mother. He would never have not come home to them.

Yet, at the same time, she couldn't help but question if he had. Had not come home to them. That he was alive and had never even attempted to contact them.

That hurt. Hurt in ways she'd never imagined. She squeezed the purse on her lap with both hands as anger filled her. How could he do that to her? To her mother? The very people he'd claimed to love.

She wanted to cry, to scream, but that wouldn't solve anything. She wanted to know why. Had to know why. That was the only reason she was on this train, but now that she was, she was also wondering if her spur of the moment decision to go to New York was the right one. If her other thoughts had been true, that Mick was working with Duane and wanted her out of town. Gone.

She was just so confused. Her mind a jumbled mess. However, of the two scenarios Mick working in cahoots with Duane was far more plausible than Tony being alive. That was part of why she'd agreed to go, to find out exactly what Duane was trying to pull.

There was money in her purse. More than enough to get her back home once she knew the truth. She'd been surprised when Mick had picked it up, and was glad that he had. He, though, would be surprised about what was in her purse at some point in the near future.

Lisa licked her lips. Not talking to him was difficult—she had plenty of questions. About many things, including him. Why was he doing this? Why would a bull from New York be helping Duane? There had to be something in it for him. Most likely money. Some men couldn't seem to get enough of it.

He'd leaned back in the seat and had closed his eyes and she eased a sigh out of her lungs, quietly, so he wouldn't hear. The back of the seat had pushed his hat forward, so it partially hid his face. A black fedora with a shiny silk band. It was as spiffy looking as his pinstriped suit. Something about him made her heart flutter in an odd way.

She really wanted to hate him. Tony had been gone

for years, and she'd gotten used to that. The idea that he was alive and had never once contacted her was so...

A chill slithered up her spine. Her house. The farm. That had to be what this was all about! It was in her name. That was the one thing her mother had insisted upon. Even before she'd had her stroke, she'd insisted that it never be put in Duane's name. Her mother and Duane had argued over that more than once, and as soon as Lisa had been old enough, the deed had been changed to her name.

Why would a cop from New York... Or maybe he wasn't a cop. Maybe that badge was stolen and he wasn't from New York any more than she was.

Lisa's thoughts went up and down many roads as the train chugged onward, stopping in nearly every small town to let people on and off. All sorts of people. She'd been on a train only the few times she'd taken one to Kansas City and she was already tired of sitting. Very tired of sitting.

"We'll get off at the next stop," Mick said.

The sound of his voice startled her. He hadn't said a word since telling her he'd told the porter she wasn't a prisoner hours ago. "Why?"

He pushed his hat back and sat up straight. "To eat. We won't arrive in Chicago until after midnight, and everything will be closed." He grinned. "There won't be a midnight bazaar like you have in Junction. That's pretty ingenious. Who came up with that idea?"

She had sworn not to talk, but that had gotten old. Fast. Maybe if she told him the truth, she'd get the truth out of him. "I did."

He didn't appear shocked. Instead he nodded, as if that was plausible, but perhaps not completely possible. "Congratulations."

"Why do you say it like that?"

"Like what?"

"Like you don't really believe me." She didn't want anything about him to bother her, but him not believing her did bother her. She'd worked hard to get the stores to participate in her idea of a marketplace at the train station. No one had thought her idea would work at first, which had made her even more determined to prove it would.

"I believe you," he said. "It's ingenious. I can see why you did it. If the entire town is benefitting, no one will want your business shut down."

Her ire increased. "That's not the reason I did it."

He lifted a brow. "Then what is?"

"The town was dying. The only customers any of the businesses had were local residents, and none of them had much money to spend. The train didn't even stop in Junction. It used to, a long time ago, but over the years, there had been no reason to stop, no one to get off or on."

"How did you make that happen? The train stopping again?"

Skepticism rose up inside her. "Why?"

Shrugging, he said, "Just curious." Then, after studying her with an intense stare, he continued, "I'm not investigating you or your joint. As long as you see your father, listen to his side of the story, I'll forget everything that I saw in Junction."

"Including my stepfather?"

"Duane Kemper."

She held her tongue and nodded, waiting for him to try and weasel his way out of not knowing Duane now.

He frowned, and then after a few moments of staring at her, laughed. "You think I'm somehow working with your stepfather, don't you?"

"I don't think. I know."

"You're wrong. I don't know your stepfather, nor do I want to, but I do know Tony, and I know how much he wants to see you again." He gave her a quick once-over glance. "He thinks you are a schoolteacher."

A shiver rippled through Lisa. That was what she'd always wanted to be, from the time she'd been little. She'd loved school and had planned on taking her state exam when her mother had become ill. Very ill. A stroke, one that left her paralyzed, bedridden. After her mother had died, the reason she hadn't completed her dream of becoming a schoolteacher was because that's what Duane had told her to do, and leave the running of the speakeasy to him.

She hadn't been willing to lose her house back then, and still wasn't now. "Why are you doing this?" she asked.

Lines formed on his forehead as he grew thoughtful. "A man, any man, deserves the chance to make things right before he dies."

Her throat burned, so did her eyes.

"I'm not lying to you, Lisa. Your father is alive."

For whatever reason, she believed him. Completely. She had spent the past ten years wishing her father was alive, and now that he was, she didn't know what to think. What to wish. "How long have you known him?"

"A few years."

She stared at him, waiting for more.

He rubbed a hand over his chin. "I met Tony while he was in prison."

"Prison?" She shifted in her seat to look at him directly. "You said he wasn't in jail."

"He's not." Lifting a brow, a hint of a grin on his face. "He got out a few months ago."

She shook her head and tried hard not to grin back at the mischievous glint in his eyes. There was nothing funny about any of this, but his admission, his show of humor of how he hadn't lied, but had stretched the truth, made him, well, human, and likeable. She didn't want him to be likeable. Didn't want to like anything about him. Glancing away, she asked, "What was he in prison for?"

"Bootlegging. He was a member of a gang my department busted in Rochester. I knew he'd have information about a rival gang and interviewed him. He agreed to help us bust the rival gang, and I agreed to find you to repay him."

"Is that why he's out of prison, because he helped you?"

"No, he's out because he served his time."

"But he's a snitch." She shook her head. To a lot of people, being a snitch was worse than being a bootlegger.

"No, he's not a snitch. He didn't work for the rival gang, and he didn't use the information he shared to keep him out of jail."

"A snitch is a snitch."

"Think what you must, but he's not in any danger, and neither are you."

"I never thought I was." Not the kind of danger he was referring to. Seeing her father did scare her because she never wanted to care about someone like she had him. Never wanted to be hurt the way he'd hurt her again. Knowing he'd forgotten all about her hurt even worse than his death had. It made her stomach knot.

She couldn't go through with this. Just couldn't. She had to find a way to escape, get back to Junction.

Chapter Six

Lisa hadn't expected the opportunity to escape to come up so quickly, but it appeared, practically out of the blue as soon as they'd finished eating. While standing in line to pay for their meal, she saw the sign to the ladies' room down a long hallway.

"Go ahead," Mick said. "This line is moving slow. I'll meet you on the boarding platform."

With little more than a nod, she walked down the hallway, and around the corner to the powder room door.

The small, cramped room was at the very end of the depot, near another door that she assumed went outside, to the back of the depot. She'd wavered between which door to open, but ultimately had chosen the powder room. Mainly because an odd sense of guilt had entered her. It wasn't as if she was betraying Mick. She had agreed to accompany him to New York, but because she had no other choice. She truly didn't want to go. Now that she figured Duane wasn't involved, she didn't want him to discover she was gone.

Leaning against the sink, she sucked in a deep breath. The depot was larger than the one in Junction, but not nearly as big as the one in Kansas City. Surely, she could find a place to hide. Mick wouldn't leave without her, though. She was sure of that, and he could call the local police to help look for her, which could cause a whole other issue.

He could also call the cops in Missouri and have the Depot busted.

Pressing a hand to her forehead, Lisa questioned what to do. She didn't want to go to New York, meet her father, but she didn't want to end up in jail, either. Not because of escaping Mick or because the Depot was busted. Everything she'd worked so hard to accomplish the past few years would be completely over then. All her work would have been for naught.

No, it wouldn't. Because she wouldn't let that happen. She'd go to New York, give her father a piece of her mind for leaving her and her mother on their own, and then return and continue to keep the town safe from Duane. She'd also find a way to keep him from knowing she was gone. As much as she didn't want to ask for his help, Mick might be able to help her in that respect.

Deciding that's what she'd have to do, she'd barely touched the knob when the door flew open, forcing her backward. Up against the wall, she froze at the sight of a man from the train. One who had stared at her until she'd closed her eyes to block him from her mind after they'd boarded in Kansas City.

"Got yourself in some trouble, doll?" he asked, entering the room and closing the door behind him.

An icy shiver rippled through her at his hoarse-sounding voice, red-rimmed eyes and yellow teeth. "No," she replied firmly, while clutching her purse against her stomach.

"I saw that bull you're traveling with." He touched

her arm. "I can help you give him the slip. Know a place we can hide."

If she hadn't already figured out that giving Mick the bum's rush here was a bad idea, she would have now. Especially upon hearing the *we* this man had used. She was used to fending off men, but usually there was a wide bar in front of her and the Hendrick boys flanking her. There was no way around this guy—he was blocking the door. Slowly, she unhooked the clasp on her purse.

His grin grew, making his eyebrows raise. "Let's blow, doll. I know what you need."

The toilet stool was on one side of her, the sink the other. Scared and trapped, she flattened against the wall to avoid his touch, and stench. Fear clawed at her throat, but she held it in as she slid her hand in her purse, found the cold metal of the gun and pulled it out. Leveling the small derringer at the thug, she said, "Get out of here! Now!"

"You aren't going to shoot me, doll."

No, she wasn't, because there weren't any bullets in the gun! Dagnabit! Not about to let him know that, she kept the gun pointed at him, until he lurched forward. With a scream, she kicked him, hard. As he let out a loud growl, doubling over and stumbling back against the door, she jumped sideways and up, landing precariously on the stool.

The door flew open, hitting the man and making him lurch forward again. With the gun still in her hand, she smacked the goon on the head, and flinched at the thud that sounded as his head struck the side of the sink.

Mick grabbed her arm, pulled her off the stool and shoved her behind him as he stepped all the way into the tiny room.

She moved further into the hallway, but didn't put the gun away because Mick leaped forward.

"Give me your scarf," Mick said as he grabbed the man and hoisted him sideways, onto the toilet stool.

Lisa didn't ask why. Her heart was pounding too hard and fast to think. She pulled the scarf off her head with one hand and gave it to him.

"Untie it," Mick instructed while positioning the thug so he was sitting on the stool with one shoulder up against the wall.

Blood trickled from the thug's forehead as his head hung limply.

She dropped the gun in her purse and untied the scarf with shaking fingers, then handed it to Mick and glanced up and down the hallway, fearful someone would see what was happening. The hall was empty and when she looked into the bathroom again, Mick was on his knees, tying the thug's legs to the base of the stool with her scarf.

Lisa's heart was still pounding. All she wanted to do was get back on the train and out of this town. She didn't know the name of the town, but they were somewhere in Illinois that she didn't want to be. "What are you doing?" she asked, glancing into the hallway again. It was still empty, but someone could come around the corner at any minute.

"Making sure he misses the train," Mick said.

The thug was slumped against the wall. "He doesn't look like he's going anywhere. Tied up or not."

"Never trust a thug. He's just stunned." Mick stood. "Are you all right?"

"I'm fine, but we need to leave before someone sees us. Sees him."

"We are leaving." He grabbed the thin linen hand

towel hanging on the small round towel rack and stepped into the hallway beside her. Then he stuffed a corner of the towel in the door latch hole and then pulled the door shut, with the towel on the inside of the door.

"Why did you do that?" she asked.

"It makes the door hard to open. People will think it's locked." He grasped her elbow. "Let's go."

She hurried down the hall beside him, her heart still thumping, but now it was pounding because of her escape. The entire episode hadn't taken more than a few minutes, but she truly hadn't been that frightened in a long time. In her line of work, she encountered unsavory men from time to time, which was why she carried the gun, but she'd never had to pull it out before.

"Where's your gun?" Mick asked.

"In my purse."

They exited the depot and hurried across the platform to the train, where Mick stepped aside so she could climb up the steps first.

She found an empty bench and took a seat.

He sat beside her. "An unloaded gun is worse than no gun."

Her spine shivered. "How do you know it's not loaded?"

His look held shrewdness.

"It could be loaded," she insisted.

"I'm sure it could be, but it's not."

She rolled her eyes and huffed out a breath. "Because I wouldn't want it to accidently go off in my purse. But the bullets are in there, too."

He turned his head, but not before she saw a grin form.

"They are," she insisted.

"I'm sure they are." He looked at her and shook his

head. "I guess I should congratulate you on your quick thinking, though you shouldn't be playing with guns."

Lisa took a moment to study him, question if he was telling the truth. Before she could conclude anything, her mind went down a different route. She found herself looking for a flaw. Not in his statement, but in his looks. He was as handsome as she'd first thought. Especially his eyes. They were cornflower blue, encircled with dark lashes and thick brows that naturally arched from the bridge of his nose to his temples. His face was narrow, his nose, cheeks and chin flawlessly defined. Even his ears were perfect. It just didn't seem right that there wasn't a thing about his looks that she didn't like. She even liked his hat. How it sat slightly cocked to the left.

The train whistle blew as the wheels began to turn and he touched her hand. "Are you all right?"

She huffed out a breath, so very thankful to be leaving this town.

Once she didn't have to speak over the noise, she said, "Yes, I'm fine, but do you think he's hurt badly? There was blood on his head."

"From where it hit the sink. He deserved what he got, so don't feel bad about it."

"Yes, he did," she agreed. She just didn't like seeing anyone hurt, not that bad.

He patted her hand and then leaned back in his seat. "He'd paid for his meal before I did, and had gone out to the platform. When I'd noticed he'd disappeared, I knew he'd followed you."

"Why would you know that?"

"Because of the way he'd been watching you on the train." He chuckled again. "I didn't expect to see you thumping him on the head with a gun when I opened that door."

"Well, I didn't expect to see you throw open the door."

"We didn't get off on the best foot," he said. "But we teamed up pretty well against that thug. Hopefully he'll think twice about cornering another woman."

"I hope so," she agreed, and also had to agree on his other comment, out of honesty if nothing more. "Due to the circumstances and all, we didn't get off on the best foot."

"Because you thought I was working for your step-father."

She wasn't sure how he knew that, just like she wasn't sure how he knew her gun hadn't had any bullets in it. "That made more sense to me than Tony being alive. That still doesn't seem possible to me."

"It's possible, because he is alive." He frowned while saying, "What doesn't make sense to me is why you'd think I was working with your stepfather."

Not wanting to think about Duane right now, she said, "Like I said, it made more sense than for you to have traveled all the way from New York to tell me that Tony wants to see me."

He stared at her for a long moment, before he said, "Tony doesn't know you're coming."

Confused, she asked, "You didn't have time to call and tell him you found me?"

He shook his head. "I never told him I was coming to get you."

Her stomach did a slight flip-flop. "But you said seeing me is his dying wish."

"It is, but he never asked me to come get you. I'd told him that I'd check into your whereabouts, find out if you were still in Junction, but when you never responded to my telegram, I decided to come find you, and surprise him."

"I told you I never got a telegram." Not overly sure that he believed her about that, she asked, "Where did you send it?"

"To Junction, but the confirmation said it had been delivered to your home first thing in the morning."

"Delivered to me or left at my door?" She shook her head. "I'm never awake first thing in the morning. For all I know, the wind could have blown it away."

He shook his head. "That's why I sent it as a telegram, so it would be delivered to a person."

She had to draw in a breath at the way her heart dropped to her stomach. The only person it could have been delivered to would have been Duane. He often oversaw the deliveries of booze to her barn in the mornings, and he wouldn't have ever told her about a telegram saying her father was alive.

"Tony didn't know about your mother's death until he was released from prison and he's worried about you," Mick said.

Lisa closed her eyes. She was worried, too. Especially now that she knew Duane knew that Tony was alive. Now she had to go to New York, just to warn her father if nothing else. Mick was in danger, too. Duane wouldn't like the fact he was a bull.

He cocked his head. "How long have you been running the Depot?"

"Three years," she answered absently, while wondering if Duane would follow her to New York. She had to return before he figured out where she was. That was all there was to it.

"Since you were eighteen?"

She nodded.

"What made you do that instead of teaching?"

A heaviness filled her chest. "My mother had a stroke. I had to take care of her."

"What about after she died?"

Lisa glanced out the window as she contemplated answering. It was growing dark, and her mind shifted to the Depot. People would be wondering why she wasn't there. That hadn't happened since the doors had opened. Duane would know by morning that she'd left, if not sooner, and be mad. It was an awful thought, but a part of her wanted things to go badly in her absence, so Duane would finally understand all that she did. But it was what he might do to the town that worried her, and she felt bad for the extra work that her absence would put on everyone else. Duane wouldn't step up to help, other than to collect the money on Sunday as usual.

She turned, looked at Mick. For whatever reason, she wanted to tell him the truth. "By the time my mother died, I didn't have a choice. Not if I wanted to keep my home."

He leaned back against the seat. "Your stepfather wanted to sell it?"

"No. It had already been put in my name. My mother saw to that as soon as I was old enough. But Duane was already using the barn as a speakeasy. He'd had one downtown until it had been busted, so when my mother had her stroke, he decided to use the barn." She shrugged. "The way he was running things, it would be busted, too, in no time, so I laid down some rules."

"You laid down some rules?"

There was humor in his tone. She understood how that could sound unbelievable. Her stepfather had thought the same thing, but she'd stuck to her guns.

Her mother had always said that once she'd made up her mind, there was no changing it, and she held on to that like a legacy. The only one she had, besides her property, which she held on to just as strongly. "Yes. It's my property, so I laid down rules. Said it would be my way or no way."

"And?"

When it came right down to it, that's what she was most proud of—how she'd proven she'd been right. "I won. Believe it or not."

Mick believed it. She was stubborn enough to make sure she'd won. Not sure how much that goon in the bathroom had upset her, he wanted to keep her talking. From what he'd surmised about her so far, he didn't expect a tearful meltdown, but he'd seen women flip, and a sobbing female was exactly what he was trying to avoid. Exactly what he had been avoiding for years.

He was also still trying to bury his own anger—at himself. He shouldn't have let her go to the powder room alone, not with the way that goon had been watching her on the train. Which was why he'd been watching the goon. The moment he'd noticed the guy had disappeared from the platform, he'd cut ahead in line, thrown bills on the counter and run down the hallway to the ladies' room. Opening that door and seeing her bashing the guy on the head with a gun had scared ten years off his life. Thank heavens that gun hadn't been loaded. It could have gone off. "What did that mean?" he asked, trying to sound normal. "You winning?"

She frowned slightly. "Well, for starters, the barn only had a small basement. From when it used to be a dairy farm and the milk was stored down there. My grandparents had died before the war, and after my father left, the dairy was too much for my mother, so she sold the herd. I had the basement expanded, so the speakeasy could be down there instead of inside the barn, and I had the tunnel built to the train station. Surprisingly, it didn't take long because half the men in town were looking for work, a way to make enough money to feed their families."

He could believe that, too. While much of the nation was seeing an economic boom, small farm communities were drying up. It was that way in New York state, too. "I see. And then you started the marketplace at midnight, once the speakeasy was built?"

"Not at first. In the beginning, I provided food for customers, but that soon became too much, so I talked to the owners of both restaurants. First, I had them bring the food in, but that didn't work out very well. People would eat and then start drinking again and they'd miss the train, so I suggested the marketplace. Within no time, the drugstore also had a table, and then the grocer, and soon, everyone in town was setting up a booth, selling their wares."

"How did you get the train to stop in Junction again?" That seemed to be the one thing that had made everything work for her.

"Fred Myers. His brother works for the railroad."

He waited for her to say more. When she didn't, he asked, "Fred is the ticket master?"

"Yes. His brother wasn't sure if he could convince the railroad to stop in Junction again, but when I promised him that I'd buy the first one hundred round trip tickets, he was willing to try."

"That was quite the investment," he told her.

"I had to make it work. Didn't have another choice." She glanced around, as if to make sure no one was listening before she leaned closer. "I gave those one hundred tickets to the Hendrick boys, had them drive to Kansas City and pass them out at the saloons. I told them to talk up the fun of drinking underground." With a glint in her eye, she added, "The fun of defying the law. Every ticket was used, and the trains have been packed ever since."

He'd already recognized her plan had been ingenious, but had to ask, "What else did you promise in order to assure all one hundred tickets would get used?"

Reading her eyes was like reading a book. Right now, they squinted as she wondered how he knew there had to be more.

He lifted a brow.

"Half-price drink tickets," she said.

Mick nodded, biting back a smile. "You are quite the entrepreneur."

"Thank you." She frowned slightly. "Why did you become a bull?"

He wasn't one for idle chatter, but it was a long ride to Rochester. "Because when I was small, my family was at a picnic near the lake and my brother became lost."

"Oh, my word!" She laid a hand on his arm. "How old was he? You found him, didn't you?"

"He was five, and yes, we found him. He'd followed a dog along the shoreline and ended up on top of a rock cluster and couldn't get down. A police officer crawled up there and got him down. I wanted to become one ever since then."

Her expression softened. "Oh. How old were you?"

"Five."

She frowned. "I thought you said your brother was five."

"He was. We're twins."

"Twins? Really? Does he look like you?"

"Some say yes, some say no."

"Which is it?"

Mick shrugged. Some people couldn't tell him and Connor apart. Others knew the difference between them right off.

Thoughtful, she sat quietly before asking, "Will I meet him?"

He hadn't thought about that. Not fully. Due to the fact that her father was staying at his house, with his mother, the likelihood of her meeting Connor was fairly high. "Probably."

She nodded. "Then I'll let you know."

"You'll let me know what?"

"If you and your brother look alike."

"All right, you do that."

"I will." She leaned into the corner of the seat and wall of the train. "Is he a police officer, too?"

"No. He owns a phone company."

"What is his name?"

"Connor."

"Are either of you married?"

Mick bit down on the tip of his tongue to keep from snapping his answer. He was over Twila, had been for years, but the way she'd turned down his marriage proposal was still alive and well inside him. He would never put himself in that position again. Ever. "No."

"Why?"

He put that back on her. "Why aren't you married?"

She covered her mouth with her hand as a yawn escaped. "I saw what marriage did to my mother, twice. I see no need in repeating that."

Mick agreed with her. There was no need to get married, but she had a need. A very different one that had nothing to do with marriage. The way she was rubbing her arms said she was cold. He leaned forward and took off his suit jacket and handed it to her. "Here. You can use this as a blanket. A small one, but it'll help some. Might as well catch sleep whenever you can. It'll be a while before we arrive in Chicago."

She glanced at his jacket. "What if you get cold?"

"My shirt has long sleeves, your dress doesn't. Besides, I'm used to the cold."

"Why do you say that?"

"Because it's colder in New York than it is in Missouri."

She looked at the jacket again. "Are you sure?"

"Yes."

She took the jacket and tucked it under her chin and over her shoulders. "Thank you. I am tired." Flashing him a coy grin, she added, "Someone rudely woke me up this morning."

He chuckled. "Rudely, huh?"

"Yes, very rudely."

He tucked the collar of his jacket under her chin. "I'll wake you when we get to Chicago."

She nodded, then without opening her eyes, asked, "Are you dating someone?"

He leaned back and closed his eyes. "No. Are you?"

"No."

"Why not?"

"I've never dated anyone."

He opened one eye to look her way. Hers were still closed. "Why not?"

"Duane insisted I was too young, and then my mother got sick, and I was too busy. Been too busy ever since then. How about you?"

He closed his eye. "I've been too busy, too."

"What about before you were a police officer?"

"I was too busy then, too."

"Doing what?"

He let out the air that had grown heavy inside his chest. "My father died when I was in high school, and I had things to take care of for him."

She sighed. "I guess we have more in common than we knew."

"I guess so," he agreed. "Get some sleep now."

"You, too," she said.

"I will," he agreed, even though he knew he wouldn't. Not when he had more on his mind than ever before. Past regrets and new worries.

Chapter Seven

The Chicago train station hadn't changed since he'd spent the night in it two days ago. Not that he'd expected it to, but with Lisa in tow, he felt a hint of guilt over the accommodations. The benches were hard wood and the train whistles never stopped blaring. Locomotives rolled in and out of town all night, except for the eastbound one they would board at six in the morning. Five hours wasn't worth finding a hotel room, but it was long enough to wear a person out.

"You can lie down here, on this bench," he suggested. "Get some sleep while we're waiting."

"I'm fine." She glanced around at all the people. Men, women and children, arriving, departing and waiting during a layover of transferring trains. "What do you think happened to that bathroom thug?"

It was the first time she'd brought it up since it had happened. "He woke up with a headache and boarded the next train leaving town." Mick didn't add that without help, the goon would have had a hell of a time getting his legs untied. There was no way he could have reached around the back of the stool to untie the scarf by himself.

"Do you think he'll arrive here?" she asked.

"Not before we are on our way east."

She nodded and kept glancing around.

"I'm sure by now he's figured out his mistake in trying to corner you." Mick held back from mentioning anything about the fact that it had been obvious that she'd been contemplating giving him the bum's rush since they'd boarded the train, and the goon had decided to take advantage of that.

"I never imagined traveling could be so dangerous."

"Traveling dangerous?" He shook his head and let out a fake laugh. "Darling, you put yourself in danger every night by working in your gin joint."

"I'm not your darling," she snapped.

She was right. He had no idea why he'd called her that. "No, you're not. But besides your gin joint, you live alone, outside of town, with doors that a child could break down."

"My home is perfectly safe."

Mick had no idea why he'd pointed all that out, other than it was the complete truth. Someone could break into her house at any time of the day or night and she'd be completely defenseless. "Do you know how to shoot that gun in your purse?"

"Yes."

"Tell me."

"Tell you what?"

"How to shoot it. Explain it to me."

She refused to look at him, instead stared straight ahead, breathing in and out of her nose. "You pull the trigger."

"How do you cock it?"

"You pull back the little notch on top. It's called the hammer, that's what falls forward, strikes the bullet and propels it out of the barrel." She picked up her purse. "Do you want me to show you how to load it?"

He pinched his lips together to keep from smiling, then gave in and released a full grin. "No. I'm glad you know how to use it and how it works."

"Why?"

"Because hitting a man over the head with a loaded gun is dangerous. It could go off."

She huffed out a breath. "I probably shouldn't have done that. I'd already kicked him hard enough to hurt him."

"Probably." The goon had been holding his crotch with both hands when he'd hit his head on the sink. "Who taught you how to shoot? Your stepfather?"

"No."

He hadn't missed how her eyes had turned cold every time her stepfather was mentioned, including now.

"My mother did. She gave me the gun on my fourteenth birthday, and she told me where to land a kick."

To many that might be considered an odd present for a fourteen-year-old girl, but to Mick it solidified what he'd been thinking. That she hadn't been safe, not even in her own home, for years.

By the time they boarded the train leaving Chicago, Lisa was so exhausted, she could barely keep her eyes open. Her tailbone hurt so badly from sitting on the hard bench, she wished they were already in New York.

Mick led her to a seat on the train. Upon sitting down, she curled into the corner and used his coat as a blanket again. It smelled good. Spicy and clean. Like him. Burying her face into his coat, she closed her eyes.

She hadn't slept on the other train when he'd given her his coat. She'd tried, but her mind had kept thinking about him. About him dating, not wanting to get married, and about him being a twin. She wanted to see his brother, wondered if Connor was as handsome as Mick.

She still wondered about that, but this time, it wasn't enough to keep her awake.

At some point, she was so chilled she woke, twisted, found warmth and fell back to sleep.

When she woke the next time, she had no idea where she was and lifted her head to glance around, blinking to clear her sleep-filled eyes. Memories formed. Returned. And she closed her eyes, realizing she'd been using Mick as a pillow, and for his warmth.

That was no longer needed. Sun was filling the passenger car. She untangled her arms from his suit coat and smoothed it out before handing it to him.

His grin was so charming, she held her breath for a moment before being able to say, "Thank you."

"How did you sleep?"

Waking up next to him, knowing that she'd used him as a pillow, gave her butterflies in her stomach. "Fine. You?"

"Fine."

Nodding, and still trying to focus on anything except for how odd he made her feel right now, she asked, "Where are we?"

"Entered Ohio about an hour ago."

Looking out the window, at the sun, she asked, "What time is it?"

"About one in the afternoon."

Surprised, she turned to look at him, make sure he wasn't teasing. "One? I slept that long?"

"Yes, you did." Grinning, he pointed to a spot on the side of his face. "You have a bit of drool on your face."

Mortified, she wiped her face with her hand, but felt

nothing. "I did not!" Shaking her head at his teasing, she asked, "What time is it, truly?"

"About one in the afternoon, truly." He stood and held out a hand. "Let's use the facilities and then visit the dining car. I'm starving."

"Dining car?"

"Yes. They serve meals. All the trains from here to Rochester have them."

She wondered if she should refuse, or pretend to be mad at him, because she wasn't supposed to be enjoying this trip, but his teasing had been good-hearted, and she hadn't had that with anyone in a long time. Her life of running the Depot, of helping the town, was too serious for joking of any kind. Furthermore, she had to go to the powder room, and her stomach growled at the thought of food. Clasping his hand, she stood and followed him into the aisle before by some unspoken mutual agreement, they released their hold on each other's hands. Thank goodness—her hand was on fire.

The facilities were at the front of the car, and after they'd each used them, they walked back through the car to the back end, and crossed through the walkway into the dining car. Her stomach growled again.

Mick's grin said he'd heard her stomach as he nodded toward an empty table.

They sat, across from each other, which wasn't as much of a relief as she'd imagined. Waking up next to him had been, well, intimate, and she'd never been intimate with anyone. Didn't want to be, either. Sitting across from him wasn't any better. In fact, now she had nowhere to look but straight at him.

That's when it dawned on her. She'd dreamed about him. Horsefeathers! She'd never dreamed about a man before. She couldn't recall exactly what her dream had been about, other than him. And it had been a good one.

The waiter arrived and provided them with menus and cups of steaming coffee.

"What looks good to you?" he asked.

"Everything," she replied.

"If nothing else, you are an honest woman, Lisa Walters."

"What do you mean, if nothing else?"

He shrugged. "It's just a saying." Frowning, he added, "You are suspicious of people, aren't you?"

She continued to read the menu and shrugged her shoulders.

"Comes with the territory, does it?"

Glancing over the menu at him, she said, "Yes, it does."

He flashed her another one of those grins and set aside his menu. "I'm going to have the fried chicken."

That was what she'd decided upon, but now wondered if she should change her mind, just so he'd know she made her own decisions.

"Did you really ask if you could do it again when you fell out of the hayloft?" he asked.

She set aside the menu. "I don't know. I honestly don't remember it happening, but wasn't allowed to go into the hayloft because I'd fallen out once."

"What do you remember about your father?" he asked.

A significant warmth filled her. "How much he loved fried chicken. We had it almost every Sunday." She sighed at the next memory that came forward. "My mother never made it after he left."

The waiter returned and as Mick handed his menu to the man, he said, "I'll have the ham steak."

Lisa frowned. "I thought you were having the chicken."

"I changed my mind."

She looked at him for a long moment and then handed her menu to the waiter. "We'll both have the fried chicken."

The waiter looked at Mick. Grinning, he nodded. "Sounds good."

"Very well," the young man said. "It'll be out shortly."

The waiter walked away and Lisa kept her gaze averted from Mick.

He was still grinning. Now at her.

Unable to ignore it any longer, she shrugged. "You were just trying to be nice by ordering the ham."

"You don't want me to be nice?" he asked.

She wasn't sure what she wanted, other than she didn't want him to feel sorry for her. To not order the chicken because of her. It might seem like a small thing, but it wasn't. Ordering the chicken for him and herself felt as if she had some control over all that was happening. "I just wanted you to have the chicken, if that's what you wanted."

"It is. Thank you."

He sounded sincere, and the devilish glint in his eyes was charming.

"I do hope your brother doesn't look like you," she said, picking up her cup of coffee.

"Why do you say that?"

She took a sip of coffee. "Because it would be a terrible thing for two men to be so homely."

He slapped a hand against his chest. "Ouch."

Lisa took another sip of coffee and fought to keep from spewing it out as she held in her laughter. She also had to look away from him. From the smile on his lips. He really was a handsome man, and for some outrageous reason, she was suddenly wondering what it would be like to kiss him. She never, ever, thought along those lines. Kissing could lead to other things. Ultimately marriage. After watching her mother go through not one, but two marriages that each had taken their toll on her, Lisa had long ago determined marriage was a farce. Something she didn't want anything to do with. Oddly enough, at one time she hadn't wanted anything to do with running a speakeasy, either.

"What are you thinking about so hard?" Mick asked.

She shook her head, dispelling the cobwebs that were catching all sorts of thoughts that truly didn't have any place in her life right now. "Nothing."

"Really?"

"Yes, really."

"You aren't thinking about how good that chicken is going to taste?" he asked, grinning all over again.

She had to shake her head again, to make sure thoughts of kissing him didn't return, even as she couldn't stop a smile from forming. "Maybe."

He laughed. "I am."

The way his eyes sparkled caused a small giggle to escape, and she was amazed at how comfortable she felt. How truly comfortable. She hadn't felt this at ease in a long time. "Is fried chicken your favorite?"

"Food in general is my favorite," he answered. "What's your favorite?"

"Chocolate cake," she said without thought. "My mother used to make one for me every year on my birthday."

"Chocolate was always Connor's favorite," he said. "Mine was vanilla."

"Was or is?"

"Is," he answered, then nodded toward the waiter walking toward their table.

The chicken was moist on the inside, crispy on the outside and tasted heavenly. They continued to talk as they ate, about foods they liked, and other things that were of little importance. Lisa couldn't remember a time when she'd enjoyed a meal more. Most of hers were eaten alone, in her kitchen, during the late afternoons and wee hours of the morning, and consisted mainly of toast and eggs because that was fast and easy.

Afterward, as they walked back to their seats, she noted something else she'd never experienced. People were looking at them with something akin to admiration.

Because of him. He carried himself in a way that people noticed, and of course they'd notice his handsomeness. A part of her felt pride in walking next to him. In being associated with him. She'd never experienced something like that before. Good heavens, that line of thinking was as odd as thoughts about kissing.

"That was close to the best meal I've ever eaten," he said as they arrived at their bench seat.

"Was it?" The food had been good, but she'd noticed his plate. It hadn't been empty.

"Yes. I'm as stuffed as a bird on Thanksgiving," he said after they'd sat down.

Because she couldn't help herself, Lisa nodded, "Yes, you are full of—"

"Cornbread stuffing," he said. "That is what you were going to say, isn't it?"

"Of course," she lied. Giggling, she changed her mind and told the truth. "And baloney. That's what you're full of. I saw how you turned up your nose at the green beans on your plate."

"I've never liked green beans," he said. "But everything else was good. Wasn't it?"

"Yes, it was." In fact, it had been the best meal she'd had in ages and that made her thoughts shift to the Depot. On how things went last night without her.

"How do you think the Depot did without you last night?" he asked a few moments later.

"How—" Lisa stopped herself from finishing the question.

He cleared his throat. "How did I know that was what you were thinking? Because you went quiet, thoughtful."

Lisa didn't know how to react to that. He was so observant, of everything she did. "I guess I'll find out when I get home," she finally said. "If I have a home to go to."

The sound of laughter rolled through the train, and she glanced over her shoulder, saw a small boy being hushed by his mother. She closed her eyes for a moment, suddenly missing her mother. No, it wasn't just missing her mother, she was suddenly wishing her life would have been different than how it had turned out.

"Why wouldn't you have a home?"

She turned back around. "Because several things could happen."

"Like what?"

"Duane could take over running the joint, which means prices would go up, entertainment would be axed and the place would be open every day of the week." Those were just a few of the things the two of them had fought about over the years.

"How many days of the week are you open now?"

"Five. We are closed on Sundays and Mondays." The complications of her being gone could go far beyond what she'd already mentioned. She'd lined up the entertainment for the rest of the month, and if Duane cancelled those, she might not be able to convince them to return. Most people wouldn't after dealing with Duane. Including the customers that she'd worked so hard to get. Many had become regulars, but that, too, could change in a heartbeat.

"Would it really matter if it was open seven days one week?"

"Yes. If people can have something every day, then they don't want it. By being closed a couple of days a week, it makes them look forward to coming again. Unlike Kansas City, Kansas, Kansas City, Missouri, has never accepted prohibition, because of Tom Pendergast. His family has run the town for years, including the saloons. He feeds the poor, provides jobs and hobnobs with the rich. When it comes to voting, he touts for people to vote early and often, for him, and they do. Therefore, because he owns a fair number of them, the saloons have been opened the entire time, just like before, but in Junction, prohibition is in full force and people from the city like the thrill of drinking underground. That's why they make the trip."

She huffed out a breath at the real truth. "Besides that, trains don't pass through Junction on Sunday, Monday or Tuesday, so it doesn't make it profitable to be open every day. Tuesdays and Wednesdays aren't busy—it's mainly locals. The trainloads don't start until Thursday night." Duane hated the marketplace, too. He'd always thought that he should be making a profit off that, too, because she was the one to come up with the idea. Money was all he was ever concerned about. "Those trains are what saved Junction from drying up and blowing away. If the people don't return, it'll all come to an end."

"It sounds to me like you're the one that kept the town from drying up and blowing away," Mick said. He knew about the Pendergast Machine, as it was known in other places of the United States and how prohibition agents completely ignored Kansas City, Missouri. A part of him was amazed at how she'd found a way to capitalize on Pendergast. He also rarely, if ever, felt guilty, and didn't appreciate the fact that a sense of guilt was rolling around in his stomach right now for forcing her to leave. Nor did he like the worry that was making the fine skin on her forehead crease with lines. This was supposed to be a simple, easy thing. Finding her and bringing her home to see Tony. So far, it hadn't been any of those things. In fact, she'd complicated things inside him that he'd thought had been long ago settled. Like dating and marriage. He'd been thinking about those things since she'd asked about them last night. Not for himself, he'd never change his mind, but for her. She wasn't like any woman he'd known. "Is there anyone you could call? Check in on things?"

"The boys, they know how to run the place, but they won't stand up to Duane." She sighed heavily. "No one will."

"Why?"

"Because he thinks he's a bimbo, a real tough guy. And he's mean. He'll fire them if they stand up to him. Those boys need their jobs at the Depot. They have families to feed. Everyone in town has families to feed. Duane could ruin it for everyone."

That fit with exactly what Tony had said about her stepfather. "Was he mean to you and your mother?"

Mick's jaw grew tight. The idea of anyone being mean to her didn't sit well with him.

She hitched one shoulder. "He didn't hit us, if that's what you're asking. He's just ornery. Always has been. He yells and he's mean-spirited. I don't know why my mother married him. He certainly didn't make her happy."

Mick knew there were many ways to be mean without hitting someone. "What did he do for work? Before the Depot?"

She looked at him and shook her head.

Her blue eyes were so sad, so despondent, he grasped her hand. "I'm not on duty, and even if I was, whatever you say to me is between us. I swear it." That wasn't like him any more than holding her hand, but he had no idea what else to do. She'd been hurt, and he didn't like that, but he did want her to tell him. "I'm not fishing for information to bust anyone."

She rubbed her nose with the back of her other hand. "He ran the saloon in town, even after prohibition hit. Until it was busted. He was in jail a few weeks, got out and…" She shrugged. "He couldn't open a speakeasy in his old saloon again, so when my mother had her stroke, he opened one in the barn, knowing she couldn't protest it."

"But you did."

She nodded.

"Until you thought you didn't have any other choice?"

She stared straight ahead for a moment, then turned, looked at him again. "No, until I realized it was my opportunity to make enough money that—" She swallowed. "That I'd finally be in charge of my life."

Mick could relate to her statement and to the determination he read in her eyes. He'd felt that way. Being in charge of his own life was why he'd become a cop. He'd wanted to become a police officer for years, but his family, especially his father, had been dead set against it. As the oldest of the twins, it had been expected he'd join the family business. More than expected. The family business had been around for years, and would continue for years, with a McCormick at the helm.

That had been what he and his father had fought over the day his father had died. It had been an argument they'd had before, and he'd thought nothing of storming out of the house that morning, stating that when he graduated that spring, he'd be going to college, and then become a police officer. That there were already enough McCormicks in the family business. Not only his father, but his uncle and his three cousins.

Madder than he'd ever been, he'd gone so far as to say he hated being a McCormick, hated his father.

There had been a snowstorm that day, and his father, while driving home from work, had gone into the ditch, crashed into a tree. They hadn't found him until the next morning. When it had been too late.

His father had died believing he hated him.

He hadn't hated his father. He'd just been mad, but never got a chance to say that. To rectify what his anger had done.

"Now you are the one who has gone thoughtful," she said. "Quiet."

"I was thinking of a plan," he said, shifting his thoughts to where they should have been. On her problem. There had to be a way that he could help her so that she didn't have to worry about the Depot right now. So she and Tony could have a chance to rectify their wrongs before it was too late.

"What sort of plan?" she asked.

"We won't have much time, but at the next stop, we'll find a phone, you can call those farm boys, tell them not to listen to Duane. That he can't fire them because you are still their boss, and that you'll be back, within a few days. They'll listen to you, won't they?"

"Yes, they'll listen to me, but Duane—"

"Won't stand a chance against all three of them, not if they believe they are following your orders. You'll have to convince them to stand up to him." Mick wanted Tony to get the chance to apologize to his daughter, make things right before he died, but Mick didn't want to ruin her life in the process.

For a moment, he questioned his own sensibility and why he was doing all of this. Tony didn't know she was on her way. The only people Mick had told were his captain, so he could have the time off work, his mother, because she was taking care of Tony at the house, and his brother Connor, so he'd stop in more regularly to check in on their mother.

"They would stand up to him, if I told them to," Lisa said, "but it would be easier if I just went back to Junction. That would truly solve it all."

"You still don't want to see your father?" he asked, realizing that he'd never actually talked with her about that. He'd been too focused on what he thought should happen, and that wasn't fair to her.

"I honestly don't know." Her face contorted as if in pain, or confusion. Or both. "I don't know what I'll say." Shrugging, she continued, "I don't even know what I feel. He's been gone for so long. Dead to me. That it still doesn't seem real that he's alive."

"That will change when you see him," Mick said, convinced of that.

The smile she offered wobbled. "Will it?" With a

heavy sigh, she shook her head, "It won't change anything."

"How do you know that? Maybe seeing him will change your life."

"Would seeing your father one last time change your life?"

Mick stiffened at the question, then forced himself to not be fazed by it and tell her the truth. "Yes. It would. I'd tell him that I love him and that I was proud to be his son." A sense of relief washed over his shoulders. As if he'd needed to admit that aloud.

"I wish you could have that opportunity," she said.

He touched her hand. "And I want you to have this opportunity."

She stared at his hand covering hers for a long moment. "But I don't know if I still love him. I just don't know."

The shift that happened inside Mick was so unexpected, so strong, he gripped her hand harder. He drew in a breath and knowing this should never have been his choice, he said, "It's up to you, Lisa. If you want to return to Missouri, we'll catch a westbound train at the next station. If you don't, we'll find a phone so you can call your friends."

She nodded and turned to stare out the window.

Chapter Eight

As he'd told her he would, Mick found a phone at the next train stop, and she called those farm boys. Following his suggestions, she told them the truth, that she was going to see her father, and that they were to tell Duane that if he tried to take over, that the place would be busted. Within a matter of minutes, they were back on the train, and it pulled away from the station, heading east again.

He was glad that had been her choice, but was also questioning if he was glad for himself, or for her.

"Thank you," she said. "Buck was happy to hear from me. He hasn't seen Duane, and no one knows I'm gone. He and the boys made sure of that so far. I told him to have Duane's money on my porch on Sunday. Maybe I'll be back before Duane knows I'm gone."

A knot formed in Mick's stomach at her going back to all that alone. It was her life, and not his job to change anything about it, but he was concerned about her, worried about her, in a way that he hadn't been about someone in a very long time. "You can call again once we get to Rochester."

"I told them I would try to."

He nodded. "Now you don't have anything to worry about."

"Except meeting my father and learning why he never once tried to contact me."

"Tony will explain all that to you." Mick balled his hand into a fist to keep from touching her again. It had become too easy. Too natural. He hoped that she and Tony got things settled quickly, because the faster he got away from Lisa, the better off he'd be. She was making him think too much. Feel too much. He wasn't comfortable with any of that. Normally, he had far more control, but sitting beside her, learning so much about her, was loosening the hold he'd always had on his emotions.

Talking with her was too easy, too. So was teasing her. He liked seeing her blush, but seeing her smile was even more enjoyable.

It was impossible to not like her, to not help her, even as he told himself that he was a cop. Saving a speakeasy should never even cross his mind.

"I don't know what there is to explain," she said. "He let us believe he was dead, all these years." She shrugged. "I guess he just didn't love us, that's all there is to it."

Tony had told him enough to make not saying much hard. It wasn't his place to explain, but maybe dropping a few things for her to think about couldn't hurt. "Maybe that's why he didn't return. Because he did love you."

She huffed a laugh. A fake one. "That truly doesn't make sense." Giving him a sincere smile, she said, "But thank you for trying."

Mick decided to change the subject. He might be

overstepping his bounds, but he was curious to know her thoughts. "Prohibition will end someday."

"Why do you say that?"

"Too many people are against it," he answered. "What will you do then?"

She frowned, and after a long, thoughtful moment, said, "I don't know. I'm sure Duane will open his saloon on Main Street again."

"What about your night-time market?" Expanding on that, he continued, "Once saloons are legal again, will you have trainloads of people coming to Junction?"

Her frown increased, tugged her brows further down. "Are you trying to convince me to not go back?"

"No." That was the last thing he'd want. The faster she went back, the faster he would be able to quit worrying about her. He was counting on the whole out of sight, out of mind thing playing in his favor as far as she was concerned. "I'm just suggesting that you think about the future."

"Why? Why would you care if I thought about the future or not?"

Why indeed? Normally, he wasn't concerned about anyone else's future. "Because everyone should think about their future." That was as good of a reply as any he could come up with at the moment.

"I suppose so."

"Maybe you could consider becoming a teacher again."

Her shoulders slumped. "I gave up that dream years ago. Everyone in town knows I run a speakeasy. They'd never let me teach school after that."

"You could teach someplace else."

"No. Junction is my home, and I found another way to help the kids, besides teaching."

Mick recalled the little boy rushing to get to the school. "By buying new playground equipment?"

"Yes, and desks, books, chalkboards, whatever they needed. The old school was taken out by straight-line winds a few years ago. Before my mother died. Between the insurance and state funds, the new school was built, but there was no money for many other things. As soon as the Depot started to turn a profit, I put a percentage aside for the school, for things they needed, and I continue to."

Mick had already gained a considerable amount of respect for her, but it grew even more. If not for her, the entire town of Junction would barely exist. "That was very nice of you."

She shrugged. "Children need the right tools in order to learn."

"They do," Mick agreed, while thinking about Riley, and the whistle in his pocket that he'd bought for the boy back home. Riley lived next door, and with few other children in their neighborhood, visited regularly.

"Part of earning my teaching certificate was helping other teachers. That's when I noticed the school needed so many things, and that no one in town had the means to help, other than Duane."

Understanding more now as to why she'd chosen to open the speakeasy, he said, "So you took it upon yourself to earn enough money to help them."

She nodded and glanced at him out of the corner of one eye. "Like you took it upon yourself to help Tony."

He couldn't deny that she was right. He had taken it upon himself. "I thought he should have the chance to say goodbye."

She nodded and then twisted in her seat to look at him squarely. "You said that my father has cancer."

"Yes, he does."

"Is he really sick?"

Mick noted the concern in her eyes. His heart took an odd tumble for her. "Some days he's worn out, tired, other days he feels pretty good."

"Is he alone?" Once again, her smile wobbled. "I mean, is someone taking care of him?"

"Yes, someone is taking care of him, but he doesn't have any family."

Blinking fast, she turned away. "Other than me."

It had been years since he'd been in a spot like this, where he was at odds with himself and his actions. He had to keep the lessons he'd learned front and center, to make sure he didn't make the same mistakes, but it was getting harder and harder.

"Can I ask you a favor?" she asked quietly.

His heart lurched. Whatever it was, he'd do it. "Of course."

"Will you go with me to see him?"

"Yes. I'll be there."

She sighed. "Thank you."

Unable not to, he took hold of her hand. "There's nothing to be afraid of."

She grimaced and nodded. "When will we arrive in Rochester?"

"Around noon tomorrow."

"Do we have to change trains again?"

"No, but we'll have stops, all night long."

Leaning her head back against the seat, she asked, "How many times have you done this before?"

"Done what?"

"Reunited families."

That's not how he'd thought of it and he shook his head. "Never."

She grinned. "Never?"

He nodded, and silently vowed that he'd never do it again. Then, as if he needed to confirm that in his mind, he released her hand.

They ate again in the dining car a short time later, used the facilities and then slept, if it could be called that, on and off throughout the long night. Long because he hadn't slept. He'd been too mesmerized by her. The way her lashes looked like folded wings on a butterfly next to her cheeks. The way she smelled, like spring flowers, and the way her lips looked as if they were as soft as flower petals.

The other thing that had kept him awake was Twila. Not necessarily her, but their relationship. How he'd thought he'd fallen in love with her, and had thought that marrying her would complete his life. Only to have it shattered instead, when she'd refused his offer of marriage. She'd said she didn't want to get married, to be tied down like that. He spent a large portion of the night reminding himself that he would never expose himself to that type of rejection again. Ever.

The next morning, after eating breakfast, they returned to their seats and talked about unimportant things, the weather, the landscape rolling past the windows, and other such topics until the train finally rolled into Rochester. Mick had been glad when he'd rolled into Junction after his trip west, but that had been nothing compared to the relief he felt upon arriving in Rochester.

He collected his bag and escorted Lisa to his car, a red and black Pontiac roadster parked in the parking lot.

Lisa let out a low whistle. "This is your car?"

"Yes." He opened the door for her.

She climbed in and rubbed the shiny leather seat. "Being a police officer must pay better in New York than it does Missouri."

"Do you know police officers in Missouri?" He couldn't help but wonder what she thought about his profession.

"Yes." She grinned. "A few of them are some of my best customers."

He closed the door. His car was only a few months old, and he still felt a thrill every time he climbed in it. Both he and Connor had loved cars since the first one their father had driven home, and probably always would. Unable to stop himself, he ran a hand over the chrome headlights as he walked around to the driver's door.

While setting his suitcase in the backseat, he thought about her, and the fact that she didn't have one. Didn't have any clothes except what she was wearing.

The stores were open, so that wasn't a problem, except for the fact that for as large as Rochester was, it was still small enough that he was well-known. His entire family. People were sure to be curious as to who Lisa was, and why he'd be buying clothes for her.

His mind searched, picturing the stores that lined the downtown area, large department stores and emporiums that specialized in ladies' clothing.

He wasn't familiar with many of them, but had heard good things about a small boutique on Lake Avenue. No one there should recognize him, and therefore, they wouldn't question who Lisa was, or why he was buying clothing for her.

Lisa had never ridden in many cars, and most certainly never one this spiffy. It smelled nice, too. Clean and fresh. Not like Duane's car. His car smelled like an ashtray. However, it was the town itself that fully captured her attention. Automobiles of all makes and models rolled up and down the streets, and buildings taller than those in Kansas City lined the streets, hosting large billboards overhead and advertising everything from hats to cigarettes and everything in between.

Someday, when she had the time, she was going to go to the city and spend the entire day just walking up and down the streets, visiting whatever store took her fancy. The few times she'd gone to Kansas City had always been for specific reasons, mainly to purchase things for the Depot, and that never allowed her enough time to just look around. To just experience the hustle and bustle. She'd never had time to experience much of anything outside of Junction. She used to dream about that. About seeing all the things she'd read about in books while studying for her teaching exam.

Not that she'd have time now to experience much this time, either. After seeing her father, she'd be back on the train. Heading west.

Her stomach burned at the thought. In the past, even though she'd been lonely, she'd also felt safe being alone, mainly because she'd been afraid of what Duane might say or do to anyone who might have been with her. After traveling with Mick from Missouri, she wasn't looking forward to returning home alone.

That was as odd as how part of her wanted to be here, in Rochester, and the other part of her didn't. Not only because of her father. Talking with Mick the past couple of days had her thinking about so many things.

He'd said prohibition would end someday, and she believed that it would, and had no idea what she would do then. She was afraid to dream, to think about the future, because whenever she had done that, something had always happened that shattered those dreams.

Not dreaming was a much better plan. That way, she wouldn't be disappointed.

Even when it came to having enough time to walk up and down the street. Right now, she was thinking about the future, but only to make a plan. It was still early in the day. She could see her father and be on a train west before nightfall. That's what she had to do, leave before Duane discovered where she'd gone and why.

She'd been watching the structures roll past while her mind had been wandering, but took a longer, harder look at the buildings when Mick pulled up next to the curb and shut off the car.

"Why are we stopping here?" Her father couldn't live in any of these buildings. They all looked to be stores to her.

"To pick you up some clothes and other essentials." He opened his door. "You've been wearing the same dress for three days."

She was well aware of that and she longed for a bath. "Are you sure there's time?"

He climbed out of the car. "Yes, there's time."

Her eyes were drawn to the store next to the car, and a light purple dress, the color of lilacs in bloom, with a drop waistline and pleated skirt hanging in the window. Purple was her favorite color.

Mick opened her door. "If you don't find what you need here, we'll stop at another store."

"I don't need much," she said. "I won't be here but a few hours. Just long enough to see my father and then I'll head back to Missouri."

He held out his hand for her. "Let's take this one step at a time."

A woman walking past looked at them, how he was holding the door open and she was sitting in the car. Mick nodded at the woman and tipped his hat slightly.

The woman smiled brightly, but it was her outfit Lisa noticed even more. A pleated skirt, with flowing-over tunic, both of olive green and embroidered with gold thread. She dreamed of being able to wear clothes like that, and the purple outfit in the window.

"I'll pay for whatever you need," Mick said.

Lisa drew her eyes off the woman and looked at him. "I have money." Taking his hand, she climbed out of the car. As they crossed the sidewalk, she contemplated the fact that there was no reason why she couldn't wear a dress like that. Here. Back home she wore the shorter flashy flapper attire because that's what was expected at the Depot. She'd been uncomfortable when she'd first started wearing her short, sleeveless dresses, but had gotten used to them quickly. It got hot behind the bar, and they were what all the women wore to speakeasies. She'd noticed that right off and had ordered several out of the catalog.

She was no longer uncomfortable in the clothes she wore—she liked them, but would enjoy wearing something more elegant, and this might be the only chance she would get. A flash of excitement filled her. She could even buy a pair of gloves, and wear them. That was impossible while working at the Depot.

"I promise I won't take long," she told Mick as he opened the door.

"Take your time, we are in no rush," he said.

The store was truly lovely. Full of all types of women's fashions. She'd never been in a store that sold nothing but women's clothing. It was amazing. Knowing

Mick was waiting, she tried to hurry, but there was so much to look at. To see.

She tried on several dresses, a black-and-gold one, as well as a green-and-yellow one before finding exactly what she was looking for. A navy blue one, with white embroidered flowers, quarter-length sleeves and a handkerchief hem. It was elegant, but simple enough for everyday wear.

Along with the dress, she bought a few accessories, a full set of underclothes, including silk stockings, and a lightweight wool jacket, blue, complete with a narrow rabbit fur collar. It might be foolish to buy it just for the trip home—because she wouldn't be able to borrow Mick's jacket—but it was too beautiful to pass up.

Smiling, she paid the female clerk who had been extremely helpful in finding what she was looking for, and collected her packages.

While she'd been shopping, Mick had taken a seat on a bench near the window, where two other men had been sitting, reading newspapers while waiting for the women they were accompanying.

"Ready?" he asked, holding his hand out to take her packages.

"Yes." Because she'd seen other women shoppers hand their packages to the men to carry for them, she handed hers to Mick. "Thank you."

They left the store and as he set her packages in the back seat of the car, she said, "I'm sorry I took so long."

He grinned while holding the door as she climbed in the passenger seat. "Actually, that was much faster than I'd expected it to be."

He closed the door and walked around to the other side, just like he'd done at the train station. The few times she had ridden in an automobile, neither Duane, nor the Hendrick boys had ever held the door open for her like Mick. They'd never carried her packages, either.

They carried things, mainly booze, down into the basement, and empty bottles back up to the barn, but so did she. Every night. It was her job to see that the shelves were restocked and ready for the following day.

Mick climbed in and started the automobile. "Did you find something you liked?"

"Yes, I did. Thank you for stopping, and waiting." She glanced at the store as he pulled away from the curb, noticing that the lovely lilac-colored dress was no longer in the window. One of the other shoppers must have purchased it. She'd considered it, but had decided that the heavier material of the blue dress would sustain traveling better.

"Is there something else you wanted?"

"No."

"We can stop at another store if you'd like."

"No. There's nothing else I need."

"If you need more money—"

"No, I don't need more money." That was true, there was still plenty in her purse. Plenty to get her back home to Missouri. At one time, she'd thought that would be all she needed. Money. That it would make everything right, but it hadn't. Sure, it had allowed her to help the school, the children, even the town, but it hadn't changed her life. Mick had done that. She had yet to determine if that was for the good or the bad.

"It's not far from here."

Her insides quivered as an icy chill rippled down her spine. "You mean my father?"

"Yes."

Lisa folded her hands in her lap and willed them to stop shaking. Years ago, she would have given up anything to see her father again. Right now, it scared the daylights out of her.

What if she discovered she did still care about him? Still loved him? She had to return home, as soon as possible. Leave this evening. Too many people back home depended on her.

This was, again, one of those times when the weight of her responsibilities was heavier than she wanted to bear. She wasn't sure how so many people had come to depend so much on her, but they had. Therefore, she'd go through with this, meet her father, and then leave.

Her stomach sank at that thought. The trip home sure would be different than the trip out here had been with Mick.

A short time later, when he pulled the car into the driveway of a large brick home with a huge front yard, white shutters and a large front porch surrounded by a bed of tulips and other flowers, she sucked in air. "This is my father's home?"

"No, this is my home."

"Your home? I thought—"

"Your father is here." Mick opened his car door. "He's been staying with my family since he got out of the hospital."

Trembling even harder, she asked, "Your family?" Oh, dear heavens, what would they think of her? Like nearly everything else in her life, this too had been thrust upon her and she was stuck dealing with it. Would it ever end?

"Yes, my family." He climbed out of the car. "Tony needed someone to take care of him. My mother offered to do that."

He closed his door, walked around the car and

opened her door. Lisa climbed out, and tried her best to act normal. It was extremely hard because inside, she felt as if she was about to enter a burning building.

Chapter Nine

If the death grip she had on his arm was any indication, Mick would say Lisa was scared out of her wits at the idea of meeting her father. He'd been fighting the way she'd made him feel and think since meeting her, and had already discovered it was nearly an impossible fight. There was so much about her that was bold and tenacious. She ran a speakeasy, had found the ability to help the entire town of Junction, yet, that was all on the outside. On the inside, she was as frightened and insecure as the young female she was. That was what was affecting him. That she was so very vulnerable.

He prided himself on remaining neutral. It was one of his best traits, something that he had to do nearly every day in the line of duty. He was surprised and irritated that he couldn't hold strong to that when it came to her. Instead of being indifferent, he was proud of her at the same time he wanted to ease her burdens. Not because he was an officer of the law, but because he was a human being. A man.

Ignoring his self-proclaimed commitment to remain aloof, he laid his hand on the one clutching his arm. "You have nothing to worry about. Your father will be happy to see you. Relieved to have this opportunity to tell you his side of what happened."

Her eyes remained locked on the house. "And that's the important thing. His happiness. His relief. Despite what I might want or feel."

"No, it's not," he said, feeling as if he'd just been punched in the gut.

"I'm not trying to convince you, I'm trying to convince myself," she said.

The desperation in her voice made him want to pull her close, hug her, and fighting it was a battle he wasn't sure he'd win.

"Mick! Mick!"

He turned and saw the hedge of bushes along the driveway shaking and a moment later, a head covered in red curls popped out near the bottom of the trimmed leaves. Riley shot out like a little rabbit leaving its burrow and leaped to his feet to run across the driveway.

"You sure were gone a long time, Mick!" the boy said.

Mick had to pull his arm from Lisa's hold to catch Riley as he jumped, expecting to be caught. "Hey, buddy," Mick said, giving the boy a quick hug.

"Where have you been?" Riley asked, hooking his arms tight around Mick's neck. "I didn't have anyone to play catch with."

Shifting Riley onto his hip, he turned to Lisa. "I went to pick up a friend of mine. Lisa, this is Riley Jansen. He's staying next door with his grandparents."

Her eyes lit up like Mick had never seen as she smiled at the boy.

"Hello, Riley," she said, holding out her hand.

Riley's freckle-covered nose wrinkled as he looked Lisa up and down. "You're a friend of Mick's?"

She glanced at him before nodding to Riley. "Yes, I am."

Riley stuck his hand out. "Well, then, any friend of Mick's is a friend of mine."

Her smile grew as she shook Riley's hand. "Thank you, I'm honored to be your friend."

Riley grinned. "She's pretty, Mick."

"Yes, she is." Mick set Riley down on his feet and dug in his pocket for the metal whistle. Handing it to the boy, he said, "I bought this for you."

"Wow, thanks, Mick!" Riley gave the whistle a test blow. "It works!"

"Yes, it does," Mick said. "But you have to promise to only blow it outside."

"I promise!"

"All right then, you run on home." Mick turned the boy around and gave him a pat on the rump. "I'll see you later."

"Bye, Mick, bye, Lisa."

"Bye, Riley," Lisa said, before looking at him. "I had no idea you had such adorable neighbors."

He'd always enjoyed Riley's company, and was thankful the boy had rushed over, because his visit appeared to ease her apprehension, and the battle he'd been fighting.

"Riley is truly adorable. We love having him next door," his mother said from where she stood on the porch stoop. In her normal, cheery way, she hurried down the steps, arms open. "Hello, Lisa, I'm so happy to meet you."

Mick stepped aside as his mother embraced Lisa with a quick hug. The hug she provided him next was met with a grin that said she hadn't forgotten him. He hadn't been worried about that, not in the least. "Hello, Mother."

"Hello, darling. I'm glad you're home." Shaking her head, she added, "I just hope Willow won't be driven crazy by that whistle."

"It's good to be home." He kissed her cheek. "Riley promised to only blow it outside." Turning to Lisa, he completed the introduction. "Lisa, this is my mother, Barbara McCormick."

Lisa nodded slightly as she graciously replied, "Hello, Mrs. McCormick."

"Please, dear, call me Barbara, or just Barb. Tony is going to be so happy." His mother's bright blue eyes dulled slightly. "He just fell asleep, though, and I think we should let him sleep for a few hours. He had a very restless night." Always willing to adapt and make the best of everything, his mother hooked her hand around Lisa's arm. "In the meantime, you can have some lunch, and a nice hot bath after all your traveling. How was the train ride? Not too uncomfortable, I hope." Without missing a beat, his mother looked at him. "Get her things, Mick, and take them up to the blue room."

He gave a nod in response as his mother led Lisa toward the door.

"We call it the blue room because it has blue carpet," his mother explained. "Has for years, I've considered having it replaced, but the room is so seldom used the carpet is still like new. This was my husband's family home. His father built it years ago, but they had a much larger family than we did, so many of the rooms go unused. Your father is in the green room, because, yes, the carpet in that room is green. Are you hungry? I made chicken and dumplings for Tony and…"

His mother's voice trailed off as she and Lisa entered

the house. Mick turned around to collect Lisa's packages out of the back seat of the car, but paused before taking a step. A smile formed as he realized that his dilemma had just been solved. Now that he was home, his mother would take over. He'd no longer need to be concerned about Lisa in any way. His mother would see to Lisa's every need, and he could go back to doing what he did best. Remain neutral. Not become involved with anything outside of his job duties of upholding the law.

With a great sense of relief, he collected Lisa's packages and his suitcase.

One additional package remained on the seat and he stared at it, wondering if he should take it in the house, or return it to the store. It had been an impulsive thing to do, but while Lisa had been trying on numerous dresses that the clerk had carried to the dressing room for her, he'd purchased a light-colored purple dress that had been hanging in the window.

He'd never purchased a dress for a woman before, and had planned on buying only a scarf to replace the one he'd used to tie up the goon on the train, but he'd pictured Lisa wearing the purple dress. At the time, he'd justified it by telling himself she could wear it on the trip home, but now wondered if he'd stepped over yet another invisible boundary that he'd sworn to never cross again.

He left the package in the car and he carried everything else into the house. He'd decide what to do with the dress later. Right now, he wanted a bath, clean clothes and some of the chicken and dumplings his mother had mentioned.

His mother's voice, chatting about the rain and spring flowers, came from the kitchen as he walked down the hallway to the stairs leading to the second floor. Up stairs, he deposited Lisa's purchases in the blue room, which did have blue carpet, along with blue curtains, bed coverings and pillows, before he walked down the hall to his room.

The house had a total of five bedrooms. The one he'd had since the day he'd been born, and the one Connor still claimed, across the hall from his room, even though his brother had purchased a home on the north end of town, closer to where his telephone company was officed. Down the hallway were the green room and the blue room, and at the far end, was Mother's room. There were also two bathing rooms. The one he and Connor had always used, and the one Mother and Father had always used.

With Tony in the green room and Lisa in the blue room, the upstairs had more occupants than it had had in a very long time.

Mick unpacked his bag, collected clean clothes and took a bath before going downstairs for lunch. Although it hadn't been something he'd consciously planned, his timing worked out well. Mother was alone in the kitchen.

"I'll fix you a plate, have a seat." She grabbed a hot pad and opened the oven door. While setting the large pot on top of the stove, she said, "Lisa ate, although not very much, and is now upstairs taking a bath. She certainly is an adorable little thing, isn't she?"

At five-foot-two, his mother was a petite woman, without a gray hair on her blond head. Lisa was at least an inch taller, but even with that, Mother was right. Lisa was adorable. Mick knew he didn't need to agree aloud, Mother had already made up her mind.

"Tony will be so surprised," she continued as she filled a plate full of steaming chicken and dumplings.

"He's wondered why he hasn't seen you the past few days." She carried the plate over and set it on the table. "I never said a word, but he might have figured it out."

"He probably did," Mick answered while blowing on a dumpling that he knew would be soft and flavorful. "I had told him that I'd check into her whereabouts." Mick popped the hot dumpling in his mouth and was not disappointed.

"Yes, you did, and you found her, brought her here for him to see." She lifted a cup out of the cupboard and filled it with coffee from the percolator. "I do hope it was for the right reasons."

Mick ignored the twinge of unease that formed in his stomach. "Tony wanted to say goodbye, to make things right."

"Did she find someone to take over her classroom while she's visiting?" Mother asked, sitting down at the table with her cup of coffee.

Mick finished chewing and swallowed. Both he and Connor had learned years ago to never withhold the truth from their mother. "She's not a schoolteacher."

"Oh." She took a sip of coffee. "When did that change?"

Mick took another bite of the savory chicken and gravy mixture, chewed and swallowed, before saying, "She never was a teacher."

"Interesting. Tony was certain that she was teaching school in Junction."

"I know, but she's not."

His mother leveled a look at Mick, waiting for him to answer her silent question. She was sure to learn sooner or later, and it might as well be from him.

"She runs a speakeasy," he said.

Mother didn't even lift a brow as she sipped her coffee. "Well, isn't that an interesting job for a young lady."

She never had been one to judge or criticize people, yet Mick felt compelled to point out. "It's also illegal."

"Yes, I'm aware of that." She stood and carried her cup to the sink. "I'm going to check on Tony while you finish eating." At the doorway, she added, "If he's awake, I'll let him know you'll be up to see him shortly."

Her way of saying that it was Mick's job to introduce Lisa to her father. He had already assumed as much, and had promised Lisa he would be with her. Suddenly, the chicken and dumplings weren't as tasty as they had been a moment ago. He finished eating and carried his plate to the sink. A sudden urge to see Lisa struck him as he wondered if his well-meaning idea of Tony being able to make things right before he died was causing more harm than good to everyone involved.

Had his own demons about how things had ended between him and his father driven him to this point? He hadn't thought that was possible, but got a sense that his mother was suggesting that moments ago. She knew the difficult time he'd had after his father had died, and had always insisted that his father had died knowing he was loved by both of his sons, and that he would be proud of him for becoming a police officer.

Mick wasn't sure of that. Would never be sure of that.

Just as he was turning to leave the room, the back door opened and a very familiar voice said, "I'm home."

Connor had entered the house saying those exact words from the time he could talk. A moment later, he walked into the kitchen.

"Do I smell chicken and dumplings?" he asked, grinning from ear to ear as always.

"Yes. It's in the oven," Mick replied.

"How was the trip?" Connor asked, walking to the cupboard for a plate.

"Fine. How were things here?"

"Good. Nothing out of the ordinary." He glanced around. "Where's the daughter?"

"Upstairs."

"And?"

Mick shrugged.

Connor laughed.

"What's funny about that?"

"You." Connor opened the oven door and pulled out the kettle. "Three days on a train, with a woman." He piled chicken and dumplings onto a plate. "That had to just about kill you."

For being twins, who looked a lot alike, the two of them were as different as night and day when it came to women. Connor had always thrived on how they flocked around him, doing all sorts of zany things to catch his attention, whereas Mick would rather keep his distance from each and every one of them. It had always been that way for him, even before Twila. Afterward, he'd decided he was far better off being alone. Be in complete control of his own life.

He'd been trying to gain control of that since the moment he'd been born, and now that he finally had it, there was no reason to change anything.

Yet, he had to admit that the trip home had been far more enjoyable than the trip to Missouri had been. Sharing meals with Lisa and passing the long hours talking with her had certainly shortened the journey. "It wasn't so bad."

Connor shut the oven door and turned, stared at him. "It wasn't?"

"No. It wasn't." Before his brother could push the subject, Mick asked, "What have you been up to?"

With a full plate in hand, Connor dug a fork out of the drawer and then walked to the table. "Working. Now that you're home, I'm going to head up state. There are a lot of farmers up that way who could use a telephone, and I'm the man who can install the lines for them."

His brother had been intrigued with telephones from the time he was old enough to talk on one. As a kid, he'd installed one in every room of the house, until their mother had made him remove most of them because she kept tripping on the lines. Connor had also designed several models of the devices. A few hadn't worked, but a couple had, and once he'd sold those, there was no stopping him. The fact he'd started his own company hadn't surprised anyone. "Another expansion?"

"Yes, all the way to Syracuse," Connor said.

All was working out well for Connor, and Mick was proud of him for that. For taking the reins and running with his dream. "When are you leaving?"

Connor scooped up a dumpling with his fork. "Right after I eat."

"How long will you be gone?"

Pausing between bites, Connor shrugged. "A couple of weeks or so. Maybe a month. Not really sure. Why? Need something?"

"No, just curious." That was a partial lie. Mick was wondering about Lisa traveling back to Missouri by herself. He wouldn't let that happen, but he couldn't ask his brother to change his plans again. He'd have to find someone else to stop in and check on his mother and Tony.

"Oh, Connor, dear, hello," Mother greeted as she walked into the room.

Mick didn't hear Connor's response because there was a swooshing sound in his ears caused by the flow of blood pounding through his veins at the sight of the woman standing next to his mother. Wearing a dark blue dress with embroidered white flowers, and a string of white pearls looped over her head, Lisa met his gaze.

He felt her unease, as if she wasn't sure of herself, and offered a genuine smile. She should be more than sure of herself. He'd seen her independence and confidence, and wished she could see that in herself, too.

The slap on his shoulder knocked his hearing back in place.

"...the better looking of the two," Connor was saying.

Mother had obviously made the introduction between Lisa and Connor and his brother was taking full advantage of it.

Mick stepped forward, blocking Connor from moving any closer to Lisa. "Are you ready to see your father?"

Her chin dipped slightly, but she quickly lifted it back up. "Yes, your mother says he's awake."

He placed a hand on her arm and turned to his brother and mother. "If you'll excuse us."

"Of course," Connor said. "We'll be right here when you come back down."

Mick's spine tingled at the undercurrent in his brother's tone, and he leveled a solid stare on Connor, one that said *stay clear of her.* Her beauty had drawn men's attention on the train, but Connor was different. He was a flirt of the worst kind. "Thought you were heading out to see some farmers."

With a grin that filled his face, Connor said, "Think I'll postpone that for a bit. Things just got a whole lot more interesting around here."

* * *

Even while attempting to maintain her composure at the idea of coming face-to-face with her father, Lisa glanced from brother to brother. She'd never seen two people look so much alike, while looking so different at the same time. Connor had the same brown hair as Mick, cut nearly the same and combed to the side so a section flopped over his forehead. His features were similar, too. Straight nose, narrow chin and wide cheeks, but he wasn't as handsome as Mick. His eyes were blue, but not the cornflower blue of Mick's. The harder she compared, the more she determined that his entire face, although similar, was different. It wasn't nearly as perfect as Mick's. Connor's was thinner, and his features were not as defined, not as refined and handsome. She now understood what Mick meant when he said some people said they looked alike and others said they didn't.

To her, they didn't. Their builds were the same. Broad shoulders, thick chest and upper arms, narrow waist and lean legs. From a distance, it would be hard to tell them apart, but up close, it certainly wasn't.

Like his brother, Connor was also a charmer. The way he grinned and greeted her in a flirty, teasing way reminded her of men she met at the speakeasy.

Mick's charm was in a much more subtle and kind way. One that she far preferred. Mick was like his mother. Barbara McCormick was a dear of a woman. Other than by her own mother, Lisa couldn't remember feeling so welcomed and being treated with such open kindness.

The hold Mick had on her arm tightened. "Ready?"

Drawing a deep breath, she nodded again. "Yes."

The faster she got this over with, the faster she could head home. Leave behind all his kindness and charm.

"You look very nice. Very pretty," Mick said as they walked down the hallway, toward the wide staircase that led upstairs.

The house was large and beautiful, with soft thick carpets covering some of the floors, and shining hardwood in other places. Brightly colored wallpaper was on nearly all of the walls, in different colors and prints, depending on the room, which were all filled with lovely wooden or upholstered furniture. "Thank you," she answered, glad that he still had hold of her arm, because her nerves were kicking in tenfold.

"Breathe," Mick whispered.

It took her a moment to let that happen. "He thinks I'm a schoolteacher," she whispered, because her voice didn't want to work. It felt as if all her steam had seeped out of her.

"You have nothing to be ashamed of, Lisa," he said. "You've made a good living for yourself and helped the entire community. You can be proud of that."

"Would you be proud of a daughter who ran a speakeasy? Would you even want to meet her?" She'd never been overly proud of running a speakeasy, and right now, felt embarrassed about it.

"Yes. I'd be proud of any child who worked as hard as you have," he answered.

He was a hard one to combat. Just when she thought she might have a solid point, it was as if he changed the rules and flipped everything back around. Especially inside her. Specifically, every time he touched her. Like now. He was merely holding her arm as they walked up the steps, but his touch made her entire arm tingle, like it had been singed by an open flame.

That had happened on the train, too, while he'd escorted her off and on, or to the dining car, or when he'd touched her hand while they'd been talking, but it had been easier to ignore then.

Probably because they hadn't been about to arrive at the door where she knew her father was on the other side. Mick's touch was doing more than making her arm tingle, it was keeping her from turning around and running the other way.

"Tony's not going to care if you're a teacher or speakeasy owner," Mick said as they arrived at the top of the stairs. "You're his daughter."

Her throat was on fire; all she could do was shake her head.

Mick released her arm and stepped in front of her. "It's going to be fine."

Fear filled her. "No, it's not, and I don't think I can do this, Mick." Glancing at the door only a few steps away, the pain and sadness she'd experienced years before renewed themselves as if it had been yesterday. "What if I'm the reason he never came back?"

Mick placed his hands on her shoulders. Squeezed them. "You can't believe that."

She did. She'd never admitted it before, but deep down, even as a small child, she'd wondered if she'd been the reason he'd gone to war. If she'd misbehaved, or been too much trouble.

"Look at me, Lisa," Mick said.

She blinked hard, keeping the tears at bay as she turned her gaze to meet his.

"You are not to blame for anything," he said. "Anything."

She glanced beyond his shoulder again, at the door, then closed her eyes.

"And you didn't ride three days on a train to turn back now," he said softly.

Opening her eyes, she asked, "Do you still have those handcuffs?"

He frowned. "Yes, why?"

Thoroughly flustered, because she had to enter the room, see her father, even though it scared her to death, she held up a wrist.

He grinned and shook his head.

She nodded and looked at the door. "I don't think I can do it on my own."

He wrapped a hand around her wrist, like his hand was a handcuff. "You aren't alone. I'm here and I'll stay as long as you want me to stay. If you want privacy, just let me know and I'll leave."

She'd never begged for anything, but did now. "Don't leave, please."

"I won't."

Chapter Ten

Lisa's throat was locked up so tight she couldn't breathe. Or maybe the air was just lodged so tight in her lungs that it couldn't get out. She remembered Tony Walters as a big, strong man. One who used to carry her around on big broad shoulders and throw her up in the air and catch her with solid strong arms. Her images of him were nothing like the man lying in the bed. He looked shriveled, worn out, old. Yet, it was her father. Though his once thick, dark hair was gray and thin, and there were wrinkles on his face, she recognized him, and she saw the tears in his dark blue eyes as he looked at her.

Her heart took a hard somersault, forcing the air out of her lungs, through her burning throat.

"Lisa," he said with a gasp as he tried to sit up.

She rushed forward to the side of the bed. "Don't. Don't move. It's not necessary." Her eyes burned and he grew blurry because of the tears that sprouted. She laid her hands on his shoulders. "Please, don't try to sit up."

He framed her face with both hands. "It is you. Oh, how I've dreamed of seeing you again."

Tears trickled out of his eyes, and hers, as she admitted, "I dreamed of seeing you again, too."

"Oh, Lisa. My sweet, little Lisa, I've missed you so, so much." He wheezed as he breathed in air.

This was him. It was her father. "I've missed you, too."

"You're so beautiful," he said, scanning her face. "Look at that hair, those eyes, that perfect little nose. You look so much like your mother. So, so much." He released her face and wiped his eyes before patting the bed beside him. "Sit. Tell me how you are."

She swiped the tears off her cheeks and saw her father look past her.

"Mick." Tony shook his head. "Oh, Mick. You found her. How can I ever thank you?"

He stood at the foot of the bed and patted one of her father's legs. "Just tell her the truth, Tony. The whole truth."

A tiny shiver rippled down Lisa's spine at the dullness that formed in her father's eyes.

He blinked several times, then nodded. "I will, Mick. I'll tell her everything."

Mick looked at her.

She felt too fragile, too fearful to be alone right now and shook her head at the silent question in his eyes.

He gave her a slight nod and sat down on the chair near the rolltop desk against the wall beside the door. His action, his silent support, filled her eyes with more tears.

"Thank you, Lisa, for coming to see me." Her father took her hand. "I'd dreamed, hoped to see you one last time, but I would have understood if you hadn't come."

She sat on the bed beside him and wrapped her other hand around their clutched ones. The initial shock of seeing him was wearing off, somewhat, and bit by bit, she felt herself returning. The grown-up Lisa. Yet, at the same time, she couldn't help but notice how frail his hand was and how weak his hold felt. Smiling at him, she teasingly said, "I have to be honest. Mick threatened to handcuff me or I wouldn't be here."

"No," her father said, looking at Mick with disdain.

She nodded and tightened her hold on his hand. "Yes. But I'm glad he did. I'm happy to see you."

"I'm so happy you are here," her father replied. "Tell me about yourself. Do you like being a teacher?"

Her heart dropped and she glanced at Mick, who winked one eye at her, along with a slight nod. She swallowed. "I'm not a teacher. I run a speakeasy."

The scorn she'd feared didn't even flash in her father's eye. Instead, humor did, and he laughed until he coughed.

Patting his chest, he apologized, "I'm sorry." After a gasp for air, he continued, "That's brilliant. You may have got your mother's beauty, but I'm happy to see you got a bit of spunk and spirit from your old man." Eyes still twinkling, he nodded. "Aw, Mick, now I understand the handcuffs."

Mick nodded, but his eyes were on her.

"He didn't bust your joint, did he?" her father asked.

Lisa shook her head. "No. But he threatened to."

Tony laughed again. Harder.

The sound of that brought back memories. Wonderful memories. She could remember that laugh filling the house. Every day. For a moment, it was as if she was eight years old again, hearing him laugh, hearing her mother laugh. Suddenly, a love she hadn't felt in years welled inside her heart.

"Oh, I wish I could have been a fly on the wall when you two met," her father said between laughs.

"You would have had to be a magician," Mick said, lifting a brow her way.

She giggled at his response. Then, perhaps because of the happiness filling her, her giggles turned into laughter. The laughter continued for some time, as her father asked her about people he'd known, Fred Myers, and Harris Hendrick, Thad and Toby's father, as well as Sean Hendrick, Buck's father, and several others. She answered each question, explaining how they were all her customers, and added some funny things that had happened over the years.

"Oh," her father said as the laughing once again died down. "I wish I could see them all."

Her heart stumbled slightly. She took a breath before asking, "Why didn't you come home? Why didn't you let us know you were alive?"

He stiffened, and patted her hand. "I couldn't, honey. I promised I wouldn't."

"Promised who?" she asked.

Waving his other hand, he asked Mick, "Will you open the bottom desk drawer and bring me the cigar box there?"

A bout of anger rose inside her. A cigar? In his condition? What had she expected? This wasn't the father she remembered. Then again, he'd have had to change over the years, just as she had. She'd grown up, and he'd grown old.

Mick walked along the other side of the bed, with the cigar box in hand. It looked as old and tattered as her father.

"Thank you," her father said. "Can you help me sit up, Mick?"

"Sure." Mick set the box on the bed and gently grasped her father by the upper arms.

Lisa stood and propped the pillows up against the headboard, and held them there until Mick gradually eased her father back against them.

"Thank you." Her father pointed at the box. "I'll take that now."

Mick handed him the cigar box and walked back to the chair. Unsure what to do, Lisa sat down on the edge of the bed again.

Her father opened the box. It didn't hold cigars, but a bundle of letters and other pieces of paper. He pulled out the letters first, a large stack tied with an old shoe string. "These are for you. They go all the way back to when I left for the war. Leaving was the hardest thing I ever did, but our country was at war. I had to go, had to defend our land and our freedom."

Lisa flinched slightly. Her mother had always said that was why he'd gone to war, to defend their land, so they'd have a home, and because of that, she'd never let anyone else have their property, and had made Lisa promise that she wouldn't, either.

She took the letters from his hand, not because she wanted them, but because he was shaking so hard, she was afraid he might drop the bundle. She was proud of him for fighting for the country, for the land, the home she still lived in. She'd held on to her home with honor over the years, just like her mother had.

Shuffling through the rest of the things in the box, her father sighed. "It's not a lot, just some military papers and such, along with my bank book." Looking at her, he handed her the box. "All that's left of my life, other than you." He smiled sadly. "It's all I have to give you."

She took the box, and set the bundle of letters back in it. "I don't want you to give me anything, other than an explanation."

He bowed his head as if shameful. "I know." Wheezing with each breath, he shook his head. "I promised her that I'd never tell you the truth. She never failed me, I failed her. I cried like a baby when I heard she'd died."

Confused, yet pretty sure who he was talking about, she asked, "My mother? You promised my mother?"

His eyes fluttered shut for a moment. "Yes. Bertha. Oh, Bertha. I remember the first time I saw her. It was at a church picnic, in Junction. She was fourteen and had just moved to town. I was sixteen and fell in love with her that day. Her father said she couldn't get married for a few more years, so we waited, and we got married on her seventeenth birthday." He took her hand again. "You were born three years later, and it was the happiest day of our lives. You were named after her sister, who had died when she was a baby. You were so smart, right from the start. Walked before you were a year old, talked before you were two, and you loved the little purple flowers that grew in the pasture. They were weeds, but not to you, and you'd get angry when the cows ate them."

Lisa knew all that. Her mother had told her all those things, yet, hearing him say them, knowing that he hadn't forgotten things about her, made her heart swell all over again.

She bowed her head, needing a moment. The letters tied with the shoe string made her frown as she recognized her mother's handwriting. For some reason, she'd thought these were letters he'd written to her, but never sent. Her frown increased when she saw the postmark date of the top one. Picking up the bundle, she examined the date closer. "This letter was written four years ago."

Her father nodded. "It was the last one she sent me. That's the one where she told me about you getting ready to take your teaching exam." Tears glistened in his eyes again. "I understand she had a stroke, and died several months later."

"She did," Lisa said, while wondering why her mother never mentioned that she'd known Tony was alive and had written to him. Unable not to, she untied the string, glanced through the stack, at other post-marks. The entire time she was growing up, believing he'd died, her mother had been writing to him. "What is this? These are all from my mother. I don't under— She never told me. Why?"

"She couldn't."

"Why?"

He closed his eyes and licked his lips before look-ing at her again. "Your mother was scared and alone, and when the army reported that I was dead, instead of missing, she didn't know what to do, so she married Duane. When I woke up in the hospital and they told me that my family had been told that I was dead, the first thing I did was write to Bertha, tell her I wasn't dead and was on my way home from France. She met me in Kansas City, told me that she'd remarried. I couldn't blame her. She'd been alone, needed someone to take care of her and you, and—"

"No. No." Shivering, Lisa stood up. "No, we didn't. She didn't have to marry Duane. Why didn't she tell me? Why didn't she tell me that she was writing to you?"

"For your own good. You were just a child. I agreed to let everyone believe I was dead, like the army had reported. It was easier that way. For everyone. I left and promised I'd never contact you."

Lisa couldn't believe what she was hearing. "Easier? Easier?"

"I'm sorry, Lisa. It was all my fault. Please don't blame her."

It couldn't be true. None of it. "I— I—" Unable to say more, to hear more, she turned and ran to the door, out it, and across the hall into her room.

Mick had stood, and was prepared to follow Lisa, yet understood she needed some time to herself. It was hard, because he wanted to go to her, tell her everything would be all right. Forcing himself to stay, he walked over to the bed. "She never received the telegram I sent."

Tony rubbed his forehead. "I shouldn't have had you send one. It was selfish. I should have left things in the past." He slowly slipped down, until he was lying on the bed again. "I'd like to be alone if you don't mind."

Mick positioned the pillows beneath Tony's head and left the room, wishing he would have left things in the past, too. For Lisa's sake, and Tony's.

Although he was mad at himself, he stopped at Lisa's door and knocked. "Lisa? Do you need anything?"

"No. I just need to be alone."

He stood there until he'd talked himself out of opening her door, and then walked down the stairs.

His mother met him at the bottom step. "How did that go?"

"Not well."

"I'm sorry, darling. Some things take time, this will be one of them."

"I shouldn't have brought her here," he admitted.

She laid a hand on his arm. "But you did, because

you believed it would help both of them. Don't give up on that belief. Not yet."

"Why? So I can make it worse?" Disgusted with himself, he shook his head. "For both of them?"

"Even the tiniest scratch takes time to heal."

"And if you keep picking at it, it never heals." He headed for the front door, needing air. Needing… Hell, he had no idea what he needed right now, other than a way to turn back time.

That's what he'd always needed. To go back and change several things.

He walked around the house to the backyard, which was immense, with numerous large trees he and Connor had had to mow around in their younger years, all the way to the back of the yard where the trees grew thicker and a steep hill led down to where the Genesee River flowed past the property. Near the large overgrown grove of trees that separated the yard from the riverbank was where the workshop sat. A solid old shed where he and Connor had spent years working on their hobbies. Connor building telephone devices, and him working on wood crafts. His last one had been a canoe, made entirely from cedar strips. It still wasn't finished.

He'd been working on it for years, because for months, years, he'd lost interest in it. His father had helped him build the frame, and in the years since his death, Mick had started attaching the long cedar strips, but still had a long way to go. It was slow, tedious work, and that's what he wanted right now, something to focus his attention on.

He opened the front and back doors of the shed, in order to fill the space with sunlight, and pulled the protective canvas off the canoe frame that sat upside down on the wooden stands.

Connor arrived while Mick was still wiping the dust off the less-than-half-built canoe. He'd worked on it only three or four times in the past eight years.

"Things didn't go well?" his brother asked.

"No." He tossed the rag onto the workbench. "I don't know why I did it, Con. Why I thought I had to help Tony."

"Because that's who you are, and why you became a cop. You've always been the first one to jump in and help others. Remember Amy White's cat? You were only seven when you climbed the tree to get that cat down."

Mick wasn't sure that was a memory that helped much. "The cat came down on its own. After I fell out of the tree and broke my arm."

"Yeah, well, it was the thought that counted."

Mick began unscrewing the clamp holding the last boards he'd glued onto the canoe. "Not this time."

Connor walked over and began to remove the clamp at the other end of the canoe. "Rome wasn't built in a day."

"Are you talking about the canoe or the mess I've made for Tony and Lisa?"

Connor shrugged and grinned. "Both."

Mick huffed out a laugh and shook his head. "I don't know what to do, Connor."

"You'll figure it out. You always do."

This time was different. He'd become too involved in something that didn't concern him and shouldn't have. That was the bottom line. He walked over to remove the weights keeping the cedar strips from warping. Once again, Connor walked over to help.

"I remember Dad helping you cut all of these pieces of wood," he said.

"Me, too," Mick answered.

"He'll be glad when it's done."

Mick frowned, looking at Connor.

His brother shrugged. "I believe he's still watching over us, and always will be." Gesturing at the wood, he picked up one end of the top piece. "Grab a hold. I'll help you put on a few pieces."

Mick took his end and set it aside so they could search the pile for the pieces he wanted to use next. Together, they picked out boards, then tacked, glued and clamped on five strips on one side of the canoe within the next couple of hours while conversing about several things, yet nothing of significance.

"Want to put a few on the other side?" Connor asked while tightening the last clamp on his end.

"Yes," Mick answered, "but you don't have to help. I know you have things to do."

Glancing out the open door, Connor nodded. "I do, and I think I will head home now. I'll stop by tomorrow."

Mick looked out the door and saw Lisa walking across the yard, toward the shed. His heart sank at the same time his pulse quickened. She'd been eye-catching the first time he'd seen her, but he swore she'd grown prettier every day since then.

He nodded at his brother as Connor slapped his shoulder while walking out the door. Mick watched as his brother paused long enough to point at the shed while answering a question Lisa asked.

Mick stepped over the threshold, and was standing there when she arrived. Her eyes were swollen, and the desire that hit, to pull her close for a hug, shocked him as much as it had earlier. No, what shocked him was his next thought. Kissing her. That was completely out of the ordinary for him. Swallowing hard, he locked his knees and kept his hands at his sides. "How are you doing?"

He flinched at the stupidity of that question as his own voice hit his ears. There just wasn't anything about this that he could get right.

Shaking her head, she said, "Fine."

He nodded and then shook his head, silently showing that her actions and words didn't match.

"It doesn't matter," she said with a half grin. "I was wondering if I could use the telephone, to call the boys again."

"Yes."

"I would have asked your mother, but she was carrying a tray into Tony's room and said you were out here." She looked around him, into the shed. "Are you building a boat?"

"Yes, a canoe."

"May I see it?"

"Sure." He stepped aside so she could enter. "It's not even half done."

She ran a hand along the side of the canoe. "You put each of these pieces of wood on one at a time?"

"Yes, be careful, you might get a sliver. I still have a lot of sanding to do."

"How do you make them stay together?" she asked while touching a clamp. "What are these?"

"Those are clamps," Mick answered, his mouth dry because the thought of kissing her was still roving around in his head. "The boards are held together with dowel pins and glue. The clamps keep it tight as they dry."

"It's beautiful wood."

He tried hard to look away from her, but couldn't.

"It is. It's eastern red cedar. My father helped me cut the slats years ago."

She walked along the side of the canoe, examining it closely. "You said he died when you were in high school. When was that?"

Finding the ability to move, Mick walked over and put the top on the can of glue. "Eight years ago. I can show you where the telephone is."

"Were you going to put more wood on this side?"

He picked up the hammer to pound the lid on tight. "I can do it later."

"No. I'm not in a hurry to call the boys. I can help you. Please. I'd like to see how it's done."

If he turned, looked at her, he knew where his thoughts would go again, so he kept his gaze averted. "You might get glue on your dress."

Her laugh was his undoing. He had to turn, look at her. A shimmer appeared in her eyes as she grinned.

"Right now, glue on a dress is the least of my worries," she said.

Her tenacity was just one of the things he admired about her, yet he asked, "You sure?"

"Very. And I'll be careful not to get any glue on me. How can I help? What do we do first?" She rubbed her hands together. "I've been sitting around for so many days, it's going to feel good to do something."

Giving in, he set down the hammer and took the lid back off the glue. "First, we pick out which slat we want to use."

"From that stack of them?"

"Yes."

"Okay." She clapped her hands. "Let's pick one out."

He laughed at her enthusiasm.

She laughed, too, and he was glad. If helping build a

canoe would make her even a little bit happy right now, he was more than willing to let her help.

They found a slat, and she held it in place as Mick tacked one end onto the frame, and then the other. Answering her questions, he explained how after tacking on the strips, glue would be brushed on and then the boards would be clamped together.

She appeared truly interested and asked other questions as they worked. Mick found enjoyment in answering her questions. Enjoyment in forgetting about the weight, not only on her shoulders, but on his for a short time. She caught on quickly, too. It felt like barely any time had passed when they were clamping several boards together.

"Now what?" she asked.

Hiding his wave of disappointment that there wasn't much more they could do on the canoe, he doubled-checked the tightness of the clamps, then walked over to the workbench and picked up the tarp. "The glue needs to dry for at least forty-eight hours before we can add more."

She took the other end of the tarp and helped him cover the canoe. "When will it be done? Completely. After all the sanding and varnishing and sealing you talked about."

He laughed. "At the rate I'm going, when I'm about fifty." He walked back to the bench, put the lid on the glue and hammered the tin lid tight. "Thanks, you were a great help."

"She lied."

He put the glue on the shelf before turning around. "Who?"

"My mother." She sighed heavily while walking around the canoe, gently smoothing the canvas covering it. "I read some of her letters. She lied to Tony in them, and she lied to me." Shaking her head, she added, "The entire time. For years, she lied to me for years."

The tears in her eyes tore at his heart, and he couldn't think of the right words. If there were any. "I'm sorry, Lisa." Giving her mother the benefit of the doubt, he added, "She must have had a reason."

She shook her head. "Because she was lonely?" She swiped at her eyes. "The entire town called him a hero, how he'd died in the war, fighting for our country. She didn't want that to end. Didn't want them to know he was alive, because she'd married Duane. The exact opposite of…" She shook her head as her words trailed off.

Mick walked over and put the weights on the strips again while he searched for a response. The desire to hold her, kiss her, was striking hard again. "It must have been a difficult situation."

"Was that a reason to lie? She told Tony that Duane was a wonderful man and taking good care of us. He wasn't. He wasn't nice and he never took care of us. He moved into our home. Tony's home. I guess that was better than us moving into his apartment above his saloon, but I don't understand why she never told me the truth. That Tony was alive. She let me believe he was dead, all these years."

The pain in her voice was so evident, the hurt in her eyes so visible, whether he wanted to admit it or not, he cared about her. "I'm sorry, Lisa. Sorry that I brought you here. Sorry that I—"

"I'm not," she said. "I'd have never known the truth if you hadn't."

"Maybe that would have been better."

"No, the truth is always best." She walked to the

open shed door. "I just need to figure out what to do about it."

His instincts about all of this had been wrong, and he'd made things worse by following those instincts. There was nothing he could do to make it right, better. It was too late for that. He walked to the back of the shed and pulled that door closed, latched it. Arriving at the front door, where she still stood, he said, "I'll show you to a phone."

She stepped outside and waited as he pulled that door closed.

"Where will you use your canoe?" She grinned slightly. "Fifty years from now."

Considering her mind had been on other things since they'd arrived, it was understandable that she didn't know the river was only a short distance away. He pointed past the shed. "The Genesee River. It's just beyond those trees."

"Will you show me?"

"Right now?"

"Yes." Meeting his gaze, she shrugged. "I'm not sure what I want to tell the boys. But I need to call them, tell them something. I know I shouldn't be putting it off, but I am."

"That's understandable." He held back the urge to take hold of her arm.

"Just not very productive," she said as they started to walk toward the trees.

"You're used to being productive, aren't you?" That was a stupid question. All she'd accomplished in her life, taking care of her mother, building and running the speakeasy, and helping the town of Junction was evidence of that. He had far less to show for his years than

that. Not that it was a competition, it just made him realize that all he'd thought he'd known, wasn't enough.

"I like being busy." They'd entered the grove of trees
and she asked, "What's that?"

Mick glanced up at what she pointed toward. It was
well hidden by the leaves. "A tree house."

"How did you get up there?"

The tree had grown since it had been built, a lot. The
boards that had been nailed to the trunk in order for him
and Connor to climb up, used to be a few feet off the
ground, now they started near his shoulders. Pointing
at the boards, he said, "Those boards. See how there is
another one every foot or so?"

"Yes. That's very ingenious."

He frowned. "Have you never seen a tree house?"

"No, never."

He looked up at the old structure that was still intact,
but unsafe for anyone to climb up or into it, otherwise
he might have helped her up, so she could see it. "Everything is pretty dilapidated now. I considered taking
it down, just so Riley couldn't climb up there, but so
far, he hasn't noticed it. But I'm sure the minute I start
tearing it down, he will."

"How old is he?"

"Five. He moved in with his grandparents in January.
His mother died when he was a baby, and his father took
a job out of town, and couldn't take Riley with him."

"And you befriended him, just like you did me." She
sighed. "You like helping people, don't you?"

He shrugged. "Riley really misses his father. I just
try to make his time away from him easier." He nodded toward the trail, for them to start walking again.

She smiled and a few steps later, asked, "Who built
the tree house?"

"Connor and I." He shook his head. "No, our father built it, Connor and I helped. We weren't very old. Seven or eight. We spent a lot of time up there when we were young, thought it was the best thing ever to spend the night up there all by ourselves."

"I bet that was fun." Her sigh echoed in the trees. "It had to have been nice having a brother to share things with."

"It was." He'd not only opened a can of worms in her life, he'd opened one in his own. The things he felt for her were so wide-ranging, and just kept growing in all directions. He couldn't stop watching her as she walked, talked. Couldn't stop thinking about how remarkable she was in so many different ways.

Because she was ahead of him on the narrow, well-worn path, he warned, "The river is just on the other side of that last row of trees. Be careful. The bank is steep and the water is deep."

"How steep? Is there a way down to the water?"

"Yes, there's a set of stairs."

Looking over her shoulder, she asked, "That your father built?"

Mick wasn't sure what struck him harder, how the sun shining through the trees haloed her, making her look more beautiful than ever, or the memories her questions evoked. Good memories of all the things he had done with his father. For the past several years, he hadn't let those memories come forward. When he allowed himself to remember his father, it had been only of his death, and the fight they'd had that morning. The fighting they'd done for two years before his father had died.

"With your and Connor's help?" she asked, her smile brighter.

"Yes. He built them. We helped," Mick answered.

"He sounds like he was a wonderful father."

Although he didn't want any more memories to come forward, Mick had to admit, "He was."

"You must have learned a lot from him. It shows in the way you treat Riley." She glanced up at him. "And others."

"He was a good man," he answered. "So is your father."

"Did you ever have someone lie to you?" she asked.

There were a lot of ways he could answer that, and he went with one that might make her smile. "I'm a police officer—people lie to me all the time," he replied with a wink.

She giggled softly. "I'm sure they do, but what about someone close to you? Someone you care about, have they lied to you?"

He'd always been a private person; not even Connor or his mother knew how things had ended between him and Twila. Yet, he was compelled to be completely honest with Lisa. "Yes."

"What did you do?"

"At first, I was hurt, then mad, and then I decided that the best thing to do was to let it go." That had been what he'd decided, but it hadn't been that easy. Within weeks of refusing to marry him, Twila had gotten married, to another actor. She'd called him, apologized, told him that being married to the actor would advance her career, and that being married to him would have scared her, because his job, being a police officer, was so dangerous.

"So you just pretended it didn't happen?"

"No," he replied. "I know it happened. I just chose to not dwell on it."

"Did that work?"

"Eventually." He hadn't dwelled on the fact Twila had lied to him. Instead, he'd decided to never open himself to let it happen again. It had worked, because until Lisa, he hadn't given a single woman a second thought. Now, he was having to remind himself of what had happened, and the commitment he'd made to himself.

Chapter Eleven

Lisa knew herself well enough to understand she was trying hard to not think about her own problems. Focusing on Mick was far easier. Trouble was, that made her think about herself, too. She liked the way he could make her smile, and she liked the idea of him being her friend. Of them being friends. She'd had friends before, but it was different with him.

No one had ever made her feel as if she wasn't alone the way he did, and she wasn't sure if that was a good thing, or a bad thing.

Stepping through the trees, her thoughts once again shifted, and she let them. The beauty before her was breathtaking. An expanse of flowing water, sparkling in the sunlight and lined by large leafed trees, was like an oasis to her mind. She stood there, just soaking up the beauty, the peacefulness.

"Careful," Mick said, taking hold of her arm. "The steps have shifted over the years, making some uneven."

Made of concrete and stone, the steps were buried into the side of the bank, and wide enough for her and Mick to walk side by side as they moved from step to step toward the water.

"I've never seen so many trees all in one place." In awe, she added, "I know we are in the city, but it doesn't feel like it." Staring at the water, she questioned her own sense of direction. The river was much larger than the creeks she'd seen back home, and the only time she'd seen the Missouri River was when the train crossed over it. "I feel like the water is flowing in the wrong direction, like it's flowing north."

"You are very perceptive. It is flowing north because we are north of the St. Lawrence Divide. Rivers flow north here. In Missouri they flow south."

"I've heard of that, of all the continental divides, but never been on the other side of one." She'd heard of many things, had studied many things while working on her teaching certificate. It all seemed so long ago. She'd forgotten about all the things she'd learned about and wanted to see someday, wanted to do someday.

They stepped off the bottom step, onto a small section of flat, hard, but slick ground from the water sloshing upon it every so often. "How deep is the water?"

His hold on her arm tightened. "Very, well over your head, and right now, it's still very cold, so be careful."

"Can we sit down for a minute?" she asked. "On the steps?"

"If you want."

She wanted to stay right here for as long as possible, wishing all her problems could flow away with the water.

He brushed sand and leaves off the step with his hand, then nodded for her to sit.

Once she had, he sat down beside her.

"It must have been wonderful growing up here, with all the beauty, with your family," she said, with a longing inside her. She had a few memories of when her father still lived with them, but most of those memories had been long ago buried by those made later, after he'd left, when she'd wished for a miracle—that he hadn't died. Never in a million years would she have even considered that her mother had been lying to her for most of that time. It hurt, it angered her and it left her wondering why. It just didn't make sense. Her mother had loved her father. Hardly a day had gone by when she hadn't said so, said that she wished he'd never gone to the army, even after she'd married Duane.

"Yeah, it was good growing up here," Mick said.

Once again, her mind shifted to him. "Why do you sound so sad?"

"Do I?" He shrugged. "I don't mean to."

Curious, she asked, "How did your father die?"

"A car accident. In the winter."

Compassion filled her. "I'm sorry. What was his name?"

"Patrick."

Recalling his given name, she said, "You were named after him? So is your name Patrick McCormick Jr.?"

He shook his head. "No, my father was junior. I'm the third."

"The third?" She grinned, having never met anyone with that in their name. Assuming that had to mean he was the firstborn, she asked, "You're older than Connor?"

He nodded. "By fifteen minutes."

That fit, him being older. She'd met Connor only briefly, but Mick seemed to be more mature, more somber. Or maybe he purposefully behaved that way, because of his profession. Believed police officers couldn't have a sensitive side.

She wasn't sure. A heavy sigh left her lungs. She wasn't sure about a lot of things.

There was one thing that she was pretty certain of. "You and Connor are different in many ways, aren't you?"

He shrugged. "Everyone is different. It would be a dull world if everyone was the same."

There he did it again. Never quite answered, yet did.

As she stared at the river, sitting there beside him, a yearning filled her. An odd one. For some crazy reason, she wanted to lean her head onto his shoulder. Something inside her said that would ease some of the sadness inside her. She didn't know how she knew that, but she did. "Do you still miss your father?"

He was silent for so long, she looked up at him, saw the frown on his forehead. "I'm sorry. I don't mean to bring up bad memories, it's just that even though I've seen my father, know he's alive, it's odd because I still miss him. Miss the man I remember. I know that sounds silly."

"No, it doesn't." He touched her hand. "And yes, I still miss my father. Every day."

"I bet he'd be proud of you, becoming a police officer." She grimaced at him. "That's far more honorable than running a speakeasy."

"You've done far more than run a speakeasy. You helped an entire town."

"I had to. I don't know why my mother married Duane, but I've always thought that he married her because of my father. The entire town considered Tony a war hero, dying for his country, and Duane wanted recognition like that. I think he thought that marrying my mother, a heartbroken widow, would make him look like a hero. It did for a while, but then he kept demanding more, like he owned the whole town and that everyone owed him. It made me so angry and I decided that if he was going to make money off the speakeasy, everyone else was, too."

"You did just that."

She'd never told anyone how deeply Duane's behavior had bothered her, not even her mother.

"Your father is proud of you."

She shook her head. "Not as proud as he would be if I'd become a teacher."

"My father didn't want me to become a police officer. It's what I wanted. If becoming a schoolteacher is what you want, it's not too late. You could still do that."

The invisible weight once again pressed heavily on her shoulders. "No. There are too many people depending on me for that to happen."

After a few quiet moments, Mick patted her hand. "Ready to go make that phone call?"

No, she wasn't ready, she wanted to sit right here, forever, but knew she couldn't, so she nodded.

He stood and held out a hand. She took it, and, figuring she might as well get the call over with as soon as possible, she stood. Too quickly. One foot slipped in the mud and for the briefest of moments, she feared she'd fall into the water.

Mick had grasped her waist with both hands, steadied her, but she still had a sense of falling. Falling deep into something. Her heart was still thumping and her hands were both clutched onto the front of his shirt, as if only he could save her.

Time appeared to stop, as they stood there, face-to-face, holding on to one another. She couldn't take her eyes off his lips, and deeply wanted to know how they would feel against hers. Warm. Nice. She was sure of that.

"Are you all right?" he asked.

She sighed and closed her eyes as she nodded. Then, because the desire she'd had before was too strong to hold back this time, she leaned forward and laid her head against the front of his shoulder.

His hands slid around to her back and pulled her closer. She slipped her hands beneath his arms, around his back, and held on. Just held on. She was no longer afraid of falling into the river, but she was afraid and just wanted to be held. By him.

Her heart thudded harder, faster, when she felt him kiss the top of her head. Softly. Sweetly, as his hold on her tightened a bit more.

One of his hands rubbed her back, in big circles, as he whispered, "It's going to be all right. I promise."

She nodded, but didn't let go. Not yet. It had been so long since she'd been hugged, and his hug was the best one ever.

After a few moments, when she felt able, capable again, she drew in a deep breath and lifted her head. "Thank you." Her cheeks warmed slightly, but still, she admitted, "Sometimes a person just needs a hug."

His smile was so charming her heart tumbled all over again.

"Yes, sometimes they do."

He took her hand and kept her steady as they walked up the steps. She thought about asking if she could stay here for a few days, long enough to talk to her father, get a few answers to her many questions, but didn't because everything depended on how things were going at the Depot. The repercussions of her being gone could ruin everything.

Shifting her thoughts, she asked, "Why didn't your father want you to become a police officer?"

"Because he wanted me to follow in his footsteps at the family business."

"You didn't want to do that?"

"No, I didn't, but I might have if he hadn't died. I was only eighteen when he died, not old enough to take over the helm, so my uncle did."

Her heart constricted. "Will you take over, now that you're older?"

"No. I have a seat on the board of directors, and will remain on the board, but I will never run the company."

"Does that make you sad?"

"No, it doesn't make me sad. I'll continue my role on the board, while continuing to be a police officer. Life throws us curve balls, and there is only so much we can do about it." He winked at her. "In my opinion, you've already done your fair share."

His sincerity touched her deeply. As deeply as his hug had. It was as if the warmth of his embrace filled her all over again.

They walked the rest of the way to the house in silence. Once inside, he led her into a large library off the living room on the main floor. Her heart fluttered slightly at all the books. Years ago, that had become her favorite pastime, reading about things, people, places and stories about great adventures with endings that made her feel happy inside.

"Have you read all of these books?" She took a deep breath while scanning the floor-to-ceiling full shelves. The room even smelled wonderful. Like books.

He stopped near a table with two chairs. "The winters here can be long and cold. If you don't have something to do, you'll start talking to the furniture and wait for it to respond."

She lifted a book off the shelf and could almost see herself sitting in one of the big armchairs with a fire blazing in the brick fireplace, reading for hours. "You have an interesting way of answering questions."

"I do?"

Flipping through the pages, not paying any attention to the words, she nodded. "Yes. Sometimes you answer in a way where there is an answer, but I have to search to find it." She set the book back on the shelf.

He chuckled. "Do you like to read?"

"I love reading."

"Well, help yourself." He then nodded at the desk. "Would you like me to get the Junction operator on the line?"

"Yes, please."

He did so, and then asked the operator to hold and handed the phone to her. She took it, asked to be connected to the Hendricks' farm.

Mick nodded at her and walked toward the door.

She wanted to ask him to stay, but Buck answered the other end of the line.

Sighing, she greeted Buck. The conversation was short. Things were fine. He'd set Duane's payment on her porch steps as told, and, as of yet, hadn't heard anything from her stepfather. Buck was curious as to when she'd be returning, and how her father was doing.

She didn't know how to answer either question. Tony was ill, that was evident, and she'd probably made it worse, the way she'd run out of his room. "I'm not sure when I'll be leaving. Within a few days. Are you all right with that?"

"We can handle things on this end, Lisa," Buck said.

"I'm glad your father is alive, I just wish I could tell people about it."

Her eyes teared up. She'd gone to school with Buck, along with Toby and Thad, and their wives. She thought about the telegram, and was certain that Duane already knew, but couldn't take a chance that he didn't. That the telegram had simply been lost. "I can't have anyone knowing. Not until I get back. I'll call again and let you know when I'll be leaving."

She hung the speaker in the cradle, and sat down in one of the chairs. The phone call hadn't been hard, it was what she had to do now. Face the facts. She'd been lied to, and now knew the truth. What happened next was all on her shoulders.

That's why it all felt so heavy.

She was still sitting there, not even sure what her choices were, when the door opened. An odd sense of disappointment occurred when it wasn't Mick.

"How are you doing?" Barbara asked.

"I'm fine," Lisa answered.

Barbara closed the door and crossed the room, sat down at the table next to her. "Tony was afraid you'd left."

Mick's mother was a pretty woman, with sky-blue eyes and blond hair, and kindness seemed to float in the air all around her. "I thought about it," Lisa admitted.

"I'm sure you did, and I'm glad you didn't." Barbara reached across the table and patted Lisa's hand. "It's hard to understand life's twists and turns, but I like to believe that there is always a silver lining. A reason that things happen the way they do."

Lisa had no idea what that reason might be for both of her parents to lie to her, for years, yet, she didn't want to hurt the other woman's feelings, so she nodded.

Barbara's smile was as gentle as her touch. "Sometimes it's a long time before we know what that reason is but, eventually, it makes sense. I just want you to know that you are welcome to stay here for as long as you wish, and if you need anything while you are here, you just let me know."

"Thank you. I do need to return home as soon as possible, so I won't stay long." She had considered one thing that she could do, and decided that was probably her best choice. "I am curious to know when Tony's doctor will be over to see him next."

"Tomorrow. George—Dr. George Bolton—comes every Monday at ten in the morning," Barbara said. "I'm sure he'll be happy to speak with you."

Lisa nodded. If the doctor said it was all right, she'd take Tony back to Missouri with her. Take care of him there, in his house, just as she had her mother. Duane wouldn't like it, but he'd have to deal with it. She'd have to hire someone to help, but Tony was her father and she couldn't just desert him.

Mick kept telling himself that Lisa going home would be the best thing all the way around. Believing what he told himself was a different task. He hadn't told anyone about his father not wanting him to be a police officer, not even Twila. Yet, like other things, telling Lisa hadn't been hard, at all.

There was more to it than that. Holding her down by the river hadn't been hard, either, and it had opened up something inside him. Something so bright and warm, and completely foreign, he knew it could never happen again.

Holding her could never happen again. She'd felt too good. Smelled too good.

He gave his head a clearing shake in order to hear what Tony was saying.

His mother had said that Tony wanted to see him, so he'd gone upstairs, and had truthfully admitted that he didn't know what Lisa would do next.

"I'm just thankful that I got to see her again," Tony said. "That in itself was a dream come true. It was too much to hope that she'd understand. I agreed with Bertha, when she said that it was best for Lisa. That she'd already lost one father, and shouldn't have to lose another one." The old man shook his head. "There wasn't any other choice. Bertha was pregnant. I had to let them live their lives. Without me."

Mick leaned forward in his chair. "Pregnant? Lisa never mentioned a sibling."

"Bertha lost the baby," Tony said. "She'd lost two babies before we had Lisa."

"Is that in the letters you gave Lisa?" Mick asked.

Tony shook his head. "No, that is the one letter I didn't give her."

"Why? Lisa needs to know. Maybe it will help her understand."

Tony shook his head again. "I've already said enough. I don't want to sully Bertha's memory. Please don't tell her, Mick. It's not necessary."

Mick didn't agree, and a heavy knot formed in his stomach. Sully Bertha's memory? What about Lisa? From the beginning of this, he hadn't been able to tell her all he'd known, and it just kept happening. He wanted it to stop. Now, before she truly hated him. Not only for starting all this, but for never telling her all he knew.

"I would like to see her again before she leaves, if you can convince her of that," Tony said.

Flustered, Mick said, "That will be her choice. I won't force her to do anything, ever again, but if you don't tell her the truth, all of it, I will." He walked to the door, and upon opening it, came face-to-face with Lisa. Her soft, almost serene smile sent his heart careening like an out-of-control car on a slippery corner.

"Is he awake?" she asked.

"Yes," Tony answered from the bed.

Mick stepped aside so Lisa could enter the room. He laid a hand on her arm and silently questioned if she wanted him to stay. When she shook her head, he felt a sense of pride at her strength and resolve.

He hoped she found pride in herself, for all she'd accomplished, but more than that, he hoped that Tony would tell her the entire truth. She deserved to know everything, needed to know everything so she could put her past behind her.

"Mick, Riley is in the kitchen," his mother said from the bottom of the stairway.

He grinned and walked down the steps.

"He has his baseball mitt," his mother said.

"Well, then, I guess I better grab mine," Mick replied.

Riley was at the table, eating a cookie, and shoved the rest of it in his mouth and jumped off the chair as Mick walked into the room.

He ruffled Riley's curls. "Come on, partner, let's play some catch."

"Gram said I wasn't supposed to interrupt if you're busy," Riley said, around the cookie he was still chewing.

Mick thought of the work that had probably piled up on his desk at the station and about the stack of mail in the library, including the report he needed to read through for next week's board meeting for the family business. Looking down at Riley's upturned face, full of hope, he grinned. "I'm not busy right now."

"Yippee! I sure did miss you, Mick."

"I missed you, too, buddy."

He collected his baseball mitt out of the back porch, and as he and Riley tossed a ball back and forth, his mind went back to years ago, when the friction between him and his father had started to grow. Because he was the oldest, it had been expected that he'd take over the helm of the family business. His name alone, Patrick Gerald McCormick the third, gave him that. His father called it a privilege. That wasn't how Mick had seen it. He'd seen it as a curse. Since he'd been twelve, he'd worked summers at the family business, as a mail boy. No family member had actually worked in the factories and packaging plants in years. Supplying America with materials and textiles would always be needed and grow along with the population, was what his grandfather and father had always said, proud of the business they'd built and continued to watch grow.

Mick had no doubt about that, but back then, he'd seen the overwhelming tension of family members vying for the helm. His father, being the oldest, had taken over the reins, and fully intended for Mick to follow in his shoes. That had caused friction because his father had four brothers, who all had sons, and they all had wanted to move up a rung of the hierarchy of the business.

All except for him.

He wouldn't say he'd been jealous of Connor for not having the same pressure put on him, because he'd never wish that on anyone, especially his brother, but he had been envious of the freedom to follow his dreams way back when Connor had been taking telephones apart just to see how they worked.

He'd wished for that same freedom and for his father to be as proud of him and his dreams as he had been of Connor. His brother wasn't to blame for any of that, and neither was his father. He was. He'd been the disappointment. The rebel.

His uncle was at the helm now, and would remain, because when their father had died, the family had decided that Mick was too young to step in. The guilt he felt over that, over disappointing his father, still lived inside him, even though he'd found a way to be active in the business while being a cop.

"Is Lisa going to live here now, with you?"

Between being lost in thought and Riley's question, Mick nearly missed the ball coming at him. He caught it, and answered, "She's going to stay here for a few days."

"Why?"

He tossed the ball to Riley. "Because Tony is her father."

Riley caught the ball, but didn't throw it back. "Is that why she's our friend?"

"No, she's our friend because she's a nice person."

"Does she know how to play catch?"

"I'm not sure if she does or not."

"We should ask her to play with us," Riley said. "Seeing how she's our friend and all, don't you think?"

Mick grinned at how simple life was at five years old. If only it could remain that simple. "She's visiting with her father right now."

Riley pointed at the house. "No, she's not. She's on the back porch, watching us."

Chapter Twelve

Lisa hadn't laughed so hard in ages, but playing keep-away from Mick with Riley had her laughing, especially when Mick overexaggerated his efforts to catch the ball when Riley threw it.

She caught the ball and tossed it over Mick's head, back to Riley. The boy caught it, but while running, tripped and fell.

Lisa rushed over to him, but Mick was already helping Riley off the ground.

"Oh, Riley," Lisa said, dropping to her knees. "Are you all right?"

"Sure, I just tripped is all."

She helped him brush the grass off his knees. "I see why. Your shoe is untied."

"Aw!" Riley huffed and stomped one foot. "Again?"

"I'll tie it for you," she offered, reaching down for the shoe strings.

"Gram says when I go to school, I'll learn how to tie my own shoes," Riley said.

"Yes, you will, you'll learn all sorts of things," she said, making sure the bow was tight.

"She's right, Riley," Mick said. "Lisa has a teaching certificate."

"You're a teacher?" Riley asked, eyes wide.

Lisa shot Mick a look. She did have her certificate, but wasn't a teacher.

Mick winked at her as he told Riley, "I bet she could even teach you how to tie your shoes."

Lisa didn't have a chance to respond when a voice shouted Riley's name.

"Sounds like it's time for your supper, bud," Mick said before shouting toward the neighboring house, "I'll send him right home, Willow!"

"Thank you, Mick!" the return shout said.

Riley ran over and grabbed his baseball mitt, but then ran back to where she and Mick were still kneeling on the ground. With a ball in one hand and a mitt in the other, he threw his arms around Mick's neck.

"I sure am glad you're home, Mick."

"I'm glad to be home, Riley," Mick answered, patting the boy's back while giving him a hug.

To her surprise, as soon as Mick released him, Riley threw his tiny arms around her. Lisa returned his hug, knowing she'd never felt anything quite so precious as those little arms around her neck.

"Could I come over tomorrow?" Riley asked. "And could you teach me to tie my shoes?"

It was impossible for Lisa to say no. "Yes, if it's all right with your grandmother."

"She'll let me." Riley said. "I already told her you were my friend, and Mick's."

"Run along home, now," Mick said.

Shooting across the yard, Riley shouted, "Bye, Mick! Bye, Lisa! See you tomorrow!"

Mick grasped her elbow and helped her stand as they both shouted goodbye.

Then, she looked at him and shook her head. "Why did you tell him that?"

"Tell him what?" He walked over and picked his baseball mitt off the ground.

She planted her hands on her hips and waited until he looked at her again. "You know. That I'm a school-teacher."

His grin was as sly as any she'd ever seen.

"You have your certificate."

"But I've never taught. I just helped."

"I bet you can teach him how to tie his shoes."

She huffed out a breath.

He stepped closer and lifted a brow. "Or maybe you can't."

She slugged him in the arm, just because he looked so smug. "Yes, I can, but that's not the point. I'm not a schoolteacher."

"You could be, if you wanted to be."

"No, I mean yes, I could, but…"

They started walking toward the house. "But what? If you want something bad enough, you find a way to make it happen."

Walking beside him, Lisa glanced up at him. "Me becoming a schoolteacher isn't like you becoming a cop."

He frowned, and then gave his head a small shake, like he was chasing aside a thought. "I wasn't talking about me. I said if *you* want something bad enough, *you'll* find a way to make it happen, just like you did in Junction. You found a way to make the Depot successful. You found a way for people to make a living. You found a way to help the school."

She would like to think that becoming a schoolteacher was still possible, but it seemed too impossible. "I did all those things because people needed me to do those things."

He stopped on the porch stoop, one hand on the screen door. "Then I'd say it was time you did something for yourself."

Barb appeared in the doorway. "I was just walking out to tell you two that supper is ready. Come and eat while it's hot."

"Smells good," Mick said.

It did smell good, and it tasted even better, but Lisa didn't pay a lot of attention to what she was eating because her mind kept going in circles about what Mick had said about her doing something for herself. That was until the conversation had turned to Riley and how she was going to teach him to tie his shoes the next day.

"Oh, Lisa, I know Willow will appreciate that," Barb said. "Riley is a good little boy, but he wears Willow and Chester out. He just has more energy than they are used to."

"How long will his father be gone?" she asked.

"Willow isn't sure," Barb said. "Riley's mother died when he was a baby. He and his father, Matt, live over by Albany, but Matt's job ended and the only one he could find was working for the railroad. He wasn't able to take Riley with him, so he brought him to stay with Willow and Chester a few months ago. Matt is their only child and they love having Riley with them, but he really misses his father. They appreciate all the attention Mick has given him—that's helped him and them."

Lisa bit her lips together at how Mick shook his head, as if embarrassed.

Patting his shoulder, his mother said, "Mick will make a wonderful father someday."

Mick cleared his throat. "I don't do that much with him. Just play ball now and again."

Lisa grinned. "And buy him gifts, like a whistle."

"I saw it at a vendor on my way to Missouri and knew he'd like it."

"And he did," she said.

Mick met her gaze across the table. "And he'll like knowing how to tie his own shoes."

She knew a challenge when she heard one, and was more than willing to accept it. "Yes, he will. Maybe I'll even teach him how to write his name."

"You'll probably have to teach him the alphabet first. He's only five."

"Then I will," she said, determined to do just that.

Mick had seen Lisa in many different situations over the past few days, but had never seen determination sparkle in her eyes like it had at the dinner table. He was happy about that. Teaching Riley a few things would be good for her. She just might find that her dream of becoming a schoolteacher hadn't completely disappeared.

He glanced around the library, where he sat sifting through his mail, but not really reading anything. He hadn't been comparing becoming a police officer to her becoming a teacher outside earlier. His thoughts had fully been on her, on all she'd accomplished and how he'd wanted her to believe she could accomplish any goal she set for herself.

Now, though, he was recalling how he had almost given up his dream of becoming a police officer. When his father had died, he'd been the first to admit he wasn't old enough to take over the helm of McCormick Textiles. Despite working for the company for years, he'd been the most ill-prepared to step into a leadership role.

He'd still had a half year of high school to complete, beside college.

However, knowing that had been his father's greatest wish, he hadn't been willing to just turn his back on it. He'd met with his uncles and cousins, and though he'd first met with differing opinions, he'd held strong with his suggestions of dividing the duties of the leadership role his father had held.

It hadn't happened overnight, nor had it been easy, but by the time he'd graduated high school, despite many sleepless nights where he'd struggled to stay awake to complete his studies, while simultaneously working on the future of McCormick Textiles, the duties of the leadership role had been equally divided between his three uncles.

Now, eight years later, the company was thriving because of the restructuring that had brought the entire family together for the common good.

The idea, at first, had been a short-term plan, until he was old enough to step into his father's shoes, but Mick had known those were shoes he could never fill. Not fully. Not ever. His father had been extraordinary. Regardless of working twelve-hour days, doing the work that three men now did, his father had always made the time for his family. He'd been a loving husband and an amazing father. He'd always had time to play catch, or build a tree house, take them fishing or swimming, or just read to them when they'd been small children.

Not just for him and Connor either. Their cousins had loved his father, as had the neighborhood children back then. It had been nothing for his father to take him and Connor along with their friends to the amusement park, or a ballgame on Saturdays.

Memories of that, and many other things about his father, flowed through Mick as he sat there.

He grinned. *All men, rich or poor, married or not, are responsible for the children of his community.* He'd heard his father say that more than once. And he'd held true to it.

That thought had crossed Mick's mind when he'd first seen Riley last winter, bundled up and trudging through the snow in Willow and Chester's yard, all by himself.

"You look awfully happy."

Mick glanced up, watched Lisa enter the room. "I was just thinking about the first time I saw Riley," he said. "He was bundled up so that nothing but his eyes showed beneath his hat and above his scarf."

"When was that?" she asked.

"Shortly after Christmas. His father had just dropped him off and he was a sad little boy."

She leaned a hip against the side of the desk. "And you decided to cheer him up."

He nodded. "Yes. Like you had decided to help the children of Junction in any way you could."

"You don't give up when you set your mind on something, do you?"

He leaned back in his chair. "Neither do you."

Her hair fluttered around her shoulders as she tossed her head back and laughed. The sight and sound were beyond lovely, beyond charming.

"I can't believe I let you goad me into teaching him how to tie his shoes."

"Because I know you can do it."

Her smile slipped away. "What if I can't?"

He didn't believe that for a moment, and leaned forward, looked her in the eye. "What if you can?"

She shook her head as a tiny smile reappeared. "Who taught you to be so confident, while remaining moral and honorable? Your father?"

He let that settle for a moment, partially because it made him wonder if he was following in his father's footsteps, in other ways than the family business. He'd never considered that before, yet, he could see that he was, and it felt good. "Yes," he said. "My father was confident, and moral and honorable."

"Just like you."

He never broke eye contact while saying, "And you."

"A bull calling a speakeasy owner moral and honorable?" She shook her head. "That's a stretch if I ever heard one."

He shrugged one shoulder. "It's true. You need to give yourself more credit for all you've accomplished."

Her expression said she didn't believe that. Holding up a hand to indicate she was done with that subject, she said, "I'm going to pick out a book, and then go say good-night to Tony. I'll see you tomorrow."

Choosing to let the subject rest for now, he said, "Good night."

A short time after she left the room, he gave up attempting to keep his attention on his mail, and went to bed. Sleep, though, evaded him. Being in his own bed after the last week of traveling, he should be sound asleep. That was if his mind hadn't been on Lisa. From the moment he'd heard about her, he'd become intent upon helping Tony and her reunite. Now, after meeting her, he was intent upon something else. He was sure Lisa needed help. She hadn't said so, but his instincts said there was something deeper going on with her stepfather. The man must have had some type of hold over her mother, and now had it over Lisa. He'd have to find out what.

The following morning, he was sitting at the table when she walked in the kitchen, looking fully refreshed and once again wearing her new blue dress.

"Good morning," she greeted. "It's been so long since the smell of coffee woke me up in the morning, I thought I was dreaming."

"Sit down and I'll get you a cup," his mother said while flipping eggs in the frying pan. "Would you like cream or sugar?"

"Thank you, but I can get it myself," Lisa said, walking to the cupboard. After taking down a cup, she went to the stove and poured herself a cup.

"How did you sleep, dear?" Mother asked her.

"Wonderful..I don't recall a bed feeling so good."

He twisted about to look at her. "That's because you'd never spent three days on a train before."

Her impish grin grew. "Probably."

"Are you ready for lessons to begin?"

She sat down across from him. "You are enjoying this."

He was, and he was hoping that she'd enjoy teaching Riley how to tie his shoes. "Perhaps, but more than that, I'm looking at the clock, and if history serves, Riley will be here in half an hour." He gave her a wink. "He always stops by to say goodbye to me before I leave for work."

"Yes, he does," his mother confirmed as she set two plates on the table. "You both better eat up so you're ready for him."

Chapter Thirteen

Lisa sighed heavily as she returned the last letter to its envelope and set it atop the pile on the bed in front of her. She'd read the entire stack, more than once, and though she had learned plenty, she still didn't know why her mother had lied. She'd clearly loved Tony. Every letter had been signed with *all my love*.

The letters had been full of things Lisa hadn't remembered until reading about them. School plays and birthdays, Christmases and Easter picnics, and many other things about her. How well she was doing in school, how tall she'd grown. Tony had known everything about her, up until her mother had had her stroke. That's when the letters had stopped.

Tony had never written one letter in return. She'd asked him why this morning. He'd said that had been part of his promise. To never bother them. The letters her mother had written had been addressed to him, at general delivery in a small town south of here.

Her father had explained that he'd never lived in that town, just knew the name of it from a man he'd been in the army with, and when he'd seen her mother in Kansas City, that had been the only place he could think to go.

A town where he'd never been. A place where no one knew him. He'd asked her to write him, let him know how they were doing, whenever she could, and she had.

The town was small, Tony said, so he didn't ever live there, but did travel through it every few months, just to collect his mail.

He'd also told her how he'd bummed around and ended up in New York City, where he'd become involved with some men, and eventually ended up here, in Rochester, working security for rumrunners.

It hadn't been an honorable job, but it had given him the money he'd needed. He'd told her more, about how the rumrunners had been busted, and how he'd gone to jail, served his time, and while there, decided he was done working on the wrong side of the law. Even before he'd been released, he'd offered his services to Mick, to help him bust other bootleggers.

Lisa stood and walked over to the window. Maybe if she hadn't been thinking about him—Mick—all day, she might have come up with a solution as to what to do now.

The doctor hadn't said that she couldn't take Tony home to Missouri, but had said that he wouldn't recommend such a long trip right now. Tony was too weak. Dr. George, a man in his late fifties or so, with a head of snow-white hair and kind green eyes, had said cancer was fickle. He'd seen people live for years with it, and others die within a week of diagnosis. Right now, Tony was recovering from the radiation treatment they'd used to treat the cancerous tumors. Within a few weeks, they'd know if more treatments were needed, or if there was nothing more they could do. At that time, depending on Tony's condition, she might be able to take him home.

Until then, he recommended they just keep Tony as comfortable as possible.

Even between seeing to Tony's needs, and teaching Riley to tie his shoes—a feat he'd accomplished with great joy—her mind had spent a large portion of every hour on Mick.

He'd given her a package before he'd left this morning, and when she'd opened it, she'd nearly cried. It had been the lilac-colored dress she'd seen in the window of the store. The very one she was wearing right now. She'd put it on before Riley had arrived, and her heart skipped a beat at how Mick had nodded when he'd seen her wearing it, as if he approved. It was odd how joyous that made her feel.

Riley's grandmother had arrived with him this morning, in time for Riley to say goodbye to Mick, which had included a promise of a game of catch this evening. The way Mick interacted with the child was so heartwarming.

So was Willow Jansen. Trim and tiny, she was older, with silvery hair and eyes that twinkled when she looked at her grandson. Graciously, Willow had shared how excited Riley was to learn to tie his shoes. She also insisted that they let her know if he became a bother while explaining that when he'd lived with his father in Albany, a neighbor with several children of her own had watched him. Now that he was living with his grandparents, he had no friends to play with, and that caused him to become bored easily.

Lisa had assured Willow that he would be fine, and he had been. He'd managed perfectly all morning. When the doctor had arrived, Riley had waited in the library, looking at picture books and practicing his shoe tying. After Dr. George had left, Lisa had taught him the alphabet song before it had been time for him to go home for lunch and a nap.

After she'd eaten lunch, she'd sat with her father until he'd fallen asleep, and then retired to her room to read all of her mother's letters again. She hadn't learned anything new from the letters, but a few other things had come to light.

She really enjoyed her time with Riley. He was a sweet boy, and teaching him to tie his shoes and then working on the alphabet had been fun and rewarding.

She enjoyed her time with her father immensely. It was as if the years that they'd been separated had faded away, except for the fact that they were both older.

She missed Mick. Today had been the first day she hadn't spent most of her waking hours with him, and more than once she found herself wanting to talk to him. That was extremely unusual for her, and brought her to the other thing that hung heavy on her mind.

Tony was her father, and she was obligated to take care of him. Mick and his mother weren't.

Where did that leave her? She couldn't take him home, but she couldn't expect Mick to let them stay here. Not for weeks.

Nor could she be away from the Depot for weeks.

That's where she really became balled up, because she wasn't ready to return to it yet. Not just the Depot, but her life there. She was surrounded by people five days of the week, and she did consider the Hendrick boys friends, other people, too, but her life as a whole was very lonely in Junction. The worst part was the idea of never seeing Mick again.

It was such a crazy, silly notion—she knew that. She'd have to go back someday, soon, and face the fact that Mick would forget about her. That was the most unsettling thing going on in her mind right now, and that concerned her. Made her worry that she'd started to like him more than she should.

That was something she was going to have to get over—liking him too much would only cause trouble.

A knock sounded on her door and she crossed the room, opened the door to reveal Barb standing there.

"I just iced the cake I baked, and am wondering if you'd like to have a piece with me?" Barb nodded toward Tony's door across the hallway. "I just checked on him and he's still sleeping."

The woman was so kind. Upon hearing the doctor's recommendations, Barb had once again said that both Lisa and Tony could stay as long as they wanted. Lisa appreciate that, but knew she couldn't take advantage of the hospitality.

"It's a cinnamon cake. A new recipe, that I'm excited to taste," Barb said with a twinkle in her eyes.

"I can smell cinnamon, and it smells delicious."

Barb hooked their arms together. "Then let's go have some."

It had been years since Lisa had had a piece of cake, and the one Barb had baked was melt-in-her-mouth delicious. She told Barb that.

"Oh, thank you," Barb said. "I got the recipe from a woman at church. She'd served it at a women's tea one afternoon and I just hadn't had a chance to bake it until today."

"I'm sorry that looking after my father has taken up so much of your time."

"Nonsense. I've enjoyed having Tony here, and now you." Barb waved a hand. "That's not why I haven't had a chance to bake it. I had other recipes to try. Up until lately, it's only been me eating them, though, with

Mick working all the time and Connor living in his own house." Grinning, she added, "And Riley informed me he likes cookies better than cakes."

Lisa laughed. "He told me that, too."

"I can't believe how quickly you taught him to tie his shoes. You are just a natural born teacher."

Lisa felt her cheeks warm at the compliment. "It'll take him a few days of practice to have it completely mastered, but he's a very smart little boy."

"He is. I have to admit, some days I'm envious of Willow, having a grandson, while I'm sitting here, twiddling my thumbs, waiting for Mick or Connor to get married."

Lisa set her fork on her empty plate and squeezed her hand shut at the odd flutter in her stomach. "Won't that be even lonelier? Or will Mick live here when he gets married?" She didn't like the thought of Mick getting married, but he was sure to, someday, even though he said he didn't want to.

"Of course, he'll live here. This is his house."

"It is? I thought it was your house. You and your husband's."

"It was. I can live here as long as I want—Mick will never kick me out, but he inherited it when his father passed away." Barb took a drink of coffee. "But being Mick, he didn't think that was fair, so he gave Connor money. Half of the value of this place. Connor used that to start his phone company."

"Why did only Mick inherit it?"

"Because he was the oldest. My husband's family was very traditional, to the point it drove me crazy at times. Patrick was the oldest son, too, so everything fell on his shoulders. The business, the family. When he died, all of that fell onto Mick. He was only eighteen and I was so worried that he'd quit school and give up his dream of being a police officer. I was so glad when he continued to pursue his dream and find a way to stay active in the family business. I shouldn't have worried, though. When Mick sets his mind to something, he makes it happen."

"I've discovered that," Lisa said.

Barb laughed. "Stubbornness is just one of the things he inherited from his father."

A knock sounded on the back door and before either of them could respond, Willow rushed into the kitchen. "Is Riley here?"

Lisa's heart lurched at the panic in the woman's voice and on her face.

"No," Barbara answered. "Why?"

"He was upset when I said he couldn't come back over here this afternoon, and now I can't find him," Willow said, wringing her hands together. "I've searched our house, and our yard, and with the river so close—" She pressed a hand to her lips.

"Calm down," Barb said. "We—"

Lisa didn't hear any more because she was already running out the back door. With her heart pounding, she raced across the backyard, toward the woods and the path that led to the river. A dozen fears filled her, as she hurried along the path, and down the steps.

While shouting Riley's name, she scanned the water, and the ground. Her and Mick's footsteps were still visible in the mud, but no others, and she prayed that meant Riley hadn't come down here.

She walked along the shoreline as far as she could, in both directions, and then climbed back up the steps in the bank and began searching the woods, shouting his name. Once she'd arrived in the yard again, she noticed the shed door was open slightly. Knowing for sure that Mick had latched it, she ran to the door and pulled it open.

A massive wave of relief washed over her because beneath the edge of the tarp covering the canoe, she saw the tips of a pair of shoes. Shoes that she had tied many times this morning. Kneeling down, she lifted the tarp. "Why didn't you answer when I called for you?" she asked.

A tear-filled urchin face looked at her. "Because I want my dad."

An image flashed in her mind, of her, sitting in the barn, crying, shortly after her father had left for the war. "Do you want to be left alone?"

"Yes." Arms crossed over his chest, Riley scooted around so his back was to her.

She remembered that feeling so well.

"All right. I'm going to go tell your grandmother that I found you, but then I will be back, and we are going to talk about what happened."

Riley didn't respond, and, keeping one eye on the shed, she hurried toward the house. Willow was on the back steps, and Lisa hurried forward. "I found him. He's in the shed."

"Oh, that little rascal!"

Lisa laid a hand on Willow's arm. "Could I talk to him for a few minutes? I was a few years older than him when my father left for the war, I think I know how he's feeling."

"Oh, you are such an angel," Willow said. "Yes, please do talk to him. I'll go tell Chester that we found him. He's still searching at our place."

"I'll bring him home shortly." Lisa hurried back to the shed. Having been watching the shed door the entire time, she knew she'd find Riley still sitting under the canoe.

Kneeling down, she once again lifted the tarp, and then climbed beneath it, to sit behind him.

Riley looked over his shoulder, but didn't say anything.

She waited for a few moments before laying a hand on his small back. "When I was little my father left."

"Tony?" he asked.

"Yes. I was eight and I missed him so much. I would cry and I would get mad, because inside I hurt."

Riley twisted and looked up at her.

"I hurt really bad." She reached over and touched his chest. "Right here."

With tear-stained cheeks, he nodded.

She held her arms open, inviting him to climb onto her lap.

He did so within an instant and buried his head against her.

Lisa wrapped her arms around him and held him close, kissing the top of his head as he cried. She could feel his pain, could remember missing her father.

When the crying stopped, she held on to him for a while longer before whispering, "I know how badly it hurts, Riley, and how angry that can make you, but hiding in here and not answering when people called for you made others hurt just as badly. Your grandma and grandpa, Barbara and me, we were all scared when we couldn't find you."

He lifted his head. "I didn't want to talk to anyone."

She wiped the tears off his cheeks with one thumb. "I know that, but you should have answered, so that we wouldn't have been scared. You could have said that you didn't want to talk to anyone."

Bowing his head, he nodded.

"You have to promise that you won't do this again," she said.

He sighed heavily and then looked up at her. "Was Tony gone a long time?"

"Yes, a very long time." She kissed his forehead. "Before he left, he told me to be good. Did your father tell you that?"

He nodded.

"I tried very hard to be good, so that when I saw him again, I could tell him that I had been good."

"Did that make him happy?" he asked.

She thought about how hard her father had laughed when he learned she'd been running a speakeasy. Not that it mattered, at this moment, she would have lied to Riley if it would keep him from running away again. Luckily, she could tell him the truth. "Yes, it did. You want your father to know you've been good, too, don't you?"

He nodded.

"Then you mustn't hide again. You always have to answer when someone calls for you."

"I will," he said.

"Promise?"

"I promise."

"You also have to apologize to your grandma and grandpa. Tell them it won't happen again."

His bottom lip quivered slightly. "Right now?"

She touched the tip of his nose and leaned close to whisper, "In a few minutes. We can sit here a while longer if you want."

He smiled.

So did she, and felt an overwhelming warmth inside her.

A moment later, the edge of the tarp was lifted. "Are you two making a tent out of my canoe?"

Every time the image of Lisa holding Riley on her lap and sitting beneath the tarp flashed in his head, Mick's breath caught. That had been five days ago, but it still affected him. He'd left the station as soon as his mother had called. By the time he'd arrived home, Lisa had found Riley and had been in the shed, under the canoe and tarp. From the doorway, he'd heard her comfort Riley, and then make him promise it wouldn't happen again, all with such compassion, he'd grown even more amazed by her.

That amazement had continued the past several days. Tony appeared to be getting better each day that she was here. Last night, he'd ventured downstairs and had supper with them at the table instead of in his room.

It was as if her presence was helping Tony to feel stronger, just like she'd taught Riley how to tie his shoes, sing the alphabet and spell his name out loud. Riley was learning how to write the letters, too. It was all so good to see.

Mick wasn't surprised. Lisa was determined to accomplish anything she set her mind to.

He shut off the car and stared at the house. It was the same house he'd come home to his entire life, yet now there was a new excitement in him when he pulled in the driveway.

It was there again tonight. A thrill at the idea of seeing Lisa, of eating supper with her, of seeing the sparkle in her eyes as she talked about the day's events, how well her father was doing and how much Riley had accomplished.

The weather had been rainy and chilly today, and

the evening air had a nip to it from a north wind that whipped around the house, rustling the leaves in the trees as he climbed out of the car.

"Hey, Mick!" Riley's voice echoed in the evening air. "Gram says I can't come over 'cause it's raining!"

Mick grinned. "Your grandmother is right. I'll see you tomorrow!"

"Did you know your name starts with an *M*?" Riley asked.

Mick walked to the back stoop. "Yes, I do know that."

"And the second letter is an *I*, just like in my name!"

"You're right about that!"

"And just like Lisa!"

"You're right about that, too!" Mick chuckled. "You best shut the door now, before you get the floor wet!"

"All right, Mick! See you tomorrow!"

"Good night, Riley!"

Laughing, Mick walked into the house. To his disappointment, Lisa wasn't in the kitchen when he entered the room. His mother was, and greeted him cheerfully, having heard his conversation with Riley, and then quickly explained that Lisa had just carried a plate up to Tony.

"I think the gloomy weather caused him to have a slight setback," she continued. "Lisa will eat up there with him tonight. We can eat as soon as you wash up."

No matter how old he got, his mother would always send him off to wash before eating. Mick told her he'd be back in a moment and went upstairs to leave his jacket and wash. Afterward, he stopped at Tony's room and knocked before opening the door.

"Good evening," he greeted, unable to pull his eyes off Lisa. She was wearing the lilac dress he'd bought her, and he couldn't help but think that she looked like springtime, especially the way her face shone, nor could he stop the way his heartbeat increased at the sight of her.

"Aw, hello, Mick," Tony said. "I'm sorry. I just haven't felt up to going downstairs today."

Shifting his attention to the man lying in the bed, Mick shook his head. "No need to be sorry." His gaze went to Lisa again, and the plate on her lap. "There's a folding table in the library. I'll go get it for you."

"There's no need to go to that trouble," Lisa said. "We're fine."

"It's no trouble," Mick said, and before she could protest further, he left Tony's room and rushed down the steps.

He collected the table that he and Connor had used for playing games, and two folding chairs, but before carrying everything upstairs, he walked into the kitchen. "I'm taking this table up to Tony's room. It's large enough for all of us to eat up there."

"That's a wonderful idea," his mother answered. "I'll fix a tray and be up momentarily."

"I'll be back to help you," he said.

Back upstairs, Lisa questioned him about the two chairs he'd carried in as he set up the table. "Mother and I will be joining the two of you up here."

"Why?" Lisa asked.

"Because it's no fun to eat alone," Mick said.

"No, it's not." Mother carried a tray into the room. "I should have thought of this earlier."

"Is there more to carry up?" Mick asked his mother.

"Yes, dear, the dessert. It's already on a tray. Oh, and I forgot the coffeepot."

Already at the door, Mick said, "I'll get it."

"The tray is already full, you can't carry both," Mother said in his wake.

A moment later, Lisa caught up with him on the stairs. "Thank you for this. Tony wanted to make it downstairs, but he's been worn out all day."

"I suppose that's expected." The moment the words were out, he wanted to retract them. "I mean, he's—"

"I know what you mean, and I know what it means for Tony to have cancer. He'll have good days and bad days, which, ironically is no different than the rest of the world. He just knows his days are numbered, but because of you, he and I have been reunited and get to spend those days together."

The desire to touch her had him balling his hand into a fist. He'd had to do that a lot the last few days, refrain from touching her.

"Thank you for that."

"You've already told me that, several times the past few days." So many times, he was growing frustrated. He may have brought her here, but she was the reason it had worked. She was the reason for a lot of things.

"Because I mean it." She stepped off the bottom step and flashed him a grin. "And I mean it when I say thank you for all you do for Riley, and your mother, and your brother. Connor said—"

Something dark snagged inside his chest. "Connor was here?" He'd never been jealous of his brother, or fearful that a woman might prefer Connor over him, but at this moment, he felt both.

"Yes. He's heading north tomorrow and stopped by to see how everyone was doing before he left."

"I thought he'd already left," Mick said.

"He said he'd waited a few days because he thought

you might need him. He sat with Tony for a short time while your mother and I went shopping this afternoon."

They entered the kitchen and he walked straight to the table to get the tray holding a pie and several plates. "Did he say how long he'll be gone?"

"No." She got a potholder and then picked the coffeepot off the stove. "He said that he's going to convince everyone between Rochester and Syracuse that they need a telephone." Once again, she flashed him a coy grin. "Considering the two of you are so alike, I'm sure he will." Walking toward the hallway, she looked over her shoulder at him. "But I doubt he'll have to resort to handcuffs."

Mick followed her out of the kitchen. "He doesn't own a pair of handcuffs."

She giggled. "Too bad for him."

"I'm sure he has other ways of convincing them."

"By telling them how much they need a telephone." She glanced at him and grimaced. "I certainly learned a lot about them."

"He gave you his sales pitch?"

Her eyes widened. "Yes. I learned more about telephones in five minutes than I'll ever need to know."

Mick laughed. "That sounds like Connor, but speaking of things to know, I was told that *I* is the second letter in my name, Riley's name and your name."

She laughed as they started up the stairway. "Riley was thrilled when he discovered that! I'd printed all three of our names on a sheet of paper and he instantly picked out the *I* in all three names."

"He sounded excited about it," Mick replied, not adding that Riley had sounded almost as excited as she sounded right now.

"We are working on numbers and colors, too."

"He's going to be too smart for school this fall."

"No, he won't be." Her chin jutted out with a bit of righteousness. "He'll just be a little bit ahead and there is nothing wrong with that."

"No, there's not," he agreed. He was glad that both she and Riley were enjoying their lessons.

"He's very excited to show his father everything that he's learned."

"I'm sure he is." Mick waited for her to enter Tony's bedroom, then followed. As they ate, he realized it had been foolish of him to be jealous of Connor. Lisa could like, or not like, anyone she chose. He had no say on that in any way.

It was just that having her stay here was far more of a challenge than he'd ever have expected. He hadn't expected a challenge at all. Especially over his own thoughts and feelings. It was as if nothing he'd known was holding true, and he couldn't stop himself from comparing Lisa to Twila. They were as different as two women could be, which had him wondering what he'd found attractive about Twila. She had been pretty—on the outside—whereas Lisa was not only pretty, she was personable, and, well, *adorable* was the word he'd use to describe her. On the inside and outside.

There was no denying how caring she was to others. One look at Tony, and at Riley, proved that. There wasn't a deceitful bone in her body, either. Even when it came to her profession of running a speakeasy, she'd been honest about that with her father and his family.

If he'd been wrong about women, that they all weren't like Twila, he couldn't help but wonder what else he'd been wrong about.

Chapter Fourteen

Lisa pushed the food around on her plate with her fork. The beef stew and buns that she'd assisted Barb in making were delicious, but she no longer felt hungry. Her father's setback was part of it, but more than that was the fact she still didn't know what she was going to do. Every day she stayed here made her not want to leave.

Mick was the main reason. She'd realized that she looked forward to him arriving home as much as Riley did. The boy adored Mick, and she could see why. There was nothing not to like about him.

Another thing that was growing stronger in her was teaching. Working with Riley every day had renewed her desire to become a teacher, and that hurt, because that was not something that could happen. The Hendrick boys couldn't keep running the Depot for much longer, and Duane was sure to have discovered her absence by now.

All of that hung heavy in her mind as they ate, while she helped Barb wash the dishes and while assisting Tony to get ready for bed.

Seeing her father had been difficult that first day. More difficult than she'd been prepared for, but she'd managed. She'd managed more than that. She'd managed to leave Junction. Leave the Depot in the hands of others. Arrive here and meet her father again. She'd made peace with her father. And in a sense, her mother, even though she still didn't know why she had been lied to for years. She'd thought about what Mick had said, about not dwelling on the reason, but she couldn't help but dwell on it. Couldn't stop wanting to know why.

One thing was for sure. She wouldn't be here, wouldn't have ever seen her father again or learned the truth, if not for Mick. She was truly grateful to him for that.

"I don't know why I'm so tired today," Tony said. "Tomorrow I'll be better again."

She smiled and kissed his cheek. "Yes, you will."

He sighed heavily. "You being here has made me want to live again. Has made me wish I had more time. That makes me want to make the most out of every day."

Maybe she hadn't managed nearly as well as she thought because tears filled her eyes. The same love she'd felt for her father as a child had fully returned—it was as if they hadn't been separated for years. She pressed her cheek against his. "That's what we will do. Make the most out of every day."

There wasn't much strength in his hug, and that, too, made more tears form. Not wanting him to see them, she kissed his cheek again and reached for the lamp. "I'll shut the light off now."

"Good night, sweetheart."

She clicked off the lamp. "Good night, Daddy."

Once in the hallway, she leaned against the door, eyes closed until the tears dried up. She stood there for several more minutes before crossing the hall and entering her room as she had done every night this week.

Back home, she wouldn't have time to worry so much. To think so much. Right now, the Depot would be full. She'd be pouring drinks, checking off cards and taking care of all the issues that arose. Running the joint. For hours yet. Once again, guilt struck, not only because of all the people back home that depended on her, but because she didn't miss any of it.

Sighing, she picked up the book she'd finished reading last night, and left the room.

The door to the library was open and she could see the blaze of the fireplace from the hallway. Sensing Mick was in the room, she paused at the doorway.

"You can come in," he said.

She entered the room and held up the book. "Just going to swap this out for another one."

He was sitting on the sofa near the fireplace.

"What are you doing?" she asked, not seeing a book in his hands.

"Nothing. Just staring into the fire." He glanced at her. "And thinking about you."

Her heart leaped inside her chest. "Why?"

"Wondering if you've talked to Buck, heard how things are going at the Depot."

"No." She put the book on the shelf before saying, "I thought I'd call him this weekend."

"It's worrying you, being gone, isn't it?"

"Yes." Resting her hands on the back of a brown leather chair, she admitted, "I don't know what to do. Tony's not well enough to travel back to Missouri with me, and I don't want to leave him here."

"You're welcome to stay as long as you need."

"I know, but you've already done so much, so has your mother." She pushed the heavy air out of her chest.

"I can't stay here much longer. I can't expect the boys to keep running the Depot by themselves."

"You're worried about Duane, too, aren't you?"

That was the one thing she'd tried hard not to think about. Duane. Because when she did, it scared her. She sucked in air, trying hard to not let that fear rise up and consume her.

Mick stood, and each step that he took closer, she fought harder to not cry. She'd never been one to feel sorry for herself, but was right now.

When he stopped beside her, and held his arms wide, she felt like Riley, when he'd leaped into her embrace inside the shed.

Mick wrapped his arms around her as she fell into them willingly, wanting someone to hang on to like she'd never wanted. Never needed. He was so strong, so solid and his hug so warm, it made her feel like she wasn't all alone. That he was here, and that he cared. Until this moment, she hadn't realized how much that meant to her.

"It's going to be all right, Lisa," he whispered.

The fear was still inside her and she shook her head. "I feel as if Duane had taken everything I'd ever loved away from me, and I'm afraid he's going to do it again."

"He won't this time. I'll help you make sure that doesn't happen."

That's what she was afraid of. That Duane would hurt him. "He's mean. So mean."

"I won't let him hurt you. I swear to you."

She lifted her head and a powerful longing rose up inside her as their eyes met. Mesmerized by the unique light blue of his eyes, by their shimmering sparkles, she couldn't look away. Couldn't think about anything other than him. How handsome he was, and how strong, confident, amazing. Utterly amazing.

When their lips met, she didn't question how that had happened, only rejoiced in the merger. As if that kiss had a sound, it echoed inside her, like her body was hollow, and was suddenly filled by the soft, repeating waves. It felt so good.

He seemed to understand that, because his head tilted, allowing their lips to merge more fully. The warmth, the tenderness, filled her so completely, so swiftly, her knees threatened to buckle beneath her.

His hold tightened, and she slid her hands upward from his waist, looping them under his arms and grasping a hold of his shoulders. There was no fear inside her, not even of her knees giving out. She was holding on because of the sensuality of the kiss. Of how it transported her, mind, body and soul, into a dreamlike state. There was no hesitancy on her part, or his, as the need to taste each other completely took over.

She wasn't overly skillful, or experienced at kissing, yet that didn't seem to matter. Mick guided her lips as if it was a dance, her heartbeat the music, and she held nothing back when his tongue prompted her lips to part.

Sensual reactions went off inside her like miniature fireworks when his tongue entered her mouth, and continued to go off as the kissing continued until she felt as if she was floating in the sky with those fireworks.

He broke the kiss with a low groan, and then held on to the back of her head, pressing her cheek firmly against his chest. She could hear his heart beating, feel her own thudding wildly, as they stood there, arms entwined and breathing heavily.

Euphoria still surrounded her, still flashed inside her. Enthralled by it, she had to know this wasn't a dream.

"Mick?"

"Yes?"

His chest rumbled beneath her ear at the same time she heard his response. She couldn't stop the giggle that rose up, escaped at knowing it wasn't a dream. Her arms were still looped under his, up his back and her hands gripping his shoulders. Tightening her hold, she said, "I'm glad you brought me here."

"I'm glad you're here."

She had to look up, had to see his face to know if he was being sincere. Even though she had no reason to doubt him. He'd been sincere, committed to his goal since entering her house that morning a week ago, yet this time, it felt far more personal.

His hold eased enough for her to lean back, see the smile on his face. Still she asked, "You are?"

"Yes, and I think you've been doing too much."

A hint of disappointment washed over her, even as confusion filled her mind. She released her hold on his shoulders, and let her hands slide down his back, to his waist, and then drop to her sides. "Doing too much of what?"

"Everything. Taking care of your father, teaching Riley, helping my mother with the house." He touched her cheek with one fingertip, ran it down along the side of her face. "I think it's time you had some fun."

"Fun?"

"Yes, fun." He grasped her hand. "Let's go get our jackets."

"Why?" she asked as he pulled her toward the door.

"Because it's still raining."

"Where are we going?"

"Have you ever seen a picture show?" he asked.

"You mean a movie theatre?"

"Yes."

"No. I've heard about them. They have a movie theatre in Kansas City."

"Then that's where we are going."

"To a movie?"

"Yes, to a movie."

"Just like that?" She felt she should protest, but truly didn't want to. She'd always wanted to see a movie, and more than that, she wanted to see one with him.

"Yes, just like that."

A hefty dose of awareness, sexual awareness, still had Mick's blood heated as he drove to the movie theatre. Once again, he was questioning if he knew what he was doing.

He was smitten by Lisa. More than smitten. Kissing her tonight had solidified that. His original motive of helping Tony was no longer something he could fall back on. Tony was grateful. Exceedingly grateful, but seeing all that Lisa was going through was gut-wrenching.

Almost as gut-wrenching as knowing what was happening to him. He was attracted to Lisa. Too attracted. There wasn't a damn thing he could do about it, either. She was too cute, too likeable and, most of all, she needed him.

He was responsible for her being here, and couldn't shirk away from that. Truth was, he didn't want to shirk away from anything about her.

"What movie are we going to see?" she asked.

"I have no idea."

"You don't?"

"We'll check out the theatres, there are two of them, and see what's playing. One's just up the block here."

"I can't believe I'm going to see a movie." She laughed. "I've wanted to, but there's just never been time."

"Sometimes, we have to make time," he said, recalling how his father had said that more than once.

"Make time? A person can't make time."

"Yes, we can. People do it all the time. When things are important, they make the time to do them, and sometimes, having fun is the most important thing of all." He turned the final corner, and pointed at the marquee lights. "There's the theatre, it's playing a war movie, we'll drive over and see what's playing at the other one."

"No, let's see this one."

"Are you sure?"

"Yes, I'm sure."

The excitement in her voice had him agreeing. "All right." He pulled into the parking lot, and bought her a bag of popcorn from a street vendor before purchasing two tickets at the ticket booth outside of the theatre's door.

Smiling up at him, she slid her hand around his arm, and a jolt of electricity shot through him as his arm bumped the side of her breast. Even though the layers of his coat and shirt, and her coat and dress separated them, his arm still felt as if it had been burned.

They found seats as the lights were being turned off. He helped her remove her jacket and sat down just as the orchestra in the pit began to play.

"This is so exciting," she whispered. "I didn't know there wouldn't be any lights."

He had, and her whisper made his heart thud harder.

She was soon engrossed in the movie. The film held his attention, too, but not completely, because when the actors were involved in airplane combat, she hid her face in his arm. Until he wrapped an arm around her shoulder.

Then when there were scenes she didn't want to see, she buried her face against his chest.

He didn't mind.

The plot was complex, with two men from the same town in love with the same woman, who ended up being billeted together when they enlisted in the air service. When one man was shot down, and presumed dead, guilt struck Mick for not checking to see what was playing at the other theatre, fearing this one was too close to her own experience with her father's service.

Especially when tears glistened on her cheeks. He dug out his handkerchief, gave it to her and held her a bit closer as she thanked him and wiped her eyes.

The man presumed dead ended up stealing a German plane and flew toward Allied lines, but the other man saw the enemy plane and took chase. He ended up shooting down the plane, believing the pilot was the one who'd killed his mate. He landed the plane to assure the enemy was dead, and discovered it hadn't been an enemy, but his mate, his best friend. The mate died, but not before forgiving his friend.

Lisa was crying again during that scene, and Mick questioned if he'd ever do anything right when it came to her.

The ending scenes showed the surviving pilot return home, apologize to the other man's parents and then marry the girl they'd both loved.

"Oh, my word," Lisa said, sniffling as the lights turned on overhead. "That was the best movie I've ever seen."

Mick used one finger to wipe a final teardrop off her cheek. "It's the only movie you've ever seen."

She giggled. "And will always be the best." Laying her hand on his arm, she shook her head. "Thank you for bringing me. I feel as if I now know more about what my father went through."

"It was just a movie," he warned.

"I know, but parts of it had been somewhat realistic, don't you think?"

He nodded. "Yes, I think so."

She sighed heavily. "It was sad, but it ended happily."

She looked so serene, the desire to kiss her struck again. Just as hard as it had at the house, but luckily, they were in public, which gave him more restraint. "Yes, it did." He stood and held up her jacket.

After sliding both arms into the coat sleeves, she turned, stretched on her toes and kissed him. A small kiss, but smack on the lips. "Thank you, again. The movie was wonderful."

Now fighting an even stronger desire to kiss her again, he took her arm and led her to the walkway. "You're welcome. I'm glad you enjoyed it."

"I did. Very much, and this place is so beautiful. The carpets, curtains and lights. It's amazing."

The theatre was fairly new, but he'd been here a few times, and couldn't say he'd noticed the thick red carpets, red velvet curtains or the glass globes encircling the lights. "We'll have to go to the other theatre now, so you can compare the two."

She giggled. "No, you don't have to do that."

"I don't have to, I want to."

Biting on her bottom lip, she nodded. "In that case, I won't say no."

He wondered if she'd say no to another kiss. Clearing

his throat, and hoping it would clear his mind as well, he asked, "Would you care for a drink?"

"A drink?" She glanced around as they stepped out of the door, onto the sidewalk. "What do you mean a drink?"

He laughed. "A beverage?"

"With alcohol?"

"Yes, with alcohol." Although she already knew it, he pointed out, "Prohibition made the manufacturing and sale of alcohol illegal, not the consumption."

"I know. But you're a cop."

"I know."

Laughing, she bumped him with her shoulder. "You know what I mean."

He loved the sound of her laughter, and wished he'd hear it more often. "Yes, I do, and I had a drink while at your establishment."

"That was different."

They arrived at the car and he opened her door. "How?"

"You were there to find me."

He laughed. "I didn't even know who you were at the time."

She flashed him a grin as she climbed in the car. "I knew you were a bull from the moment you walked through the door."

"I could tell," he answered and closed her door.

Feeling happier than he had in some time, he hurried around the front of the car, knowing exactly where he would take her. Rochester had many speakeasies, from the worst of the worst to the best of the best. Pinion's Supper Club was the best of the best.

"How could you tell?" she asked once he'd climbed in and started the car.

"People get a certain look in their eyes when they realize I'm a police officer."

She giggled. "And a knot in their stomach."

His stomach sank as he recalled Twila's comment about not wanting to marry him because he was a cop, because his job was too dangerous. "I give you a knot in your stomach?"

She giggled again. "No. You only did that night, because I thought you were going to bust the place." She let out a soft sigh. "Now, I'm proud of you. Proud to be your friend."

He pulled into the parking lot of the large brick building. Pinon's was a well-known restaurant, and the back room was known to host some of the largest weddings and other parties in the state.

"I'm proud to be your friend, too," he said while turning off the car.

She leaned over and planted a quick kiss on his cheek. "I'm glad."

He gave her a wink. "Me, too."

A few moments later, as they walked toward the large canvas awning over the double doorway, she asked, "You're sure they aren't going to think they are being raided?"

Laughing, he asked, "What would you do if that happened?"

"Run." Looking around, she shrugged. "But only as far as your car because I have no idea how to get back to your house from here."

With his happiness fully restored, he laughed. Her honesty was something else he loved.

They entered the building and were immediately met by the gray-haired Nelson Pinion, a man Mick knew well. The Pinion family had owned the Supper Club for generations and since prohibition had hit, the family claimed all the alcohol they served had been stored in their basement since prior to the law going into effect. No one believed that, but like several other states, some prominent New Yorkers had determined a few years into prohibition that tonic water without gin wasn't worth drinking. Therefore, there were places where the alcohol served was deemed legal.

Pinion's was one of them. Mick sympathized with prohibition agents and how they had to work with one hand tied behind their backs.

"Mick! Mick! Who is this beauty?" Nelson grasped both of Lisa's hands and made a show of kissing the back of one. "Please tell me you didn't marry this scallywag!"

"No," Lisa said, laughing and shaking her head. "We're not married."

"Yet," Nelson said with a wink. "And the wedding party will be here! It's a must. All the McCormicks have their wedding party here. Mick's parents did. Come, I will give you a tour."

"No tour is needed, Nelson," Mick said.

With what looked like a knowing nod, Nelson smiled at Lisa. "I will call Barb and set up an appointment."

"No call is necessary, either," Mick assured, before he took the time to make introductions. "Lisa, this is Nelson Pinion, the owner of this fine establishment. Nelson, this is Lisa Walters."

"Aw, Lisa, Lisa, such a beautiful name. Almost as beautiful as you, my dear." Nelson kissed the back of her hand again before releasing both of her hands and taking a hold of her elbow. "Come, let me escort you to the back room. It is where we host large parties, such as weddings."

Looking over her shoulder at him, Lisa grinned as she walked beside Nelson.

Shaking his head, Mick followed. He should have known that Nelson would fawn over Lisa. He was also wondering why he'd merely found humor in Nelson's marriage talk rather than irritation.

Chapter Fifteen

After showing them to a table, Nelson spoke to a waitress. Mick knew the man had just ordered them drinks, and told Lisa.

"What will our drinks be?" she asked.

"Probably champagne."

"But that's only for special occasions."

"You can order something different."

She was looking around the room while speaking. "No, I like champagne. I serve it on New Year's Eve. Only at midnight. This is a gorgeous room."

The room was large, with dark blue wallpaper embossed with gold swirls between painted murals of various local landscapes, and several sparkling, crystal chandeliers hanging down from the tiled ceiling. A large varnished bar sat along one wall, with brass foot rails and end posts, a piano player sat behind a large grand piano and the tables were all covered with white linen tablecloths.

"Thank you," Mick said to the waitress who set down two short-stemmed glasses.

"You're welcome, Mr. McCormick."

Lisa waited until the woman walked away. "Do you know her?"

"No. Why?"

Glancing in the waitress's wake, she asked, "Don't you need to pay? Or buy a card?"

"No."

She lifted a brow as she sat back in her chair. "Then how do they make money? Because there is money behind this place."

"I'm a member of the supper club."

A tiny scowl formed between her eyes. "A member? What does that mean?"

"I pay for a membership yearly, which means I can request the use of this room, and receive other member-only benefits."

"Like free drinks?"

He picked up his glass and nodded for her to do the same. When she did, he clinked his glass against hers. "Cheers."

She took a sip, grinned and took another drink. "That is good champagne. Much better than what I serve." After another sip, she asked, "What are the other benefits?"

He laughed at how he could almost see the wheels turning in her head. "Only members know that."

She shrugged. "Fine. I'll ask your mother."

He laughed. "Be careful with that."

"With what?"

"You don't want my mother thinking along the same lines as Nelson." He picked up his glass and took a drink. Champagne had never been one of his favorites, but this one was good. Or maybe it was simply the company.

"That sure was wonderful how those two got married at the end of that movie," she said. "I think he was the one she was in love with all along, but she was too kind to tell the other guy that."

"Really? I think it went the other way. That she was in love with the mate, but didn't want to hurt this man's feelings."

"Nope." She emptied her glass. "I could tell by the way she looked at him, right from the beginning of the movie."

The waitress arrived with two more glasses. "Thank you," Mick said, before replying to Lisa. "When she was kissing the other guy?"

"That was only for show."

He nodded.

She laughed. "That's how it works sometimes."

"Oh, how do you know that?"

Sipping her champagne, she shrugged. "I just do."

"If you say so."

She laughed. "I do." Her expression changed slightly. "Will you have your wedding here?"

He shrugged and took a drink to keep from having to provide a more thorough explanation.

"I bet you will, and that it'll be beautiful."

Swallowing, he set his glass down. "You'd lose that bet."

She shook her head. "I don't think so."

"I know so."

"How do you know that?"

"Because it almost happened once." Mick wasn't sure who was more surprised. Him when his own answer hit his ears, or her.

Her eyes were wide and her mouth had fallen open. She closed it quickly, but the look of surprise was still in her eyes.

"What happened?" she asked.

Oddly, he felt no animosity about telling her. Twila was in the past, more so than ever before. "She said no."

She laid a hand on his arm. "No? You asked her to marry you and she said no?"

He nodded.

"Why?"

"Because she didn't want to be married to a police officer. She thought my job was too dangerous."

Her smile grew slowly, then she giggled. "How silly is that? I mean, I'm sure that there are times that your job is dangerous, but a job wouldn't make a difference if you really loved someone."

"It wouldn't?" he asked.

Her cheeks flushed red. "No. When you love someone, you love them, no matter what they do for a job."

"Even a bull?"

"Yes, even a bull." She frowned then. "Is she who you were talking about when you said someone had lied to you?"

"Yes." It was odd, but there was no heaviness inside him. Or anger. "When I asked her, she said she didn't want to get married, but then she did, a month later."

"To whom?"

"An actor. She was an actress, and the two of them left town shortly afterward, went to California."

It was amazing how simple that sounded. Now. Back then, he'd struggled with it all.

"Do you still miss her?"

"No," he answered honestly. Which meant he also never really loved Twila. He'd just thought that was the next step in his life. To get married, start a family. After he'd worked with his uncles to get the family business thriving without his father, and to become a police officer, he'd thought it was time. He realized now how wrong that thinking had been. "I hope she and her husband are happy. Who knows, maybe we'll see them in a movie one day."

"That's very kind of you." She propped an elbow on the table and rested her chin in her palm. "I've tried not dwelling on being lied to, but I'm not finding it as easy as you did."

He shook his head, and stood. "We are here to have fun. Not dwell on anything." Holding out his hand, he said, "Dance with me."

She looked at him for a moment, and then grinned. Laying her hand in his, she stood. "All right, Rupert."

The fact she remembered calling him that the night they met thrilled him far more than it should. Actually, everything about her thrilled him far more than it should. Right now, he didn't want that to end. Not yet.

Lisa lay in bed that night, staring at the moon outside the window as her mind jumped between the events of the evening. It was impossible to determine what she'd enjoyed more. The kiss, Mick's arm around her at the movie, or drinking champagne and dancing with him. Each one was as special as the other, and filled her with such joy she couldn't stop smiling.

She didn't want to, either. It had been a long time since she'd felt so happy. So content.

Mick was such a remarkable man. She couldn't imagine someone saying no to a marriage proposal from him. He made her stomach fill with butterflies every time she looked at him, and thinking about him made her lips tingle.

That had been happening for days now, she just hadn't allowed herself to admit it.

A shiver rippled down her spine.

She could never marry him. Not because he was a police officer, that did make her proud, but because she had to return home. Soon. But right now, she was going to overlook that, and just bask in the evening's events. It had been her first date. She had not been allowed to date while in school, and then never had time afterward. That hadn't really mattered. There had never been anyone she'd wanted to date. Dating led to marriage, and marriage… She'd seen how sad her mother had been while being married to Duane, but since being here, she'd remembered more and more about what life had been like before Tony had left for the war. They'd been happy then. All three of them.

She imagined that's what being married to Mick would be like. A life of happiness.

An amazing warmth filled her as she closed her eyes, snuggled deeper into the soft bed, and let her mind relive each moment as sleep slowly took over.

The following day, she spent most of the morning talking to her father about the movie she'd seen, and having him confirm some of what had been displayed in the movie matched what he'd experienced. He hadn't wanted to talk about it at first, but she'd coaxed it out of him. Even the part about how his plane had been shot down, behind enemy lines, which was why he'd been reported as deceased. A family had found him, doctored him and taken him to safety once he was well enough to travel.

She would forever be grateful for those people, whoever they were, and that made her think about Mick again. He was another person she'd forever be grateful for. He'd given her and her father the chance to be together again, to heal old wounds and make up for lost time. It made her sad that he would never get a chance to see his father one last time.

Because it was Saturday, he wasn't working. Not as a police officer. Instead, he was working on the canoe in the shed. When her father grew tired, she left the room and made her way outside.

The sun was bright and warm today, and she was wearing another new dress she'd purchased when shopping with Barb. A white-and-yellow-striped dress, with handkerchief sleeves and an angled hem. In her hand, she carried an old shirt so she could help him with the canoe again without the worry of getting glue on her dress.

The door was open, and even before stepping inside, her smile grew at the sound of two voices. Mick's and Riley's. "Hello," she greeted while entering the building. "Is there room for one more helper?" Holding up the shirt, she told Mick, "I borrowed one of your old shirts to protect my dress."

His grin sent her heart pitter-pattering. She tried to ignore it as she slid her arms in the shirt sleeves.

"What do you think, Riley?" Mick asked. "Do we need her help?"

"Yes," Riley said from where he sat on the workbench. "We have a lot of work to do."

"You are right about that." With a slight scowl, Mick looked at her and shook his head. "But that's not an old shirt. It's one of my favorites."

"Oh!" Troubled, she glanced down at the shirt. "Your mother gave me this one because it has a stain she can't get—" His laughter stopped her. Biting back a smile at his teasing, she walked over and slapped his shoulder. "You goof!"

The scent of his aftershave filled her nose, and she drew in a deep breath, loving how good it smelled.

"It's not going to help if you don't button it." He reached down and buttoned the top button. Then the next one.

No man had ever made her feel the things he made her feel. Inside. Womanly things. Like the way her breasts tingled right now because of his nearness, and the way warmth pooled deep inside her. She'd spent most of her life dealing with men and always kept her distance. That's the way she'd wanted it. With him, it was the exact opposite. She had the strongest desire to be as close to him as possible.

His hands stilled as their eyes met, locked.

Her heartbeat increased as his gaze slid down to her mouth, making her lips tingle. It was as if he was kissing her with his eyes and that stole her breath away.

She bit down on her bottom lip as warmth spread throughout her system so strongly she wobbled slightly.

His hand slid around, gripping her side and the wink he gave her was almost her complete undoing. If Riley hadn't been sitting an arm's length away, she would have caught hold of Mick around the neck and held on while kissing him long and hard. She'd never have thought she'd be so forward, but that was exactly what she wanted to do.

Mick leaned closer and whispered, "Hold that thought."

The smile on his face thrilled her, but also sent a blush onto her cheeks to think he'd read her mind about kissing him.

He then tapped the end of her nose with a single fingertip and turned to Riley. "How are you doing with that rope?"

It took Lisa a moment to get her wits and breathing back in order. Stepping closer, she examined the ropes that Riley had tied into several knots.

"Mick's gonna need these later, for the canoe," Riley explained with pride.

"I'm sure he is," she said, hiding her knowledge that no one would ever need a rope with that many knots for any reason. Mick had merely given Riley a job, one he most likely had proclaimed was greatly needed.

Whatever had been growing inside her for Mick, grew a bit more, and a moment later, a very real fear trickled through her as a scene from the movie they'd seen last night entered her mind. She'd known which man that woman had been in love with because she'd recognized something inside the actress that she felt herself.

The chill rippling through her ran deep. She couldn't be falling in love with Mick. That would never do. Dreaming was one thing, but actually falling in love would open her up for intense disappointment. She had to return to Missouri, and he had to stay here.

"Are you all right?" he asked.

"Yes, I'm fine," she answered, trying to sound normal. "Just…uh, wondering how I can help."

Mick lifted Riley off the bench. "We are almost ready to put clamps on this side."

"I have to make sure it's straight first!" Riley exclaimed, ducking beneath the canoe that sat on two sawhorses.

Because the canoe frame was upside down, and only half of each side had wooden slats on it, the top was open and Riley's head was well below the frame boards as he slowly walked along the inside of the canoe, examining the slats carefully.

The look Lisa shared with Mick confirmed this was another job he'd found for Riley to believe he was helping. Call her hopeless, but she found the way he treated the boy so endearing.

Once Riley gave his approval, she put pressure on the slat while Mick put on the clamps and together, the three of them picked out slats to attach to the other side.

For the next hour or so, they worked together, and laughed. Riley was very inquisitive, and his never-ending questions, as well as how Mick answered each and every one of them with unending patience, was beyond delightful. She couldn't help but compare the three of them to herself when she was little, when she'd been a part of a family that had been full of fun, and love.

And that made her wonder if she'd been wrong about not wanting to get married.

For a moment. Then she remembered that her happy family hadn't lasted.

As she was contemplating that, Riley's grandmother shouted for him.

"Sounds like it's time for your lunch, bud," Mick said.

"But we aren't done," Riley said, clearly disappointed.

Mick lifted him out from the center of the canoe. "We are for today. The glue now has to dry for two days before we can do any more." He set Riley on the floor. "Run on home and have your lunch."

Riley agreed, a bit grudgingly, and then shot out the door as if he couldn't wait to get home, while shouting goodbye.

Lisa couldn't help but laugh.

Mick was in awe at how adorable she looked, eyes sparkling and laughing. There was nothing new about that. He'd been in awe of her for days. Their conversation last night about Twila had left him thinking long into the night. About several things. Including his father, and how he'd accepted the idea of never getting married, of having a family, because he'd never want to put the pressures on a child that he'd had put on him.

The trouble with that, was the more time he spent with Lisa and Riley, the three of them together, the more he remembered all the good times with his father. Those memories had become so strong, he hardly remembered the others. The ones he'd thought he'd never forget.

"Should we cover the canoe with the tarp?" she asked.

He turned, watched her walk over to the tarp, and his smile grew because he'd never forget today, working on the canoe with her and Riley. There were so many things that he'd never forget about her. Good things. New memories. A warmth curled around his heart. It was as if she'd used some of the same magic she'd used on her father and Riley, on him.

He walked over, lifted the tarp.

As they laid it over the canoe, she asked, "Why did you wait so long to work on the canoe again?"

He could say because it had been too cold during the winter months, or that he'd been too busy, or a number of other excuses, but that's exactly what they'd be. Excuses. "I'm not sure. I just never felt like working on it before."

"Why did you want to build it?" She began to unbutton the shirt over her dress.

He had to pull his eyes off her hands, off the buttons he'd fastened earlier, when her eyes had begged him to kiss her. If Riley hadn't been watching them, Mick would have kissed her. Riley wasn't here now. He shook his head and cleared his throat. "My father suggested it. I think it was his way for us to do something where we could get along." He shut the back door, and latched it.

"That had to have been nice," she said as they walked out of the front door.

He pulled the door closed, latched it, and then leaned a board against it. He'd put the extra board there just in case Riley ever considered hiding in there again. "It was." That was the truth. For a long time, he hadn't even looked at the canoe, but now, he was excited to see it done. That was just one of the things that had changed inside him.

He met her gaze. She was the reason. It was as if meeting her had somehow put his past truly in the past. Made him realize he'd been wrong about things.

She laid a hand on his upper arm. "I wish I could give you what you've given me. The chance to say goodbye to your father. I know he would have been so proud of you. Of how you found a way to become a police officer and a part of the family business, how you've taken care of your mother and others, including Riley. The way you gave him things to do so he was truly a part of working on the canoe today must be something you learned from your father."

It was. Memories of all the things his father had done with him and Connor was what he'd drawn on since Riley had arrived next door. He just hadn't given those memories credit. She was the one who deserved the credit for how she'd made him see things differently. Truthfully.

"It's something Riley will never forget." She closed her eyes for a moment and let out a soft sigh, before adding, "I won't either."

He touched the side of her face, let his finger trail

along the curve of her cheek. "I won't forget how you helped," he said. "I won't forget anything about you."

Licking her lips, she stared at him for a long, silent moment. "What's happening, Mick?"

He bit the inside of his lip to stop him from suggesting that he didn't know what she was referring to, but he did. How could he not?

"You know what I'm talking about," she said. "We started out hating each other, and now..." She shrugged and grimaced.

"I never hated you," he declared.

"You didn't like me."

He shook his head. "That's not true either."

Her grin was so coy, so sassy, he couldn't stop his own. The effect she had on him was uncanny.

She glanced toward the house and closed her eyes before turning, looking at him again. "I think I'm starting to like you too much, Mick McCormick, and I don't want to."

He'd always known she was honest, but she might as well have kicked him in the gut with the way she'd just laid that on the line. "Why?"

"Because I have to go home, run the Depot and you have to stay here, be a cop."

"So?"

"So? You know that as much as I do, so you shouldn't—" She huffed out a breath.

"Shouldn't what?"

She threw her hands up in the air. "Make me want to kiss you."

He had to fight to keep from laughing at the bolt of happiness that struck him. "You want to kiss me?"

"I didn't say that."

He lifted a brow.

She pressed a hand to her chest while sucking in air, and let out a cute little growl as she let the air out. "Oh, you...scoundrel!"

He slid his hands inside the shirt covering her dress, cupped her hips and pulled her closer. "You think I'm a scoundrel?"

Her cheeks pinkened. "No. I think you're very nice."

"I think you are very nice, too."

As she gazed up at him, a smile formed. "You're going to kiss me again, aren't you?"

Ever since she'd walked into the shed, kissing her had been the main thing on his mind. He nodded.

"Dagnabit!" She looped her arms around his neck while stretching on her toes so their lips could meet.

She had the ability to render him helpless. In more ways than one, but her kisses were definitely one of the ways. She responded to them with such passion, it filled him in ways he'd never been filled. Nothing else mattered. Not his past. Not his father. Just him and her.

"What the hell is going on here?"

Mick broke the kiss and instantly stepped in front of Lisa, shielding her with his body against whoever was yelling.

A short, stocky man with black hair was barreling his way across the backyard, closely followed by a uniformed officer.

"Get the hell away from my daughter!" the man yelled.

"Duane?" Lisa said from behind him.

Mick kept his arm in front of her as Lisa stepped up beside him.

She wrapped her hands around his biceps. "That's Duane, my stepfather."

"I figured that out," Mick answered.

"Arrest him!" her stepfather shouted. "He's the man who kidnapped her!"

"He didn't kidnap me!" Lisa shouted in return.

Recognizing the beanpole police officer, because he'd worked with him for years, Mick nodded as the men stopped a few feet away. "Hello, Roger."

"Mick," Roger Williams replied before he tipped his hat at Lisa. "Miss." Obviously nervous, Roger shifted from foot to foot. "This man claims you were kidnapped, is that true?"

"No, it's not true, officer." Looking at her stepfather, she asked, "Didn't the boys tell you why I came here?"

"What boys?"

Mick clenched his teeth to hold back from responding to the way her stepfather barked at her. The man had an air about him that said he was used to yelling at people, and at getting his way. Mick would gladly let him know that wasn't going to work for him here. Especially when it came to Lisa.

"The Hendricks," she replied. "Thad, Buck and Toby."

Her stepfather puffed out his chest. "I haven't talked to those buffoons. When I was in Kansas City, Lefty Gordon told me he saw you getting on an eastbound train with a man. Him!"

Mick returned the man's glare eyeball for eyeball.

"Is that true, Mick? You went to Missouri and brought her here?" Roger asked.

Chapter Sixteen

"No!" Lisa answered, but it was at the exact same time Mick said yes.

She still had her hands wrapped around his arm, and squeezed, while looking at him and shaking her head. Duane could hurt him for bringing her here, and that was exactly what she'd been afraid of.

Mick gave her a slight smile before telling the officer, "Yes, I did."

"But I came willingly," she interjected. "By choice. To see my father."

"Your father?" Duane let out a scoff. "He's in prison, where he belongs!"

Lisa's spine quivered. "How do you know that?" If he knew Tony had been in prison, he knew he'd been alive. All this time, he'd known, too. "How did you find me?"

Duane stuck his hands behind his thick suspenders. "I have my ways."

"The railroad would have told him that I bought two tickets to Rochester, and he'd could have gotten my name off the hotel registry," Mick said. "Or from the telegram I'd sent, asking you to contact me."

Lisa's heart sank. Duane had intercepted the telegram. She was sure of it.

"He flagged me down at the rail station," the officer said. "Asked if I'd ever heard of you and where you lived. He didn't tell me more until we arrived in the backyard."

Lisa had known he'd come looking for her sooner or later. She'd just foolishly hoped it wouldn't happen. She wrapped her hands tighter around Mick's arm. "You have no business here, Duane."

"I'd say I do, especially after what I just saw."

He was referring to her and Mick, kissing. She wasn't going to explain that, or apologize for it.

"Mick, invite Roger and his friend to stay for lunch!" Barb shouted from the back steps of the house. "It's roasted pork!"

Mick pulled his arm out of her hold, wrapped it around her back and took a step forward.

Stunned that he was agreeing to his mother's invitation, Lisa looked at him and shook her head.

He nodded. "This way," he told the men while walking around them.

She walked beside him. "Are you out of your mind?"

"No. We have to answer his questions. He came all this way to find you."

Lisa didn't miss how he said we, but she didn't want to answer any questions. How could she when she didn't even have answers to her own questions? Not just about everyone letting her believe her father was dead for years, but about Mick, and her, and how his kisses made her not want to go home.

The officer stepped up on Mick's other side. "Do you want me to make him leave?"

"No," Mick replied.

Irritated, Lisa said, "Yes."

Mick's arm around her tightened, but the squeal of pain that escaped her was from the way Duane grabbed her arm.

"I want this man arrested!" Duane shouted while trying to pull her away from Mick. "Now!"

Mick stepped in front of her and wrenched Duane's hand off her arm. "Touch her again," he said with a low, stern tone, "and you will be arrested."

Duane pulled his hand out of Mick's hold. "For what?"

"I'll start with trespassing, but won't stop there. By the time I'm done, your little manufacturing site will be shut down and you'll be in prison. The state pen, not the local jail."

Mick had said all that casually, but Lisa knew he was far from casual right now. The anger in Duane's eyes said he knew Mick was serious, too.

Duane snarled at her. "You're as ungrateful as your mother."

Seeing Mick's hand ball into a fist, she grabbed his arm, but tired, so very tired of Duane's cruelty, she challenged him, "What did we have to be grateful for?"

The wide nostrils on Duane's hawklike nose flared as he glared at her.

Mick wrapped his arm around her again and started walking to the house, leaving Duane to decide on his own to follow or not. She hoped he wouldn't, but knew he would. At the same time, she knew with Mick at her side, Duane didn't stand a chance.

That gave her a whisper of added strength. She lifted her chin and, knowing Duane was watching, she wrapped her arm around Mick's back.

Barb met them in the kitchen, as welcoming as ever,

even to Duane. The woman's attitude didn't change even after Mick introduced him as her stepfather.

With a smile that never wavered, Barb said, "Welcome, there is a washroom down the hallway, where you can wash before eating." With her smile still bright, she told Lisa, "I've set the table in the dining room. Tony is up to joining us."

"Thank you," Lisa replied, as her heart sank. The last two people she would ever want to be in the room when they met were Tony and Duane. "I'll go help him."

"There's no need, he's already in the dining room," Barb said.

"Tony?" Duane barked. "Tony Walters is here?"

Before Lisa or anyone else could answer, Barb was already shaking a finger in front of Duane's nose. Mick's mother might be small, and sweet, but she'd kept her twin boys in line for years and wasn't afraid to do the same to others.

"See here, we do not shout in this house," Barb said sternly. "Now, as I said, the washroom is down the hall. Use it."

Lisa pinched her lips together at how Duane's neck and face turned beet red. He glanced at Mick, the officer and her. Knowing he was outnumbered, he let out a muffled huff, and walked down the hallway.

Removing the old shirt still over her dress, Lisa hung it on the back of a kitchen chair and used the kitchen sink to wash her hands. Mick used that sink, too—so did the officer. They were all in the dining room, along with Tony, when Duane walked into the room.

Seeing Tony, her stepfather stiffened.

Tony offered a slow smile. "Hello, Duane," he greeted.

Lisa had started to tell her father about Duane's arrival, but he'd shaken his head, and said he'd already known. He'd seen him out the window in his bedroom.

"I thought you were in prison," Duane said, in a much quieter tone than normal.

"Mr. Kemper, you may have a seat right there," Barb said, indicating the open chair beside Roger, the police officer. Her leveled gaze also let Duane know that was not a topic of conversation she would tolerate at the table.

An eerie sensation rippled over Lisa as Mick held a chair for her to sit. Nothing good could come of this. Nothing at all. She glanced at Mick as he laid a hand on her shoulder and gave it a gentle squeeze.

The meal proceeded with a heavy silence. Other than comments of praise for the delicious meal, hardly a word was spoken. As soon as he was done, the officer excused himself, claiming he needed to get back to work, unless Mick needed him to stay.

Mick assured him all would be fine, and suggested the rest of them move into the living room.

Barb silently excluded herself and began clearing the table. Lisa felt guilty leaving all the cleaning up and dishes, or maybe she wanted to put off the confrontation that was sure to become explosive.

As if Barb understood her thoughts, she smiled. "Don't you worry. It's all going to be fine. Mick will be with you the entire time."

That was part of what she was worrying about. Mick. Duane was sure to mention that he'd seen them kissing. What would her father think of that? What would Barb think of that?

With her stomach churning, she walked down the hall and into the living room. Knowing once again that nothing good could come out of this.

"I thought you were still in prison," Duane said before everyone was seated.

"I served my time," Tony replied as he sat in one of the armchairs.

"Just like you did," Lisa added as she sat down on the sofa. If her father wasn't going to stand up for himself, she would. And let Duane know that he was no one to point fingers.

Mick sat down beside her. "I'm assuming you are here for a reason," he said to Duane.

"Hell, yes, you kidnapped my daughter!"

"He didn't kidnap me," Lisa said.

At the same time that Tony said, "I asked him to find her."

"Why?" Duane barked. "To fill her head with lies? She knows you never wanted her. That you skipped out on her and her mother."

Annoyed, Lisa shook her head. "He didn't skip out on us. He went to the war, served his country, and when he returned, his wife had married someone else."

Duane let out a bitter laugh before he leveled a sneer on her. He hadn't sat down, instead paced the floor. "After all I've done for you, this is the thanks I get? Get your stuff, we're leaving."

She shook her head. "I'm not ready to go home yet."

"Get your stuff!"

"No." Not willing to point out what Duane apparently didn't see—that Tony was gravely ill—she said, "I don't want to leave yet."

"You don't want to?" He let out another bitter laugh. "Did it ever occur to you that I didn't want to raise someone else's brat? An ungrateful one at that! You wouldn't have anything if it wasn't for me!"

Disgust filled her, but she wasn't going to get in a

shouting match with him. She'd seen her mother do that
far too often and how it had never settled anything. It
would just happen again the next day.

"I believe it's time for you to leave," Mick said to
Duane.

"Yes, it is." Duane reached over to grab her arm, but
Mick stopped him.

"She said she's not leaving, and she's not," Mick said.

With a condescending glare at Lisa, Duane said,
"You're just like your mother. Well, don't come running to me when you're pregnant with no place to go
like she did."

Mick shoved Duane toward the doorway, and didn't
let the man pause or look back.

As she watched them disappear, an odd ringing filled
Lisa's ears. Upon hearing the slam of the front door, she
looked at Tony. His downcast eyes gave her the answer,
yet she needed it confirmed. "My mother was pregnant—that's why she married Duane?"

With his eyes cast downward, he gave a slight nod.

Her mind swirled, but there was no memory of her
mother being pregnant.

"She lost the baby," her father said.

She'd known there had been miscarriages before
she'd been born, but if her mother had had one while
being married to Duane, she must have shielded her
from knowing about it. "Why did she stay married to
him?" Lisa asked, mostly to herself.

"Because it was best for you. She didn't want you to
lose another father."

"Another father?" She could barely believe her ears.

"Our life wasn't like what she told you in her letters.
Duane was exactly what you saw today. He shouted,

demanded, and left when he didn't get his way. Just to come back and do it all over again."

"I was afraid of that," he said. "That's why I sent money."

"Payments." Her throat burned at the memory that formed. Of Duane asking her mother if his payment had arrived and demanding that it should have been more. A shiver rippled over her skin. Suddenly she knew there was a lot more to all of this than she'd read in the letters, and that hurt. "Where are the rest of the letters?"

Mick paused in the doorway, glancing between Lisa and Tony. The air in the room was as charged as it had been moments ago, before he'd escorted Duane out of the house and pointed in the direction of the rail station.

"You only gave me the ones you wanted me to read." Lisa shook her head as she stared at Tony. "Where are the rest? Why tell me anything if you aren't going to tell me everything? Why…" She pinched her lips together and blinked as if holding back tears.

Mick walked toward the sofa. "She has a point, Tony."

"A point?" She frowned, then her eyes widened. "You've known all along, haven't you? And like him, didn't bother to tell me. Didn't think I deserved to know."

He wanted to shake his head, but couldn't lie to her. She'd been lied to far too much already. "I—"

"Don't!" Holding up one hand, she stood. "Just don't."

"Lisa—" Tony started.

"I don't want to hear anything that either of you has to say. Not right now." Walking toward the door, she said, "I wish I'd never have come here."

Having had enough, Mick looked at Tony. The man looked older, more tired, sicker, yet he asked, "Whose baby was it? The one that Bertha lost?"

Tony shook his head.

Anger rose inside Mick. "I'd think you'd want to save what you've rediscovered the past few days. The love of your daughter." He waited until Tony looked up at him. "The only way to do that is to tell her the truth. The entire truth."

"I can't."

"Why not?"

"Because I don't know who the father was, other than it wasn't Duane. Bertha said that it had been a drifter who had done some work for her. By the time she discovered she was pregnant, he was gone. She'd asked Duane to marry her, and he had."

"Why are you afraid to tell Lisa that?"

"Bertha didn't want her to know. She didn't want anyone to know." Tony shook his head. "Junction's a small town—if anyone had found out, they would have shunned them."

"Shunned them?" Disgust rose up inside him. "Do you have any idea how much Lisa has given that town, done for that town?" Mick shook his head. "You've been trying to protect her from the wrong thing."

Mick left the room and went straight upstairs to Lisa's room and knocked on the door. He didn't wait for her to answer, figuring she wouldn't. Opening the door, he stepped into the room. "What are you doing?"

She finished folding the blue dress in her hands and set it atop the pile of clothes on the bed. "I'm leaving."

He closed the door. She was hurt, he understood that, and why, but he also knew he didn't want her going anywhere. "So, you're packing?"

She pulled another dress out of the closet. The purple one he'd bought for her, and carried it to the bed. "Yes."

"Without a suitcase." It wasn't a question, merely an observation.

"Yes."

"You are just going to carry all that in your arms?"

She planted her hands on her hips. "I'm going to borrow one from your mother, if you must know."

"I have one you could use." He stepped closer to the bed. "Do you want me to go get it for you?" His question went deeper than a suitcase.

Turning away from him, she whispered, "I have to get out of here."

On some level, he agreed with her. This was all more than she wanted to deal with, but leaving wouldn't solve anything. "No, you don't."

"Yes, I do."

"And go where?"

She shrugged. "Home."

"Is that what you want?"

Her face was turned away from him, but he could hear her tears in her voice.

The ache to take her in his arms, to hold her, kiss her, tell her that he'd help her make everything all right, was too strong to deny. He grasped her arms, and slowly turned her about. He gently wiped aside the tears on her cheeks, then pulled her up against him. Held her as she laid her head on his chest. She didn't sob, but he felt her crying deep inside and held her, rubbed her back.

"I'm so tired of being lied to," she whispered. "So tired of all of it."

He kissed the top of her head. "I know you are, and I'm sorry."

"You knew my mother was pregnant, didn't you?"

"Tony told me the other day. I told him to tell you, and hoped he would."

She lifted her head, looked up at him. "You could have told me."

He'd never held as much regret as he did at that moment. "I could have, and should have, even though he'd asked me not to." He hooked a lock of her hair behind her ear and then ran a knuckle down the side of her cheek. "I'm sorry. Deeply sorry. I thought this was all between the two of you and didn't want to interfere."

A hint of amusement flashed in her eyes. "Interfere?"

He couldn't deny he'd been doing that since the beginning.

"Isn't that what you did by bringing me here?" she asked.

"Yes, it was, before I realized how capable you are of making your own decisions. Of how independent, strong and resourceful you are. You've been taking care of yourself for so long, you don't need someone to do that for you." He hadn't fully realized that until now, nor had he realized just how much like his father he was in believing he knew what was best for her. That's what his father had done to him, by pressuring him into following in his footsteps rather than making his own.

"Are you trying to make me feel better?"

He lifted her chin. "I'm telling you the truth. You are a smart, determined woman. Duane knows that, too. He's tried to control you like he did your mother, but you've refused to let that happen. You've stood up for yourself and the town. He's afraid of you."

She frowned. "Afraid of me?"

He nodded. "Why do you think he followed you here? He knows you can win, and that he'll lose."

Her expression turned thoughtful and he hoped she

believed him, because it was the truth. He'd seen that in Duane's eyes.

"Just now, downstairs, Tony told me your mother wasn't pregnant with Duane's baby," he said.

A deep frown filled her face. "Then who—"

"Tony said it was a drifter, who had moved on by the time she realized she was pregnant."

She turned stock still, except for her chin, which dropped. "Freddie?" she asked.

"I don't know a name." He rubbed her arm, feeling her trembles. "Who's Freddie?"

"Freddie lived with us for a few months. Mother sold the dairy cows after he was gone, and…" She swallowed, covered her mouth with one hand, and whispered behind it, "And she married Duane."

He felt her going weak and guided her over to sit on the edge of the bed.

"You never saw Freddie again?"

Her face was nearly colorless when she looked at him. "He was killed. They found his body north of town, when the pond had dried up, shortly after my mother married Duane. He'd been shot. They never found who did it."

Mick knew. In that instant. He knew.

Chapter Seventeen

The following week was a waiting game that drove Mick insane. As soon as Lisa had told him about the murder of the drifter—Freddie Jones—he'd gone in search of Duane's whereabouts, and continued to tail him, with the help of other officers.

Doing his due diligence, he discovered the killing of Freddie had long ago been written off, and without solid proof that Duane was the perpetrator, the case wouldn't be reopened. The only guarantee that Duane would be made to pay for his past deeds was to catch him in the act of another crime.

Since his arrival in town, Duane hadn't done much except take a hotel room downtown, visit gin joints and hire bimbos to watch Lisa's every move. She was the ticket to Duane's success and he wasn't going to give her up easily.

Neither was Mick. She'd come to mean too much to him.

He had men guarding his house, and nothing happened in this town without him knowing about it, but he was still worried that something could go wrong. That Lisa could be hurt.

She'd become so solemn this past week. On the outside, she pretended she was fine, even still insisted upon working on lessons with Riley, but the shine had gone out of her eyes, which told him just how troubled her thoughts were on the inside.

A truck had arrived from Missouri this morning, and the crates in the back marked flour were stocked full of moonshine. Duane's brew from Junction. There was a buyer lined up. A joint on Fourth Avenue, where Duane had been boasting about his brew and visited daily.

The owner of the joint, Al Brooks, was happy to comply, as were prohibition agents. They'd learned from their Missouri counterparts that they'd been after Duane for some time, but he was slick. They knew he delivered moonshine to Lisa's farm, but had yet to find his manufacturing site.

Mick knew why. Duane was operating under the umbrella of the Pendergast Machine, but that wouldn't save him here in New York.

"The truck's pulling in," Roger whispered.

Mick nodded from where he and Roger crouched behind a couple of barrels at the other end of the alleyway. They were there to back up the agents inside the back room of the joint. Once the deal went down, Duane would be arrested, and eventually hauled back to Missouri to face murder charges. Mick would get a confession out of him. Had to. It was time for this all to end.

The truck rolled to a stop a few feet away and two men jumped out of the back, while one got out of the passenger seat.

Mick waited for the driver to get out. None of the other men were Duane. When the driver's door finally opened, Mick's heart shot into his throat.

It wasn't Duane.

Damn it!

Duane was nowhere in sight.

Still awake, staring at a book but not seeing the words, Lisa thought the thump she heard on the back porch was Mick coming home. He'd been gone all day, hadn't even come home for supper, and it was after midnight.

She set aside the book and, tying the robe tighter around her waist, she left the library to take the plate of food out of the refrigerator and warm it in the oven for him. He'd been working long hours this last week, because of her. Duane had bimbos watching the house for her every move, and Mick had assigned an officer to be out front during the hours he was gone.

It was all her fault. Mick had been right about Duane trying to control her, and how she'd fought against that—right down to that being the reason she hadn't become a teacher. Because that's what he'd wanted her to do and she'd been determined to never do what Duane wanted.

Mick had been wrong about Duane being afraid of her. He was too much of a bully to be afraid of anyone.

Another thump came from the back porch as she entered the kitchen. Wondering if Mick had forgotten his key, she went to the door, and peeked out of the curtain.

It was pitch black, but she heard something again.

Suddenly afraid it might be Riley, she unlocked the door and stepped out onto the porch.

"Hello, Lisa."

She jumped backward, but wasn't fast enough. Duane grabbed her.

A wicked gleam filled his eyes as he pulled her off the porch and wrapped a thick arm around her throat from behind as he shoved her forward. "You conniving vamp! Thought you could ruin it all! Everything I worked so hard to build!"

She twisted, kicked and scratched at his arm, trying to break his hold around her neck. It was so tight she couldn't breathe. All she could think about was Mick, coming home and finding her gone. She couldn't let that happen, threw her head backward, felt it connect with Duane's face.

The pain made her see stars for a moment, but Duane's hold eased enough for her to catch her breath, and her wits. She dipped her head and buried her teeth in his forearm, and when his hold lessened, she broke loose.

A scream ripped from her throat when he caught hold of her hair and yanked her backward before she'd taken more than two steps. A crippling pain shot up her leg as he delivered a kick to the back of her shin.

She pinched her lips together to keep from crying out again. He thrived on hurting people and she wouldn't give him that satisfaction.

He grabbed her arm, ripping the sleeve of her housecoat as he harshly spun her around. "You can scream, shout, no one will come to your rescue. Especially not your precious cop."

Her heart lurched, and panic filled her to the point she couldn't breathe.

"That's right," he sneered. "Your cop friend will soon have a little accident, just like your friend Freddie did all those years ago."

Her blood ran cold as terror coiled inside her.

"Your mother was pregnant with his brat, was going to marry him. I couldn't let that happen."

The evilness of his tone, on his face, was like a flash-back. She'd seen him look that way, sound that way to her mother.

"No one else in the county had what she had. Money. But it was all wrapped up in her cows. Getting rid of Freddie gave me what I needed, for years, just like getting rid of your cop will do."

A firestorm of rage rose up inside her.

Duane let out anther evil laugh. "He's downtown, planning to bust me, but won't because I'm untouchable. Have been ever since I bought in with the Pendergast Machine." His hold on her dug in tighter. "With your mother's money. She was my pot of gold. All she had to do was write a letter, and your daddy sent her more money. For me." His laugh echoed in the night air.

She had to get Mick, somehow! A newfound strength filled her, and she lashed out, kicking and slapping at him until her efforts were enough to break out of Duane's grip.

She ran, blindly at first, but then headed toward the shed, remembering how Riley had hidden in there, but Duane was too close—he'd find her! She had to lose him and get back to the house, call Mick. Call the police. Call someone!

Her heart pounded, echoed in her ears and so did the thudding of the ground, from her feet hitting it, and from Duane's. He was close behind her. Shouting he'd catch her.

She couldn't let that happen. Pain shot up her leg with every step from where he'd kicked her, but she didn't let it slow her down.

The grass was wet with nighttime dew and her bare feet slipped on the damp grass as she ran past the shed. She grabbed the board Mick had leaned against the door and threw it to the ground before running into the woods. A grunt and crash sounded, suggesting Duane had tripped over the board, but she didn't slow down to check. She had to lose him and then find Mick. He couldn't be dead. She refused to believe that, even as the thought made tears burn her eyes.

Combatting the fear inside her, she told herself that Mick was too smart to be tricked by Duane. Far too smart.

Hot, sharp pain had her gritting her teeth together as a stick or stone impaled her foot. Holding her breath against the agony, she grabbed the closest tree to check her foot. She held her breath to keep from making a sound as she pulled out a stick. The pain was excruciating, and the warmth that spread along the bottom of her foot said she was bleeding.

The moonlight couldn't penetrate through the canopy of the trees, making it too dark for her to tell where she was, how close to the river or to the house.

Her heart thudded as she glanced up, saw the boards nailed to the tree. It was her only choice. Reaching up, she grasped the board and, hoping it would hold her weight, pulled herself upward. Digging her toes into the bark of the tree, she used one hand to search for, then grasp the next board. She pulled herself upward and, feeling the blood drip from her foot, climbed faster from board to board.

It felt like there were a hundred boards that she had to climb up before her head bumped the bottom of the tree house. Feeling her way, she found the opening and climbed up into the small structure.

The boards creaked and bowed beneath her as she scrambled up against one wall. Hearing the rustle of leaves, the thud of footsteps, she cupped a hand over her mouth and nose to smother the sound of her breathing.

"She couldn't have gotten far!"

Lisa squeezed her eyes shut at the sound of Duane's voice. He was close, too close. Her entire body shook and blood was pooling beneath her foot. Carefully, she eased the hem of her housecoat beneath her foot.

"Did you check the river?" someone asked. "Maybe she found our boat."

"Go see!" Duane hissed. "Damn it! We can't let her get away!"

More thuds and rustling. She had no idea how many people were with Duane, and knew she wouldn't come out of this alive if he found her.

Yes, she would! For Mick! She had to get word to him, somehow!

He wouldn't get caught in Duane's trap. Not Mick.

She forced herself to believe that, even as she wondered what happened to the police officer who had been watching the house.

"Spread out! She has to be in these woods someplace!"

Duane again. They must have checked the river, and were now back. It would only be a matter of time before they found her.

"You can't hide from me, Lisa! I know you're out here!" he shouted.

She searched the tree house, forcing her eyes to adjust to the dim light. Leaves and twigs covered the floor, as well as a few boards that had fallen down from the ceiling overhead. There were also cut-out openings on all four walls, windows with no glass.

Cautiously, she scooted over to the closest one. She could see the ground, but only a small section of it.

A light flashed across the ground and she leaned

back. Flashlights! If they shone them up in the air, into the trees, they'd see the tree house.

Scooting a bit further along the wall, pausing when the floorboards sagged beneath her weight, she grabbed one of the boards that had fallen from the roof. Then she eased her way forward to the opening in the floor, and with both hands wrapped around the board, she held it over her shoulder, ready to strike anyone who came through the hole.

Along with her thudding heart, more rustling and footsteps echoed in her ears. Then shouts, followed by gunshots.

"Don't return fire! Don't return fire!"

Lisa's heart leaped inside her chest and tears poured from her eyes at the sound of Mick's voice. "Mick! Mick!"

"Lisa?" he shouted.

More gunshots went off.

She swallowed a sob while shouting his name again.

"Lisa, where are you?"

"The tree house! I'm in the tree house!"

"Good girl!" he shouted. "Stay there! I'm coming!"

"Duane has a boat! At the river!"

"The river!" he shouted. "Pursue!"

There was a mass of thudding footsteps, then a light shone up through the hole in the floor.

"Lisa!"

She dropped the board and leaned over the opening. "Mick!" Happy tears now fell from her eyes.

"I'm coming to get you!"

"No! The boards won't hold you!"

"Are you all right?"

The pain in her leg and foot were nothing compared

to the joy of knowing he was alive. "Yes. I can climb down."

"I'll shine the lights on the boards, so you can see where to step. Be careful and go slow."

She twisted to climb down, but before doing so, asked, "Where's Duane?"

"Officers are pursuing him, they'll catch him. Don't worry."

"He's part of the Pendergast Machine," she said, while lowering herself through the opening. "He bought in with them with money he got from my mother."

"I know," he answered. "I know all about the blackmail, and his connections. Don't worry, just climb down. Can you see the boards?"

"Yes." Seeing the light shining on the board nailed to the tree near her foot, she stepped on it, then the next one.

The relief that had filled him at hearing Lisa's voice left as Mick saw the blood on the boards. It was on her clothes, too. The anger that had filled him earlier returned with a vengeance. As soon as she was close enough to touch, he dropped the flashlight and grabbed her with both arms. One around her back and one beneath her knees.

"Where are you hurt? Where's the blood from?"

"My foot. I stepped on a stick. But I can walk."

"No, I'll carry you."

"But Duane—"

He stopped her protest with a kiss. He'd never been as frightened as he'd been tonight. The fear of her being hurt, or worse, had been beyond anything he'd ever known.

So thankful to be holding her in his arms, he would

have gone on kissing her if the noise of people coming along the trail hadn't forced him to stop.

Within a few minutes, the elation of knowing his fellow officers had captured Duane and his bimbos faded because it meant he had to leave her, go to the station to assist with the bookings and paperwork. For the first time in his life, he wished he wasn't a police officer because he wanted to be with her, yet, he also wanted Duane in jail for the rest of his life.

Mick told his mother to call the doctor as he carried Lisa up to her room, and once she was settled in bed, he promised to be back as soon as possible before he kissed her forehead and left.

The sun was coming up by the time the arrest reports had been completed. He'd also gone to check on the officer who'd been guarding the house, now recovering in the hospital after being knocked out by Duane's goons.

As he drove home, the frustration of being separated from Lisa when she'd needed him at her side made him fully admit that being a police officer wasn't the most important thing in his life. It may never have been— he'd just thought it was, or at least thought it should be. That was no longer the case. Family, the people he cared about, were the most important, and always would be.

"George said it was good that her foot bled so much, but he still had to dig out some splinters and put in stitches," his mother whispered as she rose from the chair beside Lisa's bed when he walked into the room.

She was asleep, with her foot bandaged and propped on a pillow.

"There's also a big bruise up the back of her leg George is concerned about," his mother continued. "He'll be back tomorrow and says we have to watch for infection, especially blood poisoning and he gave her something to sleep." Patting his shoulder, she added, "Enough so she'll sleep until at least noon. Why don't you go get some sleep, too?"

He nodded, but made no effort to move.

"Are you hungry?"

"No," he replied. "I'll sit with her for a while."

"All right." His mother kissed his cheek before walking out of the room and closing the door.

Mick removed his coat as he crossed the room, and draped it over the back of the chair. A dozen images flashed across his mind as he stared at the bed. Of Lisa. At the Depot. At her house when he'd barged in that morning. Then later, when he'd told her about Tony and insisted that she come to New York with him.

The images continued. Them on the train, eating in the dining car, the thug in the powder room, her sleeping under his coat. Even more formed of them here, at his house, the movie theatre, Pinion's Supper Club, working on the canoe with Riley.

With every image, his heart swelled a bit more, until, when the image became what he was looking at right now, her sleeping, his heart felt oversized. Full.

He knew love. He'd lived with it his entire life, and right now, he didn't know why he'd fought against wanting it, of giving it.

He took off his shoes and quietly walked around the side of the bed. Careful to not disturb her, he climbed on the bed and slipped an arm beneath her pillow, while gently placing the other arm across her stomach.

She mumbled softly, turned her head so it was against his shoulder and sighed.

Chapter Eighteen

With the sensation of being watched, Mick opened one eye, and then the other at seeing Lisa's sweet smile. The desire to kiss her, deeply, fully, had his breath catching inside his chest. Holding back, he brushed several long hairs that were caught on her eyelashes while asking, "How are you feeling?"

Her eyelids fluttered shut for a moment as she sighed. "Fine."

Sunlight filled the room, but he wasn't sure if it had been only an hour since he'd laid down beside her, or several. "How does your foot feel?"

The soft sound she made was somewhere between a chuckle and a groan. "It hurts."

He placed a soft kiss on her forehead. "Can I get you anything?"

She rubbed one eye and sighed. "No." Grasping his hand with both of hers, she held it beneath her chin. "I'm sorry for all the trouble I caused."

He hurt for her, for all she'd been through over the years and wished he could take it all away. All of her pain. All of her suffering. He lifted their clutched hands, kissed her knuckles. "You haven't caused any trouble."

Her smile wobbled slightly. "Yes, I have. Is Duane in jail?"

Squeezing her fingers, he nodded. "Yes, and will remain there."

"The Pendergast—"

"This isn't Kansas City," he interrupted. "It's Rochester, New York, and the only time Duane will get out of jail is when they transfer him to prison."

She let out a ragged sigh. "I can't believe I was so blind. I remember him and my mother fighting, that the money wasn't enough. That his payments needed to be bigger."

He tugged her closer to him with the arm still under her neck. "It's over now, and you don't have to worry about it."

"That was money Tony was sending to her. In her letters, she made it sound like it was money for the farm. There was no farming. It was all for Duane."

"Your mother was protecting you," he said, angry again at how Duane had threatened her life, right up until he'd been put behind bars. "You'll never have to worry about him again."

"But how will I ever right all his wrongs?"

He shifted slightly to look her in the face. "You don't have to right any of his wrongs."

She sighed and closed her eyes.

He watched as she bit her lips together and squeezed her eyes closed tighter. "Don't blame yourself, honey, and don't take responsibility for any of it. Just let it go."

"I can't help it." She opened her eyes and looked at him with deep compassion. "Just like you can't help blaming yourself for having fought with your father the day he died."

He took a deep breath. Usually when that topic came

up, he'd clam up or leave the room. Neither of which he could do right now. Strangely, that didn't bother him. "I regret having fought with my father that morning. I wish it hadn't happened, and I wish he hadn't died that day." That was the most honest he'd ever been when it came to his father's death. "Who knows, given the time, I might have enjoyed following in his footsteps, working with him, for him, but it didn't work out that way."

"That's why you wanted me to see Tony before he died, so I wouldn't have regrets, wasn't it?"

He thought about that for a moment. "I felt bad for Tony when he told me the story of how he'd returned from the war and no longer had a family, but when he told me about you, about an adorable little girl who had grown up to be a schoolteacher…" Mick shook his head, remembering the images that had formed in his mind of a young girl who thought her father dead. "I wanted you to know that your father was alive and had always loved you."

"Just like you keep telling Riley."

He nodded.

"And just like your father had loved you."

That struck like a bullet. All his regrets and blame had tarnished so many memories. So many wonderful memories. It certainly hadn't done him any good. Hadn't done anyone any good. Others had pointed that out, but he hadn't been ready to hear it. Until she'd come along and opened his heart to caring again. "Yes. Just like my father had loved me."

"He sure built a solid tree fort for you and Connor," she said.

"Yes, he did."

She closed her eyes. "I was so scared when I found

that tree house. So afraid something had happened to you."

He kissed her forehead. "I was fine. I just wish I would have gotten here ten minutes earlier."

"You've done so much for me, more than anyone ever has. I don't know how I can ever repay you."

He touched the side of her face, traced the line of her chin. "Just be happy, Lisa. You deserve that." He meant that, completely. And he meant what else that meant. That she was capable of making her own decisions, whatever those decisions might be. Even if that meant she'd return to Junction and run her speakeasy.

Lisa held back the tears pressing to get out. Despite all that had happened, waking up with him lying next to her had filled her with a happiness that she'd never known. But it wasn't a happiness that she deserved. If anyone deserved to be happy, it was Mick. She wished she knew a way for that to happen. He'd make such a wonderful father. She hoped that someday, he'd see that, and get married. Marry a woman who loved him fully, completely, and would see that being married to a policeman was something to be proud of, not fear.

A knock sounded on the door, and Mick brushed his lips against her forehead before he eased off the bed and walked to the door.

"Someone has been patiently waiting to see Lisa for hours."

Lisa recognized Barb's voice and nodded for Mick to open the door further when he looked at her.

With a grin, he pulled the door all the way open, and Lisa pressed a hand over her heart at the sight in the doorway.

Riley, holding a wilted bouquet of yellow dandelions, said, "I picked you some flowers."

"Thank you, they are beautiful," she answered, pulling herself up to a sitting position. "So very beautiful."

"Here's a vase for her flowers," Barb said, handing Mick a crystal vase. "Riley didn't want to put them in it until he gave them to her."

Mick took the vase and carried it to the table beside the bed, and then propped the pillows behind her. "You best bring those flowers over here, Riley," he said. "So we can get them in water."

Riley crossed the room and held out his hand full of drooping dandelions. "Does your foot hurt real bad?"

She took the crushed stems from his hand and acted as if the blossoms smelled as lovely as roses. In her heart, they did. "These flowers make me so happy, my foot doesn't hurt at all."

Riley's face lit up. "They do?"

"Yes, they do. They are the prettiest flowers I've ever seen."

"I knew you'd like them," he said proudly.

"I do, very much." She turned to Mick. He picked up the vase and held it as she lowered the stems into the water. As Mick set the vase back on the table, she told Riley, "They will make me smile every time I look at them."

"Barb said you stepped on a stick," Riley said, leaning against her bed and examining the bandage on her foot.

"I did."

"Why weren't you wearing any shoes?"

"Because I didn't plan on going outside. I was just going to peek out the door. That wasn't very smart of me," she said.

"You're the smartest person I know," he answered. "Being a schoolteacher. Except for Mick. He's smart, too."

She managed to stop herself from laughing aloud. "Yes, he is, and so are you."

He nodded, then frowned. "Can you walk?"

"Yes."

"No," Mick answered at the same time. Lifting a brow as he looked at her, he continued, "She needs to stay off her foot for a few days."

"I can do that in the library, while Riley and I read a book," she said.

Mick looked at her and then at Riley, and grinned, while saying, "I'll carry you down there."

"I need to get dressed first," she said.

"I can help with that," Barb said from the doorway. "You two run along. I'll let you know when she's ready to go downstairs."

Mick hoisted Riley into his arms. "Come on, buddy." He picked up his shoes on the way out the door.

"You have quite the little admirer there," Barb said once the door was closed.

"He is so adorable." Lisa flipped the blanket off her and eased her foot off the pillow.

"And the older admirer is handsome, if you ask me."

Lisa bit her lip for as long as she could, then let out a giggle. "Yes, he is."

Barb walked over to the closet and opened the door. "Sometimes life breaks our hearts, and it appears as if there's nothing we can do about it. That nothing will ever make it whole again." She took a hanger holding a dress out of the closet and closed the door. "I know, and I discovered that the best thing we can do is keep living. Live right through the pain. Cry when we need to, but also laugh, and sing and dance, and when the moment is right, love. Love like our hearts were never broken because that is what will make us whole again." Holding up the dress, she asked, "Is this one all right?"

Lisa nodded about the dress, while thinking about Barb's words. It sounded simple enough, but Lisa knew that Barb was talking about her and Mick, and she wasn't sure that could happen. She could love him. She didn't doubt that, but he lived in New York. She lived in Missouri. A place that she had to return to, even more so now that Duane had been arrested. The town, the Hendricks, would all be wondering what happened, and what would happen to the Depot.

Furthermore, Mick didn't want to get married, and if her time here had taught her anything, it was that she had started to want that. Had started to want having a family. Being a part of a family again.

"How is my father doing today?" Lisa asked. She wanted to know, but also wanted to change the subject.

"Fine. He's been downstairs all morning, waiting to see you." Barb grinned. "He's been a bit more patient than Riley has been."

Lisa stood on one foot to remove her nightgown. "I'm sorry if they were disturbing you."

Barb helped her pull the nightgown over her head. "Disturbing me? Goodness, this house hasn't been so full of life in years. I love every minute. It's just been Mick and me the past few years, so having a houseful, it's like having family again."

Lisa flinched inwardly, having just had those same thoughts. She loved waking up to having others in the house. Although she'd been busy with the Depot the past few years, she had hated going home to an empty house every night. She didn't want to return to that lonely life.

"Arms up," Barb said, holding the purple dress.

Once she was dressed, minus shoes, Lisa said she could walk downstairs, but Barb wouldn't let that happen and shouted for Mick.

He arrived instantly, and carried her downstairs.

Lisa tried to hold her breath, because he smelled so good. Felt so good. His simplest touch filled her with such happiness. If things were different, if there weren't so many people depending on her back home and if he… She shook her head. That wasn't a possibility. There was no reason for her to believe she could change his mind on marriage, so there was no use thinking about it.

He carried her into the living room, and set her down on the sofa, where she could keep her leg propped up, per doctor's orders. Barb brought her in soup, which she ate, while she and Mick, as well as her father and Barb, all listened to Riley sing the alphabet and recite the spelling of his name, along with other things that had them all chuckling.

Riley's grandmother arrived before long, and much to his disappointment, insisted it was time for him to come home.

Afterward, Mick told them all what had led up to Duane's arrest, and how there were enough charges against him to have him imprisoned for years. Tony had tears in his eyes as he apologized to her, over and over again.

Lisa insisted it wasn't his fault, because it wasn't, and that she forgave him. She did. She forgave her mother, too. Now that Duane had been arrested it was over. Except for her going home. The thought made her stomach sink.

"Do you want me to carry you back upstairs?" Mick asked.

Holding in a sigh, she shook her head. "No. I'm fine."

"Well, I have some things to see to in the kitchen," Barb said.

The next moment, her father stood. "I'm going to sit on the front porch for a while."

"Would you like me to get you a pillow and blanket, so you can take a nap here?" Mick asked.

"No. I'm fine. You can leave, too. I don't need anyone to sit with me."

"There's nothing I need to do."

She leaned her head back and let out the sigh that had been pressing hard to be released. "I suppose I should call Buck, tell him what happened to Duane so they won't have to put any money on my front porch tomorrow."

"I can carry you into the library, if you want to call him."

She shook her head. "No. He'll have other questions and I won't know how to answer them."

"About a new distributor?"

Frowning, she looked at him, and admitted, "I hadn't even thought about that." She hadn't. She'd been thinking about Buck asking when she'd be home.

"Do they have enough of a supply to stay open for a while?"

"They should, as long as the deliveries have continued while I've been gone. Buck never said they'd stopped, so I assume they hadn't." If she'd been at home, that would be a real concern, but here, she didn't even want to think about it. It was as if she didn't care enough to want to think about it. "Why do I feel like things are so different?"

"Because a lot has happened," Mick said. "A lot of things have changed."

"But not me. I haven't."

"Haven't you?"

"No." Or had she? Is that why she felt so different? She closed her eyes and huffed out a breath. Or maybe it was just because she was here. Once she returned home, she wouldn't feel different. Maybe she wouldn't want to get married again, either, once she got back home. Away from him.

Mick knew why she was saying no. Everything she'd ever known had changed over the past few weeks, and that had to have changed her, too. The way she thought about things, felt about things, even looked at things. All that was confusing.

He knew because a lot of things had changed for him, too. On the inside. Too many things. The idea of her going back to Missouri settled worse now than it had before, because he'd started to think harder about going back with her. Not just so she'd be safe during the trip.

He wanted her to be safe forever. To not have to do everything all on her own. To have a partner. Someone to share the good things and the bad, because that was what he'd started to want, too. It was all so unusual, that he couldn't quite get his entire mind around it.

In some ways.

In other ways, he didn't want to wrap his mind around it. Just because that's what he now wanted, didn't mean that was what she wanted.

He stood, and unable to not touch her, laid his hand on her shoulder. "I'm going to get you a pillow and blanket."

"I'm not tired."

"Doesn't matter. You'll be more comfortable with a pillow behind you and a blanket over your legs."

"My legs aren't cold."

Grinning, because she was covering a yawn, he leaned down and kissed her forehead. "They will be once you fall asleep."

Chapter Nineteen

Mick returned with the pillow and blanket and wasn't surprised when she said that she might take a nap, after all. He left the room, and seeing Tony on the front porch, he walked out of the screen door.

"I really failed them, Mick. Really failed them. Both Lisa and Bertha," Tony said solemnly.

Mick sat down in the other chair, understanding the man had things he wanted to get off his chest.

"I should have known Duane wasn't anything like what Bertha described in her letters. I did question it, at times, but only to myself, and then I'd figured it was just jealousy. He had what I wanted, so I had reason to hate him. Had I known he was a murderer..." Tony shook his head.

Knowing Duane was behind bars, and would be forever, was a great relief to Mick, and he hoped in time, it would be to Tony, too. "You didn't know. We all have things that we didn't know, and would have done things differently if we had," Mick said.

Tony shook his head. "I would have killed him, Mick. I know I would have had I known."

Mick didn't doubt that. If he'd known then what he

knew now, he would have searched out Duane rather than just bringing Lisa home with him. "But you hadn't known—that's the difference."

Tony sighed. "Thank the Lord you found her, got her out of there."

He was thankful for that, and he was thankful for far more than that. "Lisa's a strong woman, Tony, and resourceful. She didn't let Duane have the upper hand. He tried, but she made him toe the line. You have to be proud of her for all she did."

"I am, Mick. I truly am," Tony said. "As proud as any father could be."

"Then don't miss this opportunity to tell her that, don't let either one of you hold on to any regrets," Mick advised.

Tony looked at him and frowned. "You sound like you're saying that from experience."

"I am. I've had my share of regrets." Mick glanced up, saw his mother standing in the doorway. Nodding at her, he said, "And they blinded me from seeing so many other things. Including what it was doing to me, and others."

His mother opened the door and carried a tray with cups of coffee and cake onto the porch. Pausing next to him, she kissed his temple. She didn't need to say anything. They both knew he'd finally put the past where it belonged. In the past.

"I thought you two might like some coffee and cake," she said.

He stood. "Thank you, but I'll let the two of you have the coffee and cake. I have some things to see to."

His mother frowned. "Will you be gone long?"

"I shouldn't be." He'd always been a man of action,

and right now, he needed to take the first steps of his future.

He bid them both farewell, and drove downtown to his office, where he talked to the goons that had arrived in town with Duane's booze, offering them leniency for their answers. Satisfied with the information he'd obtained, he left.

Along the way home, he saw a man selling flowers on the street corner, and pulled over to buy a bouquet for Lisa, but then, knowing her as well as he did, he bypassed the flowers and entered the nearby store. There he bought a new housecoat to replace the one that had been torn and stained last night, and a package of gum. Then drove home.

She was awake, reclined on the sofa with her foot on a pillow, and reading a book to Riley, who sat on the floor next to her. Her smile made Mick acknowledge something else about himself. His insides no longer felt dark and heavy. Instead, there was a lightness inside him. A freedom of sorts.

He leaned against the door frame and listened as she continued to read, changing her voice for each character in the story, and her expressions to match the actions she read, making it all more intriguing for Riley. When she ended the story and closed the book, Mick stayed in the doorway, listening as she and Riley discussed the tale, so the boy would fully understand the moral.

"Hey, Mick!" Riley jumped to his feet, noticing him when their discussion had ended.

Mick entered the room and nodded toward another bouquet of dandelions on the coffee table. "I see you found more flowers."

Riley beamed with pride as he explained, "Yeah, I

picked her some new ones 'cause the other ones were kinda hanging their heads. These ones aren't."

Lisa was beaming, too. "Aren't they beautiful?"

"Yes, they are," Mick answered. Though many looked at dandelions as weeds, they were the exact reason he hadn't bought her flowers. To her, those flowers from Riley were more beautiful than any of the ones the man had been selling. The other reason had been Riley. The boy was proud of his gift, and Mick was proud of Riley's thoughtfulness. He dug in his pocket and handed Riley the package of gum he'd bought.

"Chewing gum! Wow, thanks, Mick. I love chewing gum!" Riley quickly opened the pack and popped a piece in his mouth. Talking around the gum, he continued, "I gotta go. Gram said I could only listen to one story or I can't come back tomorrow."

"Then you better head home," Mick replied, tousling the boy's curls.

As he ran from the room, Riley shouted, "Bye, Lisa, thanks for the story. Bye, Mick, thanks for the gum! See you tomorrow!"

Lisa looked up at him after they'd both bid farewell and heard the front screen door slam shut. With a thoughtful gaze, she asked, "What are you going to do when he moves back home with his father?"

"Miss him," he answered while taking a seat in the chair next to the sofa and settling the box holding her gift on his lap. "And be happy for him."

"He does miss his father," she said.

"I'm sure his father misses him just as much," he said.

She nodded, making the hair tumbling around her

shoulders flutter. "I'm sure he does, and I'm sure he'll appreciate how you befriended Riley."

"You, too," he said. "The things you've taught him will be with him forever. Just like a teacher."

She stared at the doorway where Riley had disappeared for a few silent moments. "Do you want to know why I wanted to become a teacher?"

"Yes."

She grinned at his quick response. Then sighed. "Because I'd decided that I was never going to get married, never going to have children of my own."

"Why?"

"Watching my mother. She'd been heartbroken when Tony left. Devastated. I was too young and sad myself to fully understand it then, but as time went on, and she was never happy, never laughed, I found that the only time I could laugh was when I was at school. Then she married Duane and she'd tell me that she wished she'd never gotten married. Not to Tony or Duane, and told me that I shouldn't. That I should become a schoolteacher. It made sense to me."

His heart constricted at the sadness that had filled her childhood. His childhood had been wonderful, and he hoped that someday she could put the bad memories behind her, as he finally had. "You would make a wonderful teacher, if that is something you still want to do."

"Until Riley, I thought I'd given up on becoming one." Leveling a gaze on him, she grinned. "Or maybe I should say until you challenged me to teach him how to tie his shoes."

He nodded. "Then you remembered how much you enjoyed it?"

"Yes."

"Is it something you want to continue to do?"

She shrugged. "As you said, prohibition won't last forever."

"No, it won't," he said. "Too many people oppose it, and the government knows it failed. It didn't have the effect they'd hoped for, and most of those who had put the law in place have been voted out of their offices and appointments. Alcohol will be legal again. Drinking establishments will no longer be hidden, they'll be on main streets with their lights on and doors open."

"Will that make you happy?"

He shrugged. "Prohibition, illegal booze, created a crime world like no one expected. It's here now, and it won't go away. The gangsters will just move on to something else once booze is no longer the top game."

"So it won't change the world."

"The world doesn't change. People do. For the good and for the bad. It's up to them."

"Do you want to know why I never became a teacher?"

He frowned because he thought he already knew the answer, and asked, "Why?"

"Because I thought that was what Duane wanted, so he could have full control of my property, do whatever he wanted. Now, I have to wonder if he'd known that I wouldn't do anything he told me to, and that's why he let me take over the speakeasy, because it gave him exactly what he wanted. Money. That's all he'd ever wanted. I was doing all the work, and he was getting the money, just like he had taken money from my mother. Tony's money."

Mick wasn't surprised at her insight. Duane had been a manipulator. "Well, either way, it's all his loss. The Depot is yours, lock, stock and barrel, to do whatever you want to do with it, and you still have the choice of becoming a teacher or not."

She nodded, but looked away, as if to contemplate that.

He picked up the box and leaned over, handing it to her. "Here, I bought you something."

"Why?"

"Because I wanted to."

She grinned and opened the box, sighing softly as she folded back the tissue paper to reveal the pale purple house coat. "Oh, it's beautiful. Thank you, but you—"

"I wanted to," he repeated.

Touching the material, she said, "Your mother already washed and mended my other one."

"Then you have two." He pulled the slip of paper out of his shirt pocket. "I also have this for you."

Her brows knit together as she took the paper and read it. "What is this?"

"Names of distributors for the Depot."

"Oh."

"I figured you can call Buck and give him those names, if they need inventory." He gestured to her foot. "You're stuck here for a while."

She lifted her chin. "It's not that bad, I can walk, travel if I need to."

Mick avoided her gaze in order to hide a grin. He'd seen grit and determination in her the moment he'd seen her pour four drinks at a time behind the bar, but he also knew just how soft and delicate she was and how precious that made her. "I'm sure you could, but I don't want you to, and I hope you don't want to, either."

"Why?"

He knew why he wanted that, but he wanted her to decide what she wanted first, because she'd had enough people influencing her decisions for too long. "Because your foot needs to heal."

She nodded. "Yes. It does."

Staring at the new purple housecoat draped over the foot of her bed, Lisa had so many thoughts roaming around in her head that they were bumping into each other before she could focus on one. Mick was included in all of them. He'd carried her up to bed tonight. She'd tried taking a few steps, but had known she'd never make it up the steps and had given in. Throughout the day, her foot had gotten uglier. Black and blue, puffy and swollen, and it was sore. Almost as sore as her heart.

As much as she'd tried to tell herself that she hadn't changed, she had. She couldn't remember specifically when, but it had happened. Deep inside her there were desires, wants and needs that had never been there before.

She had fallen in love. Was sure of that now, but that didn't mean Mick had fallen in love with her. Didn't mean he wanted a family. A house full of people. Full of love and laughter.

A knock sounded, and, assuming it was Barb with the glass of water she'd promised to bring up after helping her change into her nightgown, Lisa said, "Come in."

Mick appeared in the doorway, with a glass of water in one hand. "I brought you some water so you can take the tablets the doctor left for pain."

"Thank you." Her heart was pounding, recalling him lying next to her in the bed earlier today, and how wonderful that had been. How wonderful her life had become since she'd met him.

He closed the door and carried the glass to the table beside her bed. "How are you feeling?"

"Fine."

"Tired?"

She shook her head—the way her mind was spinning it would be hours before she fell asleep.

He reached behind his back and pulled out a book. "Good thing I brought a book with me."

She pointed toward the table. "I have a book."

"I can read from that one if you want."

"Read from that one?"

He nodded.

"You are going to read to me?"

"Yes, I am, until you fall asleep." He opened the bottle of pills, dumped two in his hand and held it out to her. "Right after you take your medicine."

She took the pills and the glass of water he handed her, and handed the glass back after swallowing the pills.

He set down the glass and then sat on the edge of the bed and opened the book.

Laughing, she laid a hand on his arm. "You can't be serious about reading to me."

"I am serious." A slow smile formed on his lips and a gleam made his eyes even bluer. "It's either that, or what I've been thinking about all day."

Her heart skipped a beat as she asked, "What is that?"

Leaning closer, he planted a hand on each side of her. "This."

Happiness bubbled deep inside her soul as Mick's lips covered hers. She grasped his arms, and held on as the kiss deepened, when he parted her lips with his tongue, and that lit up all of those wondrous womanly desires.

She could kiss him like this forever. It filled her with such joy. It was as real and tangible as anything she'd ever touched, ever held in her hands, yet it wasn't. It was invisible. That's what scared her. There was nothing she could actually hold on to that proved he might have changed his mind. Might be falling in love with her.

Mick teasingly sucked on her bottom lip as he broke the kiss.

She kept her eyes closed, wondering if it would be worth taking the chance.

"I need to leave," he whispered. "Otherwise, I'm going to keep kissing you. All night."

She nodded, knowing if he stayed, she'd want him to keep kissing her. All night.

In the days that followed, Mick was almost irredeemable in the way he countered her best efforts to not fall deeper in love with him. He was so caring, so charming and so perfect, that she could feel herself slipping deeper and deeper. She'd thought about asking him, yet she was afraid of what the answer might be.

Her stitches had been removed a few days ago, and this morning, Dr. George said if she was still interested in taking Tony to Missouri, it should happen soon. He was doing much better right now. Well enough to make the trip.

The doctor had left a short time ago, after having cake and coffee with Barb as George was known to do, and she found her father outside.

Much stronger, and looking healthier, he was in bed only at night these days. Right now, he was weeding the large flower garden beside the front porch. She knelt down beside him. "What do you think about going home with me? Back to Missouri?"

Without looking up, he shook his head. "Oh, honey, I'm proud of what you've done back there, very proud, but that hasn't been my home for years, and I can't go back there. I won't stop you from going, if that's what you really want to do."

She had hoped that he'd say yes, making her decision easier, because truth was, she was having a hard time convincing herself that she couldn't stay here. "It's what I have to do," she said. "People there depend on me."

He set aside the small hand hoe and sat back on his haunches. "Is that all you want? For people to depend on you?"

No, it wasn't. Her life here was so different from what she'd always known and she felt guilty about not wanting to give that up. Mick was the main reason. She couldn't help but dream that if she stayed longer, maybe someday, he might change his mind about getting married. It was foolish of her, but that's what was living in her mind right now, and her heart.

"Home," her father said, "is where your heart is. It's not a piece of property. It can be anywhere in the world, as long as there is love in your heart." He took her hand. "I've made a lot of mistakes in my life. So, so many. If I could go back, I would change many things. The only two I wouldn't change, would be marrying your mother and having you."

"Even though your marriage didn't work out?"

"Yes. I'd rather have had the few years I did have with you and your mother than none." He squeezed her hand. "I wouldn't have had anything to live for then."

A car pulled into the driveway. Mick's car. Lisa's

heart skipped a beat, and the fluttering continued as he climbed out, walked toward them.

"You have your entire life ahead of you, honey." Her father picked up his hand hoe and stood. "And the opportunity to make it be whatever you want it to be. I won't beg you to stay. I don't have that right, but I do want you to be happy." He kissed her cheek before he stood and walked away before Mick arrived.

Her heart pounded harder as Mick stopped before her and held out his hand to help her up from where she was still kneeling on the ground. She laid her hand in his, and that's all it took for that special awakening to happen inside her. She had fallen in love with him. Was sure about that, and didn't know what to do about it.

Her knees felt weak as she rose to her feet and she had to lock them in place to keep from swaying against him.

"Lunch isn't ready yet," she said, trying to sound normal. It was hard. He still had hold of her hand, making her body tingle, her heart thud.

"I know." He glanced at the house. "My mother called me."

"Oh." Her heart sank. "And told you what the doctor said."

Frowning, he asked, "What did George say?"

She looked at him, searched his face. It appeared that he didn't know. "That I could take Tony to Missouri." For whatever reason, she quickly added, "But he doesn't want to go with me."

"I see." He scratched the back of his neck. "No, she hadn't told me that."

"Then why did she call you?"

He glanced across the driveway, at the house next door. "Because Willow called her. Riley's father called.

He'll be here to pick him up tonight and take him home to Albany."

Her heart constricted. "I was wondering why he hadn't come over yet." She blinked several times. "I—I..." Her throat locked up.

Mick pulled her into a hug.

She buried her face in his chest and held on. Held on tight. "He must be so happy about that."

"I'm sure he is, and his father."

It was several minutes before she felt composed enough to lift her head. "I'm going to miss him."

Mick kissed her forehead. "I know."

He would miss Riley, too. She stretched up on her toes and kissed his lips, then gave him a hard hug. "So will you."

He nodded. "I will. How is your foot?"

She held on to him for a moment longer before stepping back. "Fine. It doesn't hurt at all."

"Are you sure?"

"Yes."

"Good, but we'll still take it easy." He took her hand and pulled her toward his car. "I took the rest of the day off so we can spend it with Riley."

Her heart soared. "You did?"

"Yes. Willow said she'd have him ready, so let's go get him."

"Where are we going?" she asked, already hurrying across the driveway.

"It's a surprise," he answered. "My parents used to take Connor and me there often, but it was opening day that we looked forward to the most. For us, it signaled summer was right around the corner."

Within minutes, they were driving downtown, with Riley sitting on the seat between them. The top was down on the car, letting the bright May sun shine on them as they drove all the way to Lake Ontario. The body of water was so large that she imagined that looking at the vast, unending water had to be what looking at the ocean was like.

When he pulled into a large parking lot, Riley squealed. "The amusement park! Yippee!"

Mick's smile was as big and bright as Riley's. "Yes. The best amusement park in the world."

"The best one in the world?" she asked, laughing as he ran around the front of the car.

Opening her door, he took her hand. "Yes, it is."

Riley leaped out of the car. "Can we go on the Jack Rabbit, Mick? Can we?"

"What's the Jack Rabbit?" she asked.

"The fastest roller coaster in the world," Mick answered.

Her heart lurched and she laid a hand on Riley's shoulder. "Is it safe?"

"Tell her it's safe, Mick, please! Me and Dad rode on the Jack Rabbit! It's so fun!"

"It's safe," Mick said, scooping Riley into one arm while grabbing her hand with his other hand.

The smell of roasted peanuts, popcorn and various other wonderful food scents mingled with other new and amazing scents as they entered the park. People were everywhere; so were rides, games and street performers.

"Do you know how roller coasters came to be?" Mick asked as they walked.

She shook her head, so did Riley.

"Back in the eighteen-hundreds, the coal mines built gravity-propelled railroads to bring the coal down the mountains. Before long, people were asking if they could pay to have the opportunity to ride in the coal carts just for the fun of it."

The sparkle in his eyes had her shaking her head. "Baloney."

"It's true." He used one hand and made an X over his heart. "Cross my heart."

She laughed. "That makes it true?"

"Yes," Riley said. "A heart can't lie. My dad crossed his heart that he'd be back to get me."

Mick grinned. "Can't argue with that." Then pulled on her hand. "No one's in the ticket line."

Before long, they stood next to the roller coaster. A monstrosity of wood and metal rails that went so high in the air she grew dizzy looking at it. "You're sure this is safe?"

Still in Mick's arms, Riley touched her shoulder. "I'll hold on to you, Lisa, make sure you won't fall out."

"So will I," Mick said.

Her heart tumbled. This could be the last day they would all have together, and she wasn't going to let it be a disappointment. "In that case, give the man the tickets, Mick!"

He laughed, handed the man their tickets and they climbed in one of the carts of the miniature train.

"The best seats in the house," Mick said, and settled Riley between them. "The very front."

The steep wooden structure in front of them looked a mile high, and she drew in a deep breath.

Mick's arm stretched past Riley's head and he cupped her shoulder tight with one hand at the same time Riley grabbed one of her arms and hugged it tight to his chest.

"Are you scared, Lisa?" Riley asked.

"Are you?" she asked.

"Nope! I'm happy!"

"Me, too," Mick said.

She laughed. "Me, three!"

The cart started to move forward, slowly, with clanks, and creaks, and clatters and bangs. It went slow enough that she relaxed a small amount.

"We're almost to the top," Mick said a few moments later.

The vastness of the lake was on one side of them— the amusement park, where the people looked like ants, and the buildings of the city beyond the park looked just as minuscule. She was about to tell Riley that, when the cart started teetering. She reached one hand across Riley, planting him tight against the seat and grabbed hold of Mick's leg as the cart plummeted downward at a speed she didn't believe possible.

The scream that left her throat came from pure terror, a panic she'd never known. Then, as the cart flew around a curve, she heard Mick and Riley. Laughing. Laughing!

"Yippee!" Riley shouted. "This is so fun!"

A laugh left her then. Not just a giggle, or a chuckle over something funny, but a real, solid laugh that rose up from her stomach at the thrill of the speed, the smoothness of the cart effortlessly careening around corners and up and down dips. "Yes, it is!" she shouted.

Her heart was racing, her breaths short and quick, and the thrill, the excitement, all consuming. Every time they topped a hill, a scream escaped, half expecting they'd topple, plummet to the ground. When that didn't happen, and they'd plunge down the hill on the wooden track, she'd laugh and cheer along with Riley and Mick.

The crowd behind them, in the other carts, were screaming and cheering, too. It was so exhilarating, while being so terrifying that her senses couldn't seem to keep up.

"Put your hands over your head," Riley shouted, releasing her arm.

"Why?" she asked.

"Cause that's what you do on roller coasters!" Riley shouted while laughing.

She stretched one arm over her head, but kept the other one in front of Riley and holding onto Mick's leg, just in case.

"Yippee!" Riley shouted again.

She laughed as a sense of euphoria filled her. From the ride as much as it was from the two sitting in the cart beside her.

That sense of euphoria remained after the car rolled to a stop and they climbed out. Happiness was bubbling inside her. The only thing she could liken it to was the feeling she got when Mick kissed her.

"What did you think of that?" he asked.

His smile was so big, so bright, she knew he'd loved that ride as much as the grinning boy walking between them. Riley looked up at her, waiting for her answer. "I think that was almost the most magnificent thing I've ever experienced," she said.

Riley jumped up and down. "Can we do it again, Mick? Can we? Please?"

"Yes, we can," he answered. "As many times as you want."

Chapter Twenty

"What is this?"

Mick laughed at the way her brows were knitted together as she stared at the food he'd set on the picnic table.

After riding the Jack Rabbit several times, as well as nearly every other ride at the park, he'd told Riley it was time to eat. "That," he pointed to the first item, "is a hot dog, with ketchup, and those," he pointed to the next paper bag, "are French fries." Waggling a brow, he picked one up, and dipped it in the paper tub of ketchup. "Which are delicious dipped in ketchup." Pulling the boy into the conversation, he asked, "Aren't they, Riley?"

"Yep!" Riley managed with his mouth full.

"Try it," Mick said as he held the French fry next to her mouth.

Lifting a brow, she opened her mouth and bit the end off the French fry.

He ate the rest of the French fry as she chewed and swallowed. "You're right. That is delicious."

Nodding at her hot dog, he said, "Wait until you try

that." He took a big bite out of his and groaned as if he'd never tasted anything better.

She laughed. "It's that good, is it?"

He nodded, and when she took a bite out of her hot dog, the way her eyes fluttered shut and she moaned, he nearly choked because she made that same little moan sound when he kissed her. The roller coaster was thrilling, but nothing on earth set his blood pounding harder through his veins than her. That little sound alone had forced him to take more than one cold dip in the bathtub over the past several weeks.

When his mother had called, told him about Riley's father returning, he'd thought that would be the worst news he'd heard for the day, but the news Lisa had given him had struck him like a bullet, straight in the heart. The way she'd said that Tony didn't want to go to Missouri with her kept echoing in his head.

With her.

Which meant that was what she was planning.

"This really is delicious," she said. "The hot dog and the French fries."

"Sure was!" Riley said, having already gobbled up his. "Can I go watch that guy?"

Mick looked to where a juggler was performing a short distance away. After scanning the area, he nodded. "Yes, just stay where you can see us at all times."

"I will, Mick!" Riley climbed off the bench and ran to where several other children were seated on the ground, watching the man juggle three red balls.

"I think someone is having the time of his life," Lisa said.

"I am," Mick replied, giving her a wink.

They were sitting next to each other on one side of a small picnic table in the shade of a big oak tree.

While glancing at where Riley was seated, she said, "I meant Riley."

"I know. How about you? Are you enjoying it?"

"Yes, I am."

Mick was certain he'd never seen anything quite as beautiful as she looked at that moment, wearing a bright yellow dress, with her hair flowing free around her shoulders, and kissed by the bits of sunlight breaking through the leaves of the tree.

"Why are you staring at me like that?"

"Because you're beautiful," he admitted freely. After making sure Riley hadn't moved, and not caring that they were in public, with hundreds of people mulling about, he kissed her. A much shorter kiss than he'd have liked, but long enough to tease the passion from her.

He broke the kiss slowly, giving her several small kisses before pulling away. He couldn't live the rest of his life without her. And wouldn't. No matter what that meant.

The way she sighed, the way her eyelids fluttered as they lifted, and the smoldering passion in her eyes spoke volumes, and gave him hope.

"Mick," she said, his name barely more than a breath.

His own breathing stopped. He loved her, wanted to take her home and show her exactly how much. Wanted that so badly it made his entire body ache, but he respected her too much to act on that want, not until they were married. It was time. Time to fully admit that was exactly what he wanted. Admit to himself and her. He touched the side of her face. "You are so beautiful."

She smiled and bowed her head. "You shouldn't kiss me like that."

"Why not?"

"Because it makes me feel like that roller coaster did."

He lifted her chin. "Dizzy? Excited? Exhilarated?"

"Yes."

"That's how it makes me feel, too."

The air between them was so charged he swore there were sparks of electricity zapping between them as they looked at each other for a long, long time.

She was the one who finally looked away, to where Riley still sat, watching and clapping with the other children.

"I—I feel other things, too, Mick."

His heart soared and he drew in a breath, braced himself to open up every part of himself. "Lisa, I—" The words stopped as instinct told him to look toward Riley.

The boy was jumping to his feet, and in a flash, took off running.

Mick leaped to his feet. "Riley!" He touched Lisa's shoulder long enough to say, "Stay here!"

Lisa's heart pounded as she watched Mick race away, disappear into the crowd. The same crowd where Riley had disappeared only a moment before. With one hand pressed to her chest, she searched the sea of people, looking for both Mick and Riley. It had happened so fast. She'd barely gotten to her feet when Mick had been swallowed up by the crowd.

She searched harder, scanning the people and trying to not run into the crowd herself. The only thing stopping her was what Mick had told Riley before they left home. He'd said if they got separated, that Riley was to stand still, not move, because that way Mick would know where to find him.

He'd told her to stay here, because Riley knew this was where they'd been sitting. He must have chased after a ball that the juggler dropped or something. There was no other reason for him to take off running like he had.

Growing frantic as panic rose inside her, she continued searching the crowd for a familiar face, shape, clothes. Even though she was having a hard time remembering what Mick or Riley had been wearing.

A white shirt. That's what Riley was wearing, with blue shorts and suspenders. Mick had on a white shirt, too, with black pants and suspenders.

Dagnabit! Nearly every man in the crowd was wearing a white shirt and black pants!

Just when frustration and fear were about to overcome her, she saw Mick emerge from the crowd. Her heart nearly doubled in size at the sight of him, but then it dropped, because he wasn't carrying Riley. She'd expected him to be carrying Riley.

As she darted around the picnic table, a familiar voice hit her ears.

"Lisa! Lisa!"

That's when she saw the man next to Mick. Tall, with red hair, carrying Riley.

Her relief was so great, her knees wobbled.

"It's my dad, Lisa! My dad's home!" Riley shouted.

Mick arrived at her side and wrapped an arm around her, as if knowing she needed his support because of how hard her legs were still shaking. She leaned against him, savoring his strength.

"This is Matt," Mick said. "Riley's father."

"I'm sorry," Matt said. "When my mother said Riley

was at the amusement park, I had to come find him. I couldn't wait another hour. It's been a long five months."

Lisa had to blink beyond the tears blurring her eyes at how Riley was holding on to his father's neck. The two were the spitting images of each other, and the love in their eyes as father and son looked at each other was enough for her to forget the fear that had filled her moments ago.

Mick's arm around her tightened as she nodded. "I can understand that," she told Matt. "He's missed you just as much."

"I can't thank you enough, both of you. Every time I talked to my mother, she told me about how you'd befriended Riley." Matt kissed Riley's forehead. "And he told me all about being able to tie his shoes and about working on the canoe, and he even sang me the alphabet song over the phone."

"We've enjoyed having him next door," Mick said. "And will look forward to each and every one of his future visits."

"I've been offered my old job back," Matt said. "So we'll be heading back to Albany tomorrow, but will visit as often as we can."

"We're going back to Albany?" Riley asked.

Matt nodded. "Yes, but not until tomorrow."

"Can we ride the roller coaster one more time? Can we, Dad? Please?"

Lisa had to laugh at Riley's priorities, which were perfect for a little boy.

"Yes," Matt said. "We can."

"Yippee!" Riley shouted.

Mick's hand caressed her side as he said, "I think Lisa and I have ridden it enough today, but you two go ahead. We'll see you tomorrow morning before you leave."

"All right, Mick! Let's go, Dad!"

Matt laughed. "We are off to ride the roller coaster, and thank you again. Both of you."

Lisa wrapped her arm around Mick's waist and leaned against him as they watched Matt and Riley walk toward the roller coaster ride.

"Riley swore he'd seen Matt walking through the gate," Mick said. "And then it took us a moment to find him."

Lisa nodded, hearing what he'd said, but she was still watching Matt and Riley, knowing full well that was what she wanted. A husband who would take their children to the amusement park, let them help build a canoe, buy them tiny gifts just for the fun of it and love them.

"I'm sorry, we—"

"Riley is where he belongs," she said. "With his father." She dropped her arm from his waist and turned away from him, toward the picnic table. "I need to throw this trash away."

Mick's hand slipped off her and he helped her collect the trash. "Are you doing all right?" he asked as they deposited the paper food wrappers in the nearby trash cans.

"Yes, I'm fine. Just thinking about how you reunited another father and child today."

He leaned down and kissed her. Longer than before, much longer. When his lips left hers, she felt as if her entire body wanted to melt into his.

"Now that I have your full attention," he said. "I want to finish saying what I started to say earlier. I love you, Lisa Walters, and I'd like to ask you to marry me. I'll move to Missouri, help you run the Depot or—"

"No!" Lisa gasped at the word that had shot out of her mouth. "I mean no, you can't move to Missouri. You live here. Your family is here. Your job is here."

"I love you more than anything that is here, but I understand if—"

"No." She growled at having said the word again. "I mean you don't understand."

"What don't I understand?"

Flustered because her heart was racing as fast as her mind was spinning, she sucked in a deep breath and told herself to concentrate. Huffing it out, she said, "First off, you don't want to get married, Mick McCormick. You told me that on the train and at Pinion's." The specific times he'd said that to her had become branded in her mind.

His hands slid up and down her arms. "I did say that, both times, but I changed my mind."

Still trying hard to concentrate because in the back of her mind, three words kept repeating over and over. *I love you. I love you.* She'd heard him say that, twice. And that alone was enough that she couldn't stop a smile from forming. "Changed your mind?"

"Yes."

"When?"

"A while ago." A slow smile rose on his lips. "When I realized I was in love with you."

The amount of love that filled her heart was beyond all she'd ever known. "I changed my mind, too, but there's something you should know."

A teasing gleam filled his eyes. "That you aren't a good traveling partner?"

Seems he remembered everything she'd told him, too. "No. I don't want to live in Missouri. I want to live here. In Rochester, because that is where a man lives, whom I love very, very much."

He lifted a brow. "Really? Do I know him?"

She laughed, then stretched on her toes so their lips almost touched as she said, "His name is Mick Mc-Cormick."

"I might have heard of him," he said.

"Good, because I'm going to marry him." Their lips met, and she kissed him with all the love filling her. All the love she'd felt for him for weeks, and would feel for the rest of her life. A life that was truly hers, and one she was going to make the most of every single day.

As the kiss ended, Mick grabbed her hand. "Come on!"

"Where to?" she asked, already running beside him.

They dodged around a large group of people, and then another before reaching the parking lot. At the car, he paused long enough to kiss her before opening the car door.

"Where are we going now?" she asked again, even though it didn't matter. As long as they were together, she didn't care.

"I didn't put handcuffs on you back in Missouri, but I'm putting one on you today!"

Laughing, and utterly thrilled because everyone called an engagement ring a handcuff, she watched as he ran around the front of the car. Once he was inside, she threw her arms around his neck and kissed him.

"I was afraid you'd never change your mind," she said as their lips parted.

"And I was afraid you'd never change yours."

She laughed. "You've been changing my mind since the moment you walked into the Depot! A man had never caught my attention the way you did."

"Because I was a bull?"

"No, because you were the most handsome man I'd ever seen."

He rubbed the tip of her nose with his. "Even more handsome than Rupert the Magnificent?"

Laughing again, she said, "Far more handsome, but you are the true magician."

He kissed her again, then started the car. "Wait until you see the tricks I have up my sleeve."

Chapter Twenty-One

The next two days were proving to be the longest in Mick's life, and he still had an hour to go before the ceremony, and several after that before he and Lisa would be alone. Sleeping down the hall from her was torturous. He wanted her in his bed, but with his mother and her father also sleeping down the hall, that couldn't happen. Not until the *I do*'s were spoken. He was extremely grateful that, like him, Lisa wanted the ceremony to happen as soon as possible.

He was also glad that his brother had returned to town last night. It would be a small ceremony, just immediate family here at the house, but not having Connor there would have been an integral missing piece.

As if his brother knew he was thinking about him, Mick heard the back door open, and instantly knew who was walking through it.

"I'm home!" Connor shouted, before walking in the kitchen.

Whatever Mick had been about to say stalled on his lips as he noticed the woman beside his brother. Then again, of course Connor would bring a date. Connor always had a woman on his arm.

"Mick, you remember Jenny Sommers," Connor said, nodding at the woman.

Mick remembered the name as a girl Connor had dated in high school. She had moved away, and that had nearly crushed Connor. His brother had never admitted that, but Mick had seen it. Right now, he saw the happiness in his brother's eyes, and Mick liked seeing that. "Yes, I do." He nodded at the woman. "Good to see you again."

"Hello," she said. "And congratulations."

"Thanks." Before he could say more, the back door opened again and he grinned, this time recognizing the speed of footsteps, and the voice.

"Mick! Lisa!"

"I believe the guest of honor just arrived," he said to Connor and Jenny.

Riley shot into the kitchen at a full run. Mick caught him midair as Riley leaped into his arms.

"Hey, buddy!" he greeted, giving the boy a solid hug.

"Me and Dad are here for your wedding!" Riley released his hold on Mick's neck to look around the room. "Where's Lisa?"

"We can't see her yet," Mick said. "She's still getting ready."

Riley shook his head. "Women."

The room filled with laughter, and the sound continued throughout the next several hours.

Mick would forever remember how beautiful Lisa looked in her gold dress, covered with swirls of embroidered flowers. Everything about her shimmered as brightly as the sun outside, especially her smile, as they'd exchanged their vows.

Everything about the day was perfect, which was exactly what he wanted for Lisa, but by the time they arrived at the secluded resort several miles west of the city, he was wound tighter than a cheap clock.

He'd driven up yesterday, paid for the cottage and collected the key. The air between him and Lisa was so charged with emotion and anticipation, sparks were flying as they entered the cabin. Want had turned into a full-grown need over the past couple of days, and it took all he had to keep from acting on it this very moment.

"I'll get the suitcases," he said, hesitating for a second.

She used that second to plaster herself against him. "The suitcases can wait. I can't." Her mouth landed on his, and, lips open, she held nothing back.

He'd never refuse her anything. Ever.

Mick tried to go slow, to be cautious of the delicate buttons of her dress, but she was as desperate as him. Somehow their clothes managed to be removed with nothing being torn, at least he hadn't heard anything. Stripped bare, time stopped for a moment as they stared at each other, gasping for air and exploring each other with nothing but their eyes.

She was gorgeous, more beautiful than he deserved, yet she was his. Forever more.

The cabin was small, just two rooms. A bathroom, and this room that held the kitchen and sitting areas, as well as the bed right behind him. He held out his hand, reaching for hers.

With a joyous laugh, she didn't take his hand. Instead, she leaped forward. Her legs wrapped around his hips as her arms looped around his neck. He caught her, held on to her with both of his palms on the lush, perfect roundness of her butt.

As she placed a wonderful, wet kiss on his lips, he leaned backward, fell onto the bed. The springs creaked and they both laughed while still kissing, their arms and legs still holding on to each other.

She planted her hands on the mattress next to his head and let out a squeal of delight. "We're married! Finally! I never dared dream this. I was too afraid it wouldn't happen."

Her hair was cascading around him, like a curtain of silk. He ran a hand through the soft, silky strands, and then down her arm. "I dreamed about it, and I wanted that dream to come true more than any other dream I've ever had."

"I love you so much, Mick McCormick."

"I love you, Lisa McCormick."

"That's me! Lisa McCormick! Mrs. Mick McCormick!"

He fondled one of her breasts as their mouths met again. When the kiss ended, he grasped her waist and scooted all the way onto the bed, then laid her beside him, where he could fully explore her beauty. He took it slow, watching her expressions, checking to make sure she was enjoying every touch as much as him.

Tentative at first, she touched him, which sent fire licking through his veins, testing him to the limit. Soon they were both on the edge, teetering like they were at the top of the roller coaster.

"Now?" she asked, little more than a whisper between gasps of air.

He had to swallow as their eyes met. He'd never known desire this strong, this all encompassing. "Yes. Just tell me if it hurts and we'll stop."

"No, we won't," she said. "I feel as if I've been waiting for this my entire life."

"Me, too." He positioned himself above her. Need, anticipation... Hell, he wasn't sure what was making his heart pound so hard, other than love. He couldn't even remember what it felt like to not love her.

At the first touch of entering her, he paused. He didn't want to hurt her, not ever, not even while showing her how much he loved her. She spread her legs wider, as an invitation. He eased forward, and the pressure, the warmth of her engulfing him stole the breath right out of his lungs.

"Still doing all right?" he managed to ask, looking into her eyes.

"Yes." She hooked her legs behind his knees. "I'm doing wonderfully. How are you doing?"

He pulled out and glided inside her again. "Wonderful."

"Then let's keep doing wonderful together," she said, kissing him.

He set a momentum, slow at first, then growing faster, quicker, all the while watching her reactions as the friction increased, the pleasure mounting with each thrust.

Reveling in her reactions, her expressions, her sounds, he continued until he was shaking with his own impending release when she gasped, her body tensed, and then shuddered, gushing warmth around him.

He lost all control at that moment. Wave after wave of the utmost pleasure rippled through him until he was completely spent, drained, but full of glorious satisfaction.

She went limp beneath him, thrusting her arms and legs out to her sides. "Now that." She sucked in air. "Was a roller coaster ride."

He laughed, kissed her lips, her neck, the top point of her breast bone. "Yes, it was."

"That's a ride I want to ride for the rest of my life."

Rolling off her, he flopped onto his back and took hold of her hand, lacing his fingers between hers. "Good, because that was the beginning of forever."

Lisa had never felt so relaxed, so utterly boneless and blissful. She wasn't just feeling euphoric, she was euphoric. Everything was wonderful. Her life was wonderful. She was Mrs. Mick McCormick. The happiness inside her had to be released.

"What are you giggling about?" Mick asked.

"You. Me." She giggled again. "Life." Flipping onto her side, she said. "If someone had told me two months ago that I'd fall in love with and marry a bull, I would have told them they were full of baloney—to tell it to Sweeny!" That was a common expression used at the Depot—tell it to Sweeny—when people thought someone was trying to fool them.

He flipped onto his side. "Are you going to miss it? The Depot?"

The sincerity in his tone, in his eyes, nearly brought a tear to her eye, only because if she said yes, he'd take her to Missouri. He loved her that much. She loved him that much, too. "No," she declared straight from the heart. She'd sold the Depot, the entire farm, to the Hendrick boys, and wasn't sure who had been more overjoyed with the deal. Her or them. She kissed Mick's chin. "I'll never miss anything about it. I have you and our future together." She ran a finger down his shoulder. "It was somewhat of a magic trick, though, don't you think? A speakeasy owner marrying a bull."

His hand rubbed her stomach, then worked its way upward, toward her breasts. "Or scandalous," he said.

A thrill shot through her at the sound of his voice and at the idea of repeating all they'd just experienced. It had been a roller coaster ride. A very fun, and magnificent one. "Oh, you're right. That does sound rather scandalous."

He laughed. "You like the sound of that, don't you?"

"Yes. And so do you."

"I like you. Everything about you, as much as I love you."

As his hand cupped one of her breasts, she looked into his eyes. Saw the desire she'd seen earlier. He did love her, and he wanted another ride, too!

And so did she!

That first ride had been amazing, but round two was even better. She knew what to expect, and that, along with knowing every ride with Mick would be an adventure, things would just keep getting better and better.

By the time their honeymoon was over, and it was time to head home, she was no longer afraid that her life would be like her mother's had been. Mick would never fail her, and she would never fail him. She knew that deep in her heart, in the very soul of her being. They would be together forever.

"We'll go see Niagara Falls again," he said.

Sitting next to him in the car, rather than near the window, she asked, "Why? We saw it."

"For all of five minutes."

She giggled and snuggled her head on his shoulder. They had driven over to Niagara Falls, but not even the gorgeous, massive wall of cascading water could distract them from what they both would rather have been doing, so they'd hopped back in the car and driven back to the cabin. Letting out a sigh filled with wonderful memories, she said, "I loved that cabin in the woods."

He kissed the top of her head. "We'll go back there, too."

"Or, we could rebuild your tree house. Then we'd have our own little cottage in the woods."

"We could do that, too," he said.

She closed her eyes, and thought of the future, of her and Mick's children playing in the tree house, along with Riley whenever he visited his grandparents.

Contentment filled her and she snuggled closer.

"Happy?" he asked.

"Yes. Happier than I've ever been in my life."

"Me, too," he said. "Me, too."

Epilogue

"Are you sure I can't hire you?" Nelson Pinion asked.

"Yes, I'm sure," Lisa answered. "I have a job teaching school." Which she loved, but she loved her family even more. "I just want everything to be perfect for this wedding." Scanning the room yet again, she searched to make sure not a single detail had been missed. The tables were each covered with a white lace tablecloth and hosted a bouquet of flowers, along with a bottle of champagne and glasses. Lace bunting ran along the bar. The long buffet was ready for the food to be carried out when the time came, and the entire room glowed from the twinkling lights of the chandeliers overhead. But the most beautiful thing was the lattice archway that Mick had built standing in the center of the dance floor. That's where the bride and groom would exchange vows.

"Everything is perfect." Nelson took her hand, and kissed the back of it. "I tell you, my dear, with you overseeing parties, people would come from as far away as California, or England, to have an event here."

She laughed. "You are almost as charming as my husband."

He kissed her hand again. "Now, that is a compliment. A true compliment."

"Nelson, every time I see you, you are kissing my wife."

"I just can't help myself, Mick," Nelson declared. "I truly can't."

"I know the feeling."

Laughing, Lisa grasped Mick's forearms as his arms wrapped around her from behind, and she turned her face so he could kiss her.

Which he did, of course.

"How are you feeling?" His hands cradled her rounded stomach.

"Wonderful." It was the solid truth. Life couldn't be more wonderful. Their first baby would arrive within a few months, and if her dreams kept coming true, her father would still be here to meet his grandchild. Tony was still doctoring, but it was as if he'd gotten a new lease on life. A second chance. Just like her. All thanks to her wonderful, loving husband.

He kissed the side of her neck. "Do you wish we'd done this? Had a big wedding here?"

She twisted around to face him. "No. This took weeks of planning. I wasn't about to wait that long." Pressing up against him wasn't necessary, he knew what she meant, yet she still did it, because she could, even with a protruding stomach. She also looped her arms around his neck. "We had a reception here. That was more than enough."

He kissed her. A solid kiss that filled her with promises of tonight, when they were alone in their bedroom.

"How is the groom doing?" she asked as their lips parted, only because if she didn't change the subject,

their petting could get out of hand. That had happened
before. She was quite sure the baby she was carrying
was conceived in the back seat of the car because they
hadn't been able to wait to get home one evening. Thank
goodness he knew all the secluded alleys in town.

"Nervous," Mick answered.

"How are you doing?" she asked.

"I'm fine."

She knew he was fine, but had been concerned when
his mother had announced that she was getting married.
She hadn't needed to be. Mick was truly happy that his
mother had found love again.

So was Lisa. Barb deserved happiness and Dr.
George was a wonderful man.

Giving Mick one last kiss, for now, she slid her arms
off his neck. "I'd better go check on the bride. It's almost time."

"All right. I'll be ready to walk her down the aisle
at your signal."

She shook her head. "My signal? I'm not the one in
charge here."

He laughed. "Yes, you are. You are always in charge.
Have been since the day you were born." His hands slid
off her waist, and he playfully gave her a kiss. "Some
things you are downright brilliant at."

Glancing around to make sure no one was looking
at them, she gave the front of his pants a solid cupping.
"You aren't so bad at some things yourself."

He grasped her waist again and pulled her tight
against him as he whispered in her ear, telling what
was going to happen tonight with such detail that her
cheeks flushed.

When he was done, she whispered, "Promise?"

"Yes." Mick winked at her. "You know I never break a promise."

He didn't. In fact, he fulfilled that promise, over and over again.

* * * * *

If you enjoyed this book, why
not check out Lauri Robinson's
Sisters of the Roaring Twenties miniseries

The Flapper's Fake Fiancé
The Flapper's Baby Scandal
The Flapper's Scandalous Elopement

And look out for the next book in the
Twins of the Twenties miniseries, coming soon!